SINS OF THE FATHERS

A Valberg Novel

DESMOND J. DOHERTY

GUILDHALL PRESS

ISBN: 978 1 906271 89 3

Copyright © Desmond J. Doherty/Guildhall Press 2014

Author's photo (inside front cover) © Mustafa Oymak

Cover image: 'The Hanserot Angel of Death Victorious' © RB photography.

A Herbal taken from *Human Chain* © Seamus Heaney and reprinted by kind permission of
Faber and Faber Ltd.

First published June 2014.

Guildhall Press
Ráth Mór Business Park
Bligh's Lane, Derry
Ireland
BT48 0LZ
00 44 28 7136 4413
info@ghpress.com
www.ghpress.com

A catalogue record for this title is available from the British Library.

Guildhall Press gratefully acknowledges the financial support of the Arts Council
of Northern Ireland as a principal funder under its Annual Funding Programme.

ACKNOWLEDGEMENTS

My heartfelt gratitude for their encouragement and support to: Gerard Brennan, Brian McGilloway, Jim Curran, Bill Vail, Andrew Eaton, Mark McCauley, Michael Doherty, Richard Moore, Jackie Hamilton and Pearse Moore.

Sincere thanks to all those at Guildhall Press and associates for a great professional job as usual: Paul Hippsley, Kevin Hippsley, Joe McAllister, Declan Carlin, Jenni Doherty, Una Downey and Peter McCartney.

A very special mention to Garbhan Downey: a consummate writer, astute editor and good friend whose advice and guidance illuminated the way.

My appreciation to the Arts Council NI for their vision in supporting publishing in general and this production in particular.

For Clare

'A nation can survive its fools, and even the ambitious. But it cannot survive treason from within. An enemy at the gates is less formidable, for he is known and carries his banner openly. But the traitor moves amongst those within the gate freely, his sly whispers rustling through all the alleys, heard in the very halls of government itself. For the traitor appears not a traitor; he speaks in accents familiar to his victims, and he wears their face and their arguments, he appeals to the baseness that lies deep in the hearts of all men.'

Marcus Tullius Cicero
Roman politician, lawyer and philosopher

PROLOGUE

Derry, 21 December 2011

The snow was coming early again. The media made sure everyone was aware of that.

As darkness fell, Josephine Valberg drove hurriedly to the City Cemetery which loomed high over Derry, arriving just before the gates were to close. She had been listening to the radio and television predicting a severe snowstorm when something snapped in her. Little Patrick would be cold. Frozen deep in the ground. A blanket would help him. It made sense.

She talked quietly to her dead son and spread the large blanket over his grave. She hugged and kissed the marble gravestone which also marked the passing of her husband Gustav just months before. The first innocent drops of white snow began to fall. Soon the blanket was covered in a thick, soft layer.

For a brief moment she remembered being on the beach in Santa Monica, California, and Patrick was making a sand-castle with his brother and father. Little Patrick was dancing and jumping up and down on the beautiful beach on that beautiful summer's day. He was so full of life. It was bursting out of him.

It was time to leave. Patrick's mother walked back to her Volkswagen Polo but discovered she had locked her keys in the ignition. She had left her mobile phone in the car as well, and the snow was getting heavier.

9

Undeterred, and almost nonchalant with the thought of that beautiful day on the beach at Santa Monica still in her head, she walked carefully down to the bottom of the cemetery facing Lone Moor Road. But the gates were locked and no-one was about. Complete desolation. As a result of the previous severe winter, everyone in Derry wisely stayed at home as soon as the heavy snow fell. It had been forecast for days. Home was the safest place to be.

Feeling a tinge of anxiety, she thought it best to make her way back to her car. She might be able to break a window and get her phone. But the climb back up the steep hill was tough for her. And it was getting darker now. Even with the glare of the snow, this was a darkness that an elderly woman would struggle to manage.

Her breath was freezing in the thin air and she was exhausted. Her body felt weak and her limbs ached. She felt pain and distress to the core and shivers gripped her. She grew weaker and didn't have the strength to call out for help. She tried. But it was no use.

Somehow she made it to her car but found it was covered in a thick layer of snow. By this time she was shaking uncontrollably and completely drained of energy. She was freezing. She faced the inevitable. She went back to the grave, dug with her hands and found the blanket she had put down earlier. She shook it out as best she could. She pulled out the Rosary beads she had on around her neck and held them tightly. Wrapping the blanket around her shoulders and praying quietly, she lay down on top of the final resting place of her husband and son.

The snow was incessant as her mobile rang in the car, and her other son's name came up on the screen. It was the only name she had stored in the phone. She only used it to contact him.

Jon.

CHAPTER 1

Sidney Rankin had no choice. In fact, he'd run out of the luxury of deciding on anything in his life for the past year; even more so in the last six months, since his ex-client, Gerard O'Driscoll, had returned to Derry.

Rankin, like most solicitors, was not recession-proof. Especially since his lucrative relationship with the crime squad at Strand Road PSNI Station had ended. No more free-and-easy clients entitled to Legal Aid. The solicitor-of-choice of the police had blotted his copy book. Murderers, rapists, arsonists, burglars and benefit fraudsters had fallen on Rankin's lap for years because he caused no fuss for the police. He caused them even less fuss when his clients came before the court. Now his life and his law firm were in meltdown.

Rankin's secretary had been providing him with a running commentary on his personal and commercial disintegration via a series of Dictaphone messages. The worst news so far was that he could not afford to renew his professional indemnity insurance for the year and the Bank of Emerald had just obtained a Repossession Order against his building in Clarendon Street. And now his secretary had left him one last audio message on his desk. He had a gnawing anxiety about what he was about to hear and dreaded it.

The only functioning equipment left in his office was an old tape cassette player, which he used for his classical music. He was about to make what would be one of the final acts of control in his life – to listen to Beethoven's *Seventh Symphony* or his *Moonlight Sonata*. After a brief but futile moment of deliberation, he decided on the latter and put the tape into his machine and pressed play. He then switched on the Dictaphone and listened to his secretary's indignant voice for the last time as he sat staring at an old brown and tattered office file on his desk: 'The Crown V. Gerard O'Driscoll'.

'Okay, Sid, here goes – the final countdown, depressing and all as it is.

'Petula Wilson phoned thirty-two times in the last few days. She says if you don't return her calls she's reporting you to the Law Society.

'Mickey Clarke phoned once. Sorry. Well, not sorry. He's a nice man. He's looking for you to get his deeds and keep them for him. He's just paid off his mortgage.

'Walter McMurray called at reception demanding his mother's deeds and says he wants them by five tomorrow or he's reporting you to the Law Society. I don't trust him at all and he gives me the creeps. He smells as well. I'm sure he was a nice child. God, he is horrible now.

'Calvin Baxter from the bank phoned and wanted to know if you'd had the Repossession Order served on you yet and if not he would do it personally. He said all your debt has been called in and the Bank of Emerald was very disappointed with you, and they are also making a formal complaint to the Law Society about you. About what, I dunno. But it's very much a recurring theme, always "disappointed". Condescending gits.

'The accountants phoned and they said if you don't pay the outstanding income tax, PAYE, VAT and National Insurance that the Crown Solicitors will start bankruptcy proceedings. The time limit on the Statutory Demand is well up and they say some female solicitor there really has it in for you. The accountants said your only chance was to produce a bank draft for the full amount by Friday – some chance of that – or it's lights out. Sorry. That was last Friday. They also said their bill was outstanding and had to be paid immediately. They said they were very disappointed with you.

'Oil man says, not that you care, no more oil will be delivered on credit, but the plumber says if you don't keep the heat on the pipes will burst, probably in the next day or so, as it's so cold – oh, and the electricity will be going off soon as well.

'I've opened your mail, but most of it's demands for this and that, usually money; but there's also a healthy smattering of complaints and letters from the Law Society about complaints.

'You were supposed to be before the Ethics Committee last week. They phoned, too, and said they were now referring you to the Council with a view to reporting you to the Solicitors' Disciplinary Tribunal. They were very cheeky and said all complaints would be dealt with at the one time. I think there are about twenty.

'Let's see here ... Aye, you're in the Magistrates' Court again first Monday after Christmas as well with your own case. That's the rates you owe. The rates vermin said they will get an order against you this time and the case will not be adjourned – unless you pay the rates.

'Sorry, but that McDonagh case became statute-barred on Friday last there at five. So the lovely clients with their crap case will now sue you. Brilliant.

'Now let me look over my notes again. Aye, right. There was another phone call from Sophie Cunningham at the bank. She started quoting the Consumer Credit Act to me, and I think she was enjoying herself. Would any of those bankers survive in the real world with a real job? She started going on about the Act and said a formal demand was being sent out requesting immediate payment of your personal overdraft. I did ask her why she was telephoning me about this but, believe it or not, she just giggled and I couldn't make out her reply. Can someone do something about those bankers? Give me a gun. I shouldn't say that, I know. But what moral authority do they have at all? I dunno.

'And now the bad news.

'The Legal Aid Department also called and said you were overpaid in the last payment and that they would be clawing it back from any future payments. And that idiot of a solicitor – whatya call him? I can see his ugly fat face. You got some of his fees and he was in here breathing hell and damnation and spittle on you. And guess what? He threatened to report you to the Law Society.

13

'On that note, and unfortunate pictorial image, I bid you *adieu.*'

It was well after 9.00am now, but Rankin had no staff left and his office door was closed. He peeked out his window at a disgruntled ex-client, Declan O'Houlihan, who was commencing his daily picket outside Rankin's office, getting his placards ready and starting chants of: 'Down with Rankin, the money-grabbing bastard. Justice for Rankin. Send him to hell.'

The mobile-phone company had cancelled his contract and were sending texts saying they would be taking him to court over his unpaid bills. Leading up to Christmas it also meant no more boxes of chocolates and bottles of cheap wine for the custody sergeants at Strand Road Station. No more invites to the PSNI Christmas office party, either. Rankin's legal career and practice boiled down to this ignominious moment. No friends, no money, and no future.

Rankin took a moment to look around his room for one last time, the room that he took so many naps in and calmly sorted out so many problems in his head. It was a room that had not changed much since Gerard O'Driscoll's case but a room O'Driscoll never made it to, as he was a remand prisoner and then a sentenced one. However, O'Driscoll's heartbroken mother Bernadette had sat in it, usually in tears, pleading for her son and pleading for mercy, under the illusion that if she did so, justice and mercy would be assured. Rankin was well aware that Mrs O'Driscoll's faith led her down what he always thought was an erroneous path as well.

Rankin remembered all this as he prepared for what he was instructed to do. He could now see Mrs O'Driscoll in floods of tears and inconsolable. She had lost her husband to a prematurely exploding IRA bomb and was now losing her son. Rankin had been a solicitor of the Supreme Court of Judicature for many years. He had witnessed much pain and suffering. But he knew his career was over now. This was the end. He had no choice but to fully comply with the final instructions he had received from Mrs O'Driscoll's son.

His only deviation from these instructions was to stand up and smash open the medal display his own father had given him before he died, which included his grandfather's original War of Independence medal. He attached the medal with a hint of pride to the lapel of the dark trench coat which he wrapped round the bulky strapping across his chest as he left to catch his pre-arranged taxi.

At the same time across the city, Detective Chief Inspector Jon Valberg was entering the witness box of courtroom number two at Bishop Street courthouse in the adjourned trial of Raymond Grimestone – now dubbed 'the Reaper' by the tabloid media.

CHAPTER 2

'And so, Detective Valberg, you were first on the scene? The first to arrive at the home of Mr and Mrs White? Correct?'

'Correct.'

'Mr … sorry … *Detective* Valberg, are you presently working undercover on some case? I mean, at least you took your sunglasses off – but your beard, long hair and army fatigue jacket—'

The trial judge – Judge Peter McCourt – interjected. 'Mr Creswell, that is neither here nor there. It is none of your business, none of *my* business and, if I may respectfully say so, members of the jury, none of yours, either. Now, Mr Creswell, kindly move on.'

'Indeed, Your Honour. If I may. I apologise.' Charlie Creswell QC didn't sound remotely sorry. 'You say in your statement you were off duty and on your way home.'

'Yes.'

'What time did you finish your shift?'

'Eight. But I worked on until midnight then left.'

'Oh, I see. Duty calls, Detective. And the brutal dictatorship of time meant nothing to you this night?'

'No.'

'Well, did you consider yourself off duty at eight o'clock?'

'No.'

'But you weren't paid, were you, for doing what you were doing between eight and midnight?'

'No. Members of the police, Mr Creswell, are seldom off duty.'

16

'Well, Detective Valberg, can you tell the jury what you were doing generally? I don't want specifics.'

Mr Creswell paused and looked at the trial judge then Valberg. 'And if it pleases the court, I will not pursue this in detail. Can you just tell us well what specifically you were up to?'

The barrister looked again up at the trial judge.

'Sorry, Your Honour. *Generally*.'

'I wanted to discuss another case with a colleague.'

'Yes, I see. And did you do that?'

'Yes.'

'For four hours?'

'No.'

'How long, then?'

'Two hours or so.'

'Yes, I see. So what did you do for the rest of the time?'

'We had sex. Not for a full two hours, though.'

The trial judge interjected again.

'Mr Creswell. Really. Is this helping any of us? What is the point of this line of questioning?'

Creswell looked apologetically at the trial judge.

'If it pleases Your Honour, it conveniently leads me on to my next question. Which is, Detective Valberg ...' Creswell looked directly at Valberg. 'Did you drink any alcohol during your ah, hmm, discussions with your colleague?'

'Yes. I did. She didn't.'

'Oh. Excuse me, Detective Valberg. The colleague was a she. I forgot to ask. I am obliged to you for that.'

'Mr Creswell.' The trial judge sat back in his seat, rolled his eyes and shook his head. 'Mr Creswell, Mr Creswell. That's not helping me at all. Or the jury. Not helping me at all, Mr Creswell. And I don't want to have to repeat myself.'

CHAPTER 3

Rankin hurried into the waiting taxi just as O'Houlihan turned to parade up Clarendon Street, shouting abuse at every step. As the car pulled off, several pipes in Rankin's office cracked and broke open, cascading water from the tanks in the loft and flooding his premises as if to cleanse them from all the sins of the past.

Just listening to the rantings of the taxi driver after directing him to the nearby Fort George branch of the Bank of Emerald was almost enough to make the lawyer scream.

Rankin thought the driver looked familiar. He furtively scanned his identity card – Thomas Thaddeus Thompson. It suddenly came to him. Thompson was a regular in the courthouse. He had had the benefit, via the Legal Aid system, of free legal advice resulting from various breaches of law and order over the last thirty years.

Rankin knew he was in the presence of a man who believed he knew everything about everything and about everyone in Derry. The one thing he and Rankin had in common with each other and the working public, however, was their understandable vitriolic hatred of banks and bankers. The driver seldom paused his verbal assault on the banks and bankers, and when he did it was only to complain about the weather. Thankfully, he did not criticise solicitors too much. Thompson began his rant.

'Fuckin' scum. Complete vermin. Thieves and liars. I hate them. Burning at the stake's too good for those morons. Fuckin' banks. Wait till I tell ye. My brother-in-law Freddie Prendergast had a great wee business, fixing TVs and all electrical stuff. Fuckin' genius. Genius, I tell yee. He had so much work he needed to move up from a wee van to a truck thing and take a couple of young fellas on. Then a lot of fuckers didn't pay him, including that toe-rag, scum-pig bastard Baxter down at Emerald. Never paid him and wouldn't give him an overdraft. Five grand. That's all poor Freddie wanted so he could pay the two boys and keep things going for a few months when cash flow was bad, but naw. Baxter blamed credit in Belfast. Fuckin' Derry. Everything revolves around Belfast. Anyway, Freddie never owed a penny in his life to anyone, couldn't handle the pressure, so he stuck his head in the gas cooker and killed himself. Bloody awful, those bankers, and they're getting away with it. I tried moving my own account and me sister's away from them scum in Emerald, but we can't get it sorted. But their day will come. Ye know, I really believe someone will blow them up some day. There will be a wave of suicide attacks on banks. Poor Freddie should have taken those scumbag, lowlife fuckers out with him.'

Rankin made no reply as he nervously shuffled in the back seat and carefully adjusted his coat. He gave Thompson a five-pound note and mumbled his thanks as he stepped out of the car.

The driver just said, 'Aye, sound man. Thanks, mucker. Tell the Nazi he's a fuckin' scumbag and Tommy Thompson will be down to see him. Those fuckers in there are like politicians. Ugly celebrities. No moral authority whatsoever. Wouldn't get a job and wouldn't survive in the real world the rest of us live in. Thanks again, mucker. Cheerio.'

CHAPTER 4

'Yes, I see, Detective, I see. So you were the first to arrive. Well, do you know what Mr and Mrs White's daughter Diana said about you?'

'About me?'

'Yes. About you. Do you know? You have read her statement, have you not? There is no surprise or trickery here, Detective.'

'Well, I'm not on trial. Your client is.'

'Detective, I am not going to dance around the head of a pin on this topic. The court and this jury seek the truth and we all seek justice.'

'Yes. Very nice, Mr Creswell. Your search for truth and justice is admirable,' said the trial judge, and rolled his eyes again. 'Let's get on with it.'

'She indicated the presence of alcohol on my breath,' said Valberg.

'The strong smell of drink is how she put it, Detective. The smell that reminded her of an old aunt she wanted to forget is also how she ... ah ... put it. And, Detective, when your other colleagues arrived on the scene, you were, if I may say so, forcibly removed by them, were you not? We have their statements, too. Shall I remind you?'

'Is that a question or are you giving evidence?'

'Detective, Detective. Come on. May I please ask you to confirm to this jury that what I have just put to you – fairly, if I may respectfully say so, and subject to Your Honour – is the truth? Can you do that or will we go through the details bit by bit? Piece by piece? Well, Detective? What do you say?'

'I wasn't drunk.'

'I have not come to that yet, Detective. But I will.'

Valberg frowned down at prosecution Junior Counsel Victor Bostridge. Valberg could see that he was fawning over his pupil Julie Seymour. Valberg noticed that the young girl was uneasy and looked as if she hated Bostridge. Hated his smell, his breath and the moisture around his mouth. Valberg was becoming increasingly irritated at Bostridge trying to look down the top of the young barrister's blouse and sneaking a peek at her legs every time she moved instead of breaking up the unnecessary cross-examination. Valberg only had Judge McCourt to protect him. Valberg looked to Bostridge but he knew Bostridge only had eyes for Julie. Valberg was at boiling point. In real life, Bostridge would never have gotten to within fifty feet of Julie Seymour. Had it not been for the fact that every year Bostridge was 'keen to help' the younger female members of the Bar he would never have known Seymour.

Bostridge left Valberg on his own. Valberg was experienced enough to know that if Seymour rose to her feet to object, it would be more about the fat creep sitting beside her than the cross-examination of Valberg.

Valberg, with his temper up, said to Creswell, 'You seem to know more about all this than I do.'

'Sadly, Detective Valberg, that isn't flattering to either of us. Now, one more time. Is it correct that not only was my client charged with a number of serious offences, but that you, as a result of what happened in the White home that evening, also ended up before the court? That is correct, is it not? And you have taken the oath. And we all must presume you believe in God, then. Can we? The truth, then, Detective Valberg. Even if the truth is inconvenient.'

The trial judge was going to interject again and help Valberg, but Valberg had had enough.

'The truth is that you have no defence. Nothing to go on and yet you choose to ridicule me. But that's okay. You proceed as you see fit. Anyway, before you combust with sarcasm, Traffic Branch followed me from the station and I was arrested for DIC at the Whites' house. Yes, charged and convicted, properly so.'

21

'Well, with Your Honour's permission, may it please the court, DIC is "drunk in charge". Drunk in charge of your motor vehicle. Isn't that right, Detective? Drunk? Correct? And they could have charged you with drink driving but decided on the lesser charge. Correct?'

CHAPTER 5

Wendy McKinnon greeted Sidney Rankin at the lavish marble and glass reception area of the Bank of Emerald with surprise.

'Mr Rankin. We weren't expecting you here today ... and you can't go in there. There's a meeting going on ... *Mr Rankin!*'

Rankin glared at her with disdain and strode on through to the room where he had received countless lectures from various junior bank officials over the last year on how to run his law firm. The receptionist hurried after him, still remonstrating.

As advised by Gerard O'Driscoll, Rankin knew that the chief executive of the Bank of Emerald, and one of the most hated men in Ireland, Sir Roger Rothschild, was in town for an early, clandestine meeting with one of the most hated men in Derry, Calvin Baxter, to discuss what customers the bank could bust in the Derry area. O'Driscoll's investigations confirmed that Rothschild was concerned that Baxter was not busting enough of them. O'Driscoll had given Rankin the access code to the main conference room to the back of the palatial bank. Rankin keyed in the numbers and entered, slamming the oak door shut behind him. Wendy McKinnon could only look on via the glass panel in the door.

In the room with Rothschild and Baxter were Sophie Cunningham and Rothschild's assistant, Stella Harper. All four had their Emerald-branded laptops out, going over names and accounts in a meeting that had been underway long before the bank opened. All four looked up with expressions of surprise and irritation. Ignoring the angry outburst of rebuke from Baxter, Rankin opened his long trench coat to reveal a metal bodice of explosives. He pressed a small device at his side and the detonators lit up like a Christmas tree. Their expressions turning to fear and confusion, the four bank members scrambled to distance themselves from the danger.

Rankin announced: 'Yes, if you are in any doubt, this is an explosives vest. There's also a small camera on my left shoulder relaying all this to the person who sent me here. I also have an earpiece through which I'll be told what to do, although I've been promised this will be kept to a minimum to allow me some control in the last moments of my life. The explosives can be detonated remotely by my advisor at any time, or as you can see, if I press this button here again we'll all be vaporised. That is what I've been told. It's just the four of you I want, so this has worked out exactly as I was told it would. All the other bank staff can leave. Isn't this nice? You all there ending people's lives with the flick of a switch and me about to do the same, so it seems.'

McKinnon was the first to run screaming from the bank. 'He's got a bomb! He's a bomb! He's going to blow them up!'

Rankin realised now that Thomas Thaddeus Thompson had predicted something correctly for all the wrong reasons. This was going to end in blood and death.

Sidney Rankin had snapped. Not only was he now falling foul of the criminal law, he was falling foul of the one piece of legislation that controlled his life, namely The Solicitors' Order. Rankin was now most definitely, in the eyes of the Law Society anyway, bringing his profession, such as it had become, into disrepute. It was the least of his worries and strangely, at this moment, he never felt more content, free and in control.

He smiled at Baxter. 'And don't you fuckin' move, you Nazi bastard.'

CHAPTER 6

Valberg was not in control. He was stuck in the witness box under the duty of an oath he did not believe in.

'Your Honour, may I address you in the absence of the jury?' said Bostridge from his seat. His large bulk made it difficult for him to get to his feet.

'Yes, Mr Bostridge, you may. And perhaps you can tell me what all this commotion is about.'

'Your Honour, if it pleases the court, may I regretfully and sadly advise that the prosecution cannot proceed in this matter.'

'Mr Bostridge, this may not sound very judicial, or polite, but I feel I am about to suck the metal fillings from my mouth and spit them at you with a vengeance, unless you say something to me that lowers my blood pressure.'

'With respect.'

'Forget the respect and get on with it, man. What is the problem?'

'Simply put, Your Honour, the prosecution is not in a position to offer any more evidence. We cannot proceed and perhaps we—'

His Honour Judge McCourt, not known for his patience, got up out of his seat and left in a rage. Inevitably, he sent his tipstaff out to summon all legal representatives to his chambers immediately.

Valberg, in a rage of his own, was left sitting in the witness box under oath, deliberately by Bostridge, who did not ask for Valberg to be excused.

Even Grimestone's defence team did not know what was going on, and the White family were in tears.

Bostridge made his way hastily from the courtroom without speaking to anyone, ignoring Valberg. Valberg knew this was on purpose to allow Bostridge safe passage to his room. When he got there with his bewildered pupil in tow, Bostridge sat down and spread his lunch out in front of him and started to eat it.

Valberg had had enough and darted from the witness box. He burst through Bostridge's door, dragged him outside into the corridor and started strangling him on the worn carpet. Julie Seymour did not call for help. Valberg thought the whole episode seemed to be exciting her and she wanted him to really harm Bostridge. Bostridge's flailing legs knocked over a metal fire bucket that clattered against his office door as he roared and struggled to fight off Valberg. The ensuing racket left Seymour with no choice but to call for help, reluctantly and faintly.

Defence counsel Charlie Creswell was first over to the prosecutor's office, having been alerted more by the sound of Bostridge's cries than Julie's unimpressive attempts at raising the alarm. He could not shift Valberg at all and Bostridge was in real danger of being choked to death. It took four uniformed police officers who were in court on other duties to loosen Valberg's grip on Bostridge.

Valberg spoke only loud enough for Bostridge to hear him clearly.

'You fucking slimedog. You fat, greedy, useless, lazy bastard.'

Valberg eventually let Bostridge go, under pressure of the uniformed officers pulling at him and when he heard Detective Sergeant Linda Wilson call at the top of her voice: 'Jon, Jon. Stop it. Stop it, Jon. Jon. Your mother's dead. Jon, please. She's dead. I'm sorry. So sorry.'

Valberg froze like the snow outside in a sudden state of anger and heartbreak.

Bostridge was still choking loudly and gasping for air. An ambulance was called while first aid was administered by the police officers. Without realising it, Valberg had made the exit of Bostridge from the court a lot easier and safer as he was stretchered away in an ambulance with all the media looking on and taking photographs.

Judge McCourt smiled ruefully when he heard what happened to Bostridge. He told his tipstaff: 'Detective Valberg is a good man. And please apologise to him on my behalf for not excusing him from the witness box. As soon as I got back, the chief clerk told me about his mother. Terrible. A good man, though. Like his father in many ways.'

CHAPTER 7

Valberg was saved from being arrested as a result of a telephone call from the Chief Constable's office that permitted him to go to the City Cemetery with Sergeant Wilson. By now, Chief Constable Anna Harte was also aware that a dangerous hostage situation was developing at the Bank of Emerald.

Wilson had ensured that the scene at the cemetery was preserved until Valberg could see it for himself instead of relying on photographs and video. Abigail Burns, an experienced Scenes of Crime Officer, was already there to give Valberg some solace that she had checked the situation and that no crime was suspected. But Valberg knew what had happened: he had heard his mother once mentioning 'Little Patrick' would need a blanket to keep warm on the cold winter nights in Derry ...

Outside the courthouse, Traffic Branch awaited in a four-wheel-drive vehicle to take Valberg up to the cemetery. Valberg knew this was not the time or place for another confrontation and graciously accepted the assistance provided. On the journey from Bishop Street to the grave, Valberg recalled, as a child, asking his mother what angels looked like in heaven.

'Jon, they are all dressed in white with wings, helping God. You can't mistake them. They all look the same.'

'Well, if they all look the same, how will I find you?'

***

Abigail Burns and her colleagues were all clad in white forensic suits around the grave, but Valberg easily identified Abigail from her shape and movement. He did not want to speak to anyone, and the only noise or movement that caught his attention was the upset groundsman and caretaker.

'I lock the gates every night at this time of year at half four,' he was saying. 'There's a big sign down there. The snow must have covered it. Mrs Valberg was here a lot recently. I always watched out for her. I never thought for a moment she'd be up at the grave yesterday in that big storm. Oh, I'm so sorry. It's really all my fault. I locked the gates. I'm really, really sorry.'

Valberg thought the angel figures on the other graves were moving and looked saddened and confused, just like him.

Abigail Burns picked her moment carefully, and Valberg was conscious of this. She offered no sympathy or handshake. He didn't want either. Valberg listened intently as she told him there was nothing more for him to see and they would remove his mother's body now with his permission. Valberg paused. Without looking at Abigail, he nodded his head. He wondered if he could just summon a gravedigger and get the burial over now to avoid the wake.

Father James Doherty stood out, wearing the same colours as Valberg. Both all in black apart from Valberg's green Canadian Army fatigue jacket. He went to sympathise with Valberg, but Valberg took little notice of him as his anger was beginning to mount.

Valberg watched from a short distance his mother's frozen body being removed as delicately as possible under the protection of a white tarpaulin tent from the top of the grave of his father and brother. The body would go for post mortem. Valberg looked around for Wilson, who was now joined by Constable Michael Bell, to take him away.

But before he could move, he could feel a wave of emotion building up inside him he had not felt since Detective Constable Finbar Callaghan's funeral many months before. He regretted his public display of grief then and was fighting doing something he believed to be stupid now. But he couldn't stop himself. He rushed to his mother and fell to his knees on the trampled snow. He knelt over her just before her body was to be covered. No-one dared stop him. Abigail signalled to everyone to move back.

Valberg got as close as he could to his mother and held her while he whispered in her ear so no-one could pick up what he was saying.

'Don't leave me. I'm begging you. Don't leave me now. I love you so much.'

***

The BBC Radio Foyle one o'clock news could be heard faintly in the four-wheel-drive vehicle Valberg had arrived in from court. It was reporting that the alleged rapist Raymond 'the Reaper' Grimestone had been released from custody following the collapse of his trial at Londonderry Crown Court that morning. That report was then swept aside to go live to the Bank of Emerald at Fort George where a hostage situation was developing. There were breaking reports that an unidentified male had strapped himself with explosives and was now holding hostage the CEO of the Bank of Emerald.

Valberg said to Linda, 'My ticket to LA is inside my jacket. I was going this time and not coming back. I wanted to help the Whites this one last time. I didn't want to have to spend another Christmas and New Year in Derry. It's not Derry. I just wanted out. I had agreed it all with the Chief Con. I'm sure you all know anyway. When I was sitting in the witness box the only thing that was keeping me going was the thought of my business-class seat on Virgin Airlines all the way to the West Coast. I shouldn't have thought about it – and walking on the beach at Marina Del-Rey. What I pleasantly imagine, I seem to destroy.'

As the news coverage of the bomb incident intensified, Valberg asked Linda and Michael to go and speak with the White family and ensure the Family Liaison Officer was assisting them.

'Keep everyone away from me and don't bother me until I get home and get all the funeral arrangements sorted.'

CHAPTER 8

'What are you doing, Rankin? Have you lost it, man?' Baxter cried out.

'Lost it? Lost it, you fuckin' wretch? You parasites. The lot of you. The misery you scum have all created. You use a wider global meltdown to empty and kill your own people. Do you want to serve your repossession order now, Baxter? The problem now is that I just might trigger this switch taking it from you.'

Cunningham began sobbing and crying in abject terror. Harper began doing the same, but not to the same extent as her younger colleague.

'Just before we start. Where did you scum all get your names from? None of you are from about these parts anyway.'

No-one answered.

'Anyway, if any of you has a spare mobile, and especially you, Baxter, stuck up your arse or wherever, I will blow us all to kingdom come. Now, which one of you two is Cunningham?'

The younger woman let out a small cry.

'You direct calls here to this room, and the phone is going to start ringing. It will be the PSNI. You answer it and you tell them the situation here as you see it. But make sure you tell them if anyone comes into this building I will blow everyone up. And tell them there's only one policeman I will talk to. His name is Jon Valberg. Detective Chief Inspector Jon Valberg of the PSNI, Strand Road, Derry fucking City. If they fob me off I will blow us up, and what's worse, even if I don't, the Necromancer will. Now when you mention the Necromancer, they will know who you are talking about. It's his new code name on their files. He said he likes this latest one. He's back. Back from the dead. Now ... type up what I am about to say and read it out to them. Tell them to publish it, and we are going to check on the internet here if they have done as instructed and the Necromancer will be checking, too. If it's not published in the media within one hour of you telling them we are all going to die. Fucking horribly, I might add. You see the stuff I'm locked into here? It's fucking awful I'm told. Nitrobenzene and God knows what else. Even if this partially explodes and you think you've survived, you'll die of a horrible cancer. I'm a walking, talking, highly toxic compound. I'm a real Provo co-op mix this morning. Whatever way this pans out, instead of begging for your miserable wretched lives, you will be begging to die. And, Baxter, by the way, you may have left your wife and children for the last time this morning. Here, Cunningham, start typing, and it can go as an email to the police as well.'

Rankin started to dictate: 'The budget should be balanced, the treasury should be refilled, public debt should be reduced, the arrogance of officialdom should be tempered and controlled, and the assistance to foreign lands should be curtailed lest Rome become bankrupt. People must again learn to work instead of living on public assistance.'

Rankin smiled as he checked the text on the laptop screen.

'That's it, just in time. There's the phone ringing now and sirens blazing outside. The police know I'm here by now anyway. Now, which of you scumbags knows where that quotation is from? Anyone? If I get a right answer, I might just spare you.'

'Cicero. From around 55BC.'

'I was waiting for you to speak, Rothschild.'

The voice in Rankin's earpiece said: 'Couldn't have done it better myself, Sidney. Excellent. All going just dandy at the moment. Stay calm and you keep doing as I tell you. Nice touch there with that War of Independence medal. Your grandfather's? Think what he must have gone through. And for what? All in the name of a piece of dirt.'

CHAPTER 9

Ian Peter Haslette only worked as a solicitor part time. At least, that was the plan until the global financial crisis also hit him to a lesser degree. Fortunately, he had taken the advice of Valberg's father years before and sold his Georgian building in Clarendon Street to Joseph Arbuckle, a young, up-and-coming solicitor, at the height of the property boom. Unfortunately for Arbuckle, he had become another victim of the Bank of Emerald. The loan he took out over the building was currently three or four times more than its present value. But the bank wanted to be paid. So Arbuckle was in financial trouble himself and under severe pressure. Haslette believed that Joseph Arbuckle was going to kill himself. Or combust. There was no talking sense to him anymore. His correspondence with his fellow members of the legal profession in Derry, as far as Haslette could detect, was becoming more and more aggressive and unprofessional, laced with threats and demands – and all signed with a huge signature. Haslette had seen it all before. He knew Arbuckle was a hostile young man under pressure with no grace. In this state he was dangerous, however.

Haslette worked from home with one secretary. A polite but reclusive solicitor, he was of a time that did not exist anymore. He was seldom seen without a glass of red wine or a cigar in his hand. He had a 1988 model JLS Jaguar car that drank petrol as much as he drank Pinot. But he loved driving it and his older Jaguar before it.

Today, Haslette sat down to read another angry letter from Arbuckle and Co Solicitors. He felt ashamed to belong

33

to a profession in which one of its members could write a letter that was so rude and unnecessary to a fellow colleague.

Arbuckle and Co seemed to be taking delight in suing him for alleged professional negligence in respect of a transaction many years ago involving a small piece of land that a property speculator purchased. It was now alleged that no sewerage serviced the site therefore it could not be sold, and Haslette was one of the people getting the blame. He had acted on behalf of the speculator then who was now himself being sued by the Bank of Emerald as all his debt was called in. One of the pieces of security that the bank had was the site. They, too, were suing Haslette, as they claimed the title to the site was defective and Haslette was to blame. None of this would be happening if money was flowing freely and banks were making credit available. The reality was that Haslette cared nothing about the action at all. It was a hazard being a solicitor. But what was upsetting was the manner in which Arbuckle and Co pursued Haslette with some relish, and the fact that Haslette was annoyed that Joseph Arbuckle might think that he was worried about the litigation at all, especially at his age and the stage his career was at.

In any event, legal actions of this type, and Haslette had a few against him, involved him depressingly having to engage in endless and futile meetings and telephone conferences with the solicitors acting on behalf of his professional indemnity insurers, some of whom were young enough to be his grandchildren. This was all time consuming, but the more the insurance solicitors could engage in meetings and telephone conferences, the more money they would make, charging it all up at an hourly rate. Haslette was a Conveyancing, Wills and Probate solicitor, in practice for nearly fifty years, and he, too, had had enough of it. He'd had enough of his colleagues, especially the younger ones, the Law Society, the Inland Revenue, courts, judges and the majority of his clients who were still alive.

Conveyancing was gone, but at least people were still dying. The long-established old-fashioned Probate Solicitor could now cash in on his dead clients just as long as he survived them. All Haslette needed was one a month to die. Perhaps two a month. That was more than enough.

34

On occasion, there would be a bumper crop when three or four might die in the one month. Haslette virtually had no overheads. Working from home, mortgage free and debt free, he was cocooned from the financial problems that existed for all his colleagues. Selling his building in Clarendon Street at the right time had been a masterstroke, and he had Gustav Valberg, his long and loyal friend, to thank for that and much more in his life.

There was always at least one funeral a week to go to now. He would arrive at the ceremonies, content in the knowledge that, as he sympathised with family members, the original will of the deceased was safely tucked in his inside jacket pocket and he was one of the executors and trustees, if needs be, of the estate. It represented certain fees and income. Steady and reliable. His secretary would fill out all the probate and tax forms, and Haslette would do all the public relations with the family. He was adept and gifted in being able to talk about the deceased in glowing terms as if he knew them personally.

He always kept in the will wallet, or envelope, his original instructions so as to remind him of the person who had died and what they talked about. His notes were meticulous and he wrote down everything his clients told him when making their will. This would include, but was not limited to, family secrets – which children were adopted, which children were to be disinherited – and suspicions about family members, spouses, brothers, sisters, cousins and even their own parents. Nothing escaped Haslette, he recorded everything, good and bad. The will would speak from death and so would Haslette's notes. He even recorded for family members which funerals a testator or testatrix would not go to if they died before them. Making their own will and the thought of their mortality either had a calming effect or made them angry. Haslette could see that many of his elderly clients, who had strong faith in the afterlife in heaven or hell, feared death but would not admit it. Their deep genuine religious beliefs, thought Haslette, contributed more to their rapid acceleration towards death as opposed to the terminal illness they may have had. Some even muttered in his presence: 'I fear I am for hell.'

Haslette always believed, no matter what the family circumstance, that a parent should leave their entire estate to their spouse and in the event of a spouse predeceasing the other then in equal shares to all surviving children. That advice, many times, caused an awkward silence in Haslette's office. Some parents hated their children and hated even more the person they had married. This hatred bewildered Haslette who had no children, but by the time the parent explained why a certain child was not to receive any bequest, Haslette understood. He had to cover himself, waiting for the disgruntled, disinherited child arriving at his reception demanding a copy of their father or mother's will, usually after they had just buried them and were on their way home from the cemetery. Haslette had to be sure he recorded a valid and cogent reason as to why a child was not mentioned in the will of their deceased parent in case the will was contested. The hatred that existed between brothers and sisters, and why some of Haslette's clients did not even want them at their funeral, was also a common feature in his wills and probate work.

However, Haslette took enormous pride in knowing that in all his years of practising as a solicitor, not one of the thousands of wills drafted by him had been successfully contested. His notes were watertight and respected by the courts.

Haslette read again the angry Arbuckle and Co letter he had just received and put it down. He stared at it thinking that – for other reasons in his life, perhaps – he deserved to be treated in such a disrespectful way by a person no-one in the legal community in Derry had any real regard for.

Then the phone rang. It was Valberg. The news Valberg conveyed about his mother shattered Haslette. He offered his sympathy and condolences and was a true professional. Valberg's parents had been very good to Haslette and they had been close friends. Haslette confirmed Valberg's mother had made a new will with him shortly after her husband died and would get a copy made available. Haslette wept quietly and said out loud after he put the phone down: 'Now they both know the truth.'

If Haslette's faith in God meant anything to him, salvation was going to be difficult. It was not certain. The dark wave that enveloped Valberg had already closed in on Haslette, too. The only way to fight it off was to fill his head with music and poetry. He listened to Dante's *La Vita Nuova* and thought of the last moments of the life of his wife, Lily.

Haslette rolled up the letter from Arbuckle and Co and threw it in the bin. He was worried that Valberg might have detected his odd, over-polite reaction to the news of the death of his mother. He wondered if Valberg ever questioned the circumstances of the death of his wife some years previously. It was accepted to have been as a result of an accident at home when she fell down the stairs.

They were a childless couple and Haslette cared for little now in life apart from his cigars, wine and literature – especially poetry, and, like Sidney Rankin, classical music.

Haslette was just waiting to die.

As *La Vita Nuova* echoed around his home, he moved to his will file cabinet and there it was.

Josephine Valberg's Last Will and Testament was dated 7 July 2011. Josephine, 'otherwise known as Josie' as confirmed in her will, appointed her son as the sole executor of her estate. However, in view of the perils of her son's job and what she believed to be his fragile mental state, she made provision for the appointment of Father James Doherty and Ian Haslette to act as her executors and trustees in place of her son if required. It was a simple will and like her, embodied with no fuss or drama if her son survived her. In the event of her son predeceasing her, however, then half of her estate was to go to Father James Doherty and the other half to a secret trust. Valberg knew nothing of this yet, as all Haslette had told him was: 'Aye, all to you, Jon, after payment of all her "Just Debts, Funeral and Testamentary Expenses". She wanted buried out of Long Tower. I remember she was quite insistent about that. Aye, Long Tower, Jon. I'm so sorry.'

CHAPTER 10

The solicitor, the priest and the undertaker were all now organised as far as Valberg was concerned. He put the phone down. He thought a glass of wine might thaw him out of his frozen state and let some of the emotion out. However, his mobile rang and it was the Chief Constable who, after sympathising at length, asked if he had heard the news about the Bank of Emerald.

'I know this is dreadful timing as always, Jon, but turn on the TV or Radio Foyle, whatever you can get there.'

Valberg put on the radio first, then stared in wonder at the television, trying to make sense of the Cicero quote as the drama at the Bank of Emerald was being relayed live via Sky. The ancient admonishing words were now in the public domain.

***

Meanwhile at the bank, Rankin could not calm Sophie Cunningham, who was getting increasingly distressed and asking to go to the bathroom. Rankin was petrified for the safety of his own family should he not follow O'Driscoll's instructions exactly. He had been warned what would happen should he disobey. He had to take the threat seriously.

Rankin told Baxter to get the details of his own personal account up on his laptop. Once this was done, he told him to find the account of the widowed Mrs Prendergast, whose first name he did not know.

What no-one, including O'Driscoll, had anticipated was

38

the huge outpouring of public support that Sidney Rankin was about to receive – despite the awful weather.

Hundreds of people had gathered as close as possible to the bank, despite the massive security operation in motion. The specialist PSNI negotiating team from Belfast found it all bewildering. The world was watching Derry again. A small, despondent solicitor seemed to have captured the public consciousness quite unintentionally.

'Now, how much is in that account of yours, Baxter? And don't have me come and look.'

'Forty-seven thousand, three hundred and ninety-four pounds and thirteen pence. I just transferred it here this morning from my interest account. It's just the proceeds from—'

'Fuck up. Transfer it all now less the thirteen pence to Mrs Prendergast's account. The widow. Her husband killed himself. You know all about it. Don't fuck with me. Do it now.'

'But I—'

Rothschild looked angrily at Baxter. 'Do it now, you fuckwit.'

'You better do as your boss tells you. Now, you, Harper, or whatever your name is, you are going to get Mrs Prendergast's number from her file there on the system and you are going to phone her and tell her that the money was discovered in her late husband's account or something like that. Say it was a life-assurance policy he had via the bank, and it was just discovered this morning. And that despite the circumstances of his death, the company still decided to pay out as a gesture of goodwill and the representations of that fucker Baxter. Fuckin' do it now. And, Cunningham, if you stop crying I'll let you use the bathroom. And if this is all done right now by your esteemed colleague I might even let you go.'

Rankin's earpiece spoke to him again.

'That wasn't in the plan, Sidney, but what can I say? Making it up as you go along. Well done. Let Cunningham go. Adapt. She's about to get even more hysterical. I'm outside watching. Make sure I see her come out the front door. Protect her dignity. Let her clean up and wear her coat. Stay with it, Sidney. The cops know we want Valberg. He'll not be long now.'

39

CHAPTER 11

'Sidney Rankin? The solicitor, Anna?' Valberg was totally bewildered.

'Aye. Him for sure, and time is not on our side. We're monitoring it all from here, Jon, and everything's in place. Negotiators, Tactical Support Team, bomb squad and marksmen, just in case. He wants you. He won't talk to anyone else. And it seems someone is directing him. But until he speaks with you personally we can't confirm it. He's let one of them go just now, a woman, but she's been taken straight to Casualty in a state of severe shock.'

'Why me? And, fuckin' Jesus, why now? Can't I even bury my mother in peace? I dunno, Anna. Enough. I've had enough.'

'Jon, I'm sorry. I wouldn't ask unless I needed you. We can't storm the bank yet. We'd like to, but the Police Ombudsman would have something to say about it. And the crowds and the media are there in force. If I could do what I want, this would be over quickly.'

'Does he have a gun or a weapon of any sort?'

'Not that we know for sure. But as I told you, he's loaded or strapped with explosives and has some kind of detonator device.'

'More bombs. A Derry solicitor with explosives strapped to him taking over a bank. Maybe we should let him blow himself up – and the bank. Who would care anyway?'

Valberg paused, looking at all the family photographs surrounding him.

'Her body isn't even here yet. And the Valbergs from Sweden are on their way – again. And what's left of her side. My mother's side, that is. My mother. Even if I could mourn, I wouldn't get peace. Ian Haslette and Father Doherty have keys for the house. I'll phone them now and make my way down. Or just Father Doherty. Perhaps in my sorrowful state I'm perfect for this. For death. For more death and mayhem. It's my life, the way my life works, Anna, isn't it? I know nothing else.'

Valberg paused again and Anna just waited for him to continue.

'Of course, you know what this has the smell of? It's sour and dangerous. And the Derry public think we fished him out of the Foyle six months ago. I can't get out and he won't let me out. He won't stop until everyone's dead. He only teased us the last time. Tell me I'm wrong, Anna, but I think the dark wave is returning.'

'I'll let Commander Everett know you are on the way. She's down there now.'

'Delightful, Anna, just fuckin' delightful. Here we go again.'

Valberg had been listening to Simon and Garfunkel's *Greatest Hits* in his car. The opening words of *The Sound Of Silence* reverberated in his head as he hummed to himself: *'Hello darkness, my old friend, I've come to talk with you again.'*

***

Sidney Rankin stared in silence at his hostages and they stared back in silent fear and terror. The bank was a lot quieter now that Cunningham had been allowed to leave. Rankin was waiting on instructions from his ex-client and on the arrival of Valberg. The crowds of support for Sidney Rankin were swelling in silence, too. They were supportive of the idea of a bank, any bank, being held to ransom.

As darkness descended, a candlelight vigil began for the hostage taker and the hostages. Valberg looked on as he drove up, thinking that if the crowd and the Derry public knew what he reckoned was going to happen in Derry in the coming days, they would have fled, and justifiably so – in abject fear and panic.

CHAPTER 12

Much to his disdain and angst, Thomas Thaddeus Thompson was in an interview room at Strand Road Police Station with DS Wilson and Constable Bell, providing a statement to help the PSNI.

As he sat there, all he could think of was the names of every informer he knew RUC Special Branch had ever employed, especially in Derry. He was very uncomfortable and sat sideways on his seat as if he could run out of the police station when it suited him.

Helping the police with their enquiries would have been enough to earn him a bullet in the head in the old days, dumped in a country lane, naked, his hands tied behind his back and a black hood over his battered skull. Is this what all the Volunteers died for? All he could say was: 'For fuck's sake. Fuckin' banks. Bastards. And I didn't know him personally. Odd sorta boy, isn't he? Rumours around the town about him for a long time now. Especially after that O'Driscoll thing. Some stories going around about him then, but look, fuck me sideways, I didn't know what he was up to. The wee fucker coulda blew me to fuck in me car. Fucker. Bastard. Selfish wee shite.'

'You got a call from him, then?' asked DS Wilson.

'Ah, naw. The dispatcher called me.'

'What's the dispatcher's name and who called him?'

Thompson was sinking, slowly but surely. Now he was a tout for sure.

'Knucker Dykes. Knucker. He's the dispatcher. He just told me to go to Rankin's office. I knew where it was. Told me to be there at ten this morning, so I was. I thought he was for court or something. I knew who he was but didn't let on and a fiver later, fuckin' here I am.'

'Well, you're on all the CCTV footage. At Clarendon Street and at the bank. And you never knew him or had any dealings with him?'

'Naw. Never. Honestly.'

'How was he? Did he have anything with him or say anything?'

'Fuck all and said fuckin' nowt. The wee bastard – gettin' into my car with a bomb.'

'Can you tell us anything to help us? What did you talk about?' asked Constable Bell.

'Well, nothing really. I just gave off about the banks. Scumbags that they are. I probably gave off about the weather as well. That's all. Nothing else. He barely spoke a word.'

'Right. Well, we have all your details now and you've already given us all the timings, which ties in with the CCTV footage,' confirmed Wilson.

'I just have one question, Mr Thompson,' said Bell.

'Aye, well, what is it?'

'If he didn't speak much, how did you know where to go?'

Thompson stared at the missing ceiling tile exposing the air-ventilation system above him and thought about climbing up inside it to escape.

'Knucker told me. He knew. He must have. Aye, Knucker told me.'

'Okay, then,' said Bell. 'We'll speak to him and get his statement. That's great, Mr Thompson. Thank you so much for helping us.'

'So that's it, then? That's all you want to know?' asked Thompson.

'Aye. Sure we have all your details now. If we need anything else, we'll call and see you if it's really urgent. That's okay with you, is it?'

'Oh, aye, surely. No bother.'

DS Wilson asked one final question.

'Just one other thing, Mr Thompson. Did he mention anything at all about bombs or explosives, or anything at all?'

Thompson looked again at the ceiling, recounting in his

43

head what he'd said to Rankin. *I really believe someone will blow them up some day.*

'Naw, nothing. Not a thing.'

Thompson felt guilty. He believed his street cred, such as it was for a Derry taxi driver, was in danger if he were spotted leaving a police station. He was more worried about leaving it than anything. What was he to say if spotted? *'It's okay. I'm not a tout. I was just in signing the Sexual Offenders' Register.'*

His worst fears were realised. Just when he walked out, Knucker Dykes was driving by and waved at him. Now when the police would arrive at Dykes's home, he would know who sent them. Neither Dykes nor Thompson had done anything wrong on this occasion but both would feel guilty.

CHAPTER 13

While Valberg was arriving outside the Bank of Emerald, Rankin was losing it inside.

Rankin was faltering. He was waiting for his faith to save him, but it did not. There was no blinding light. No revelation. Rankin started to think about all the injustices that he had contributed to over the course of his legal career. All as a result of greed. The greed that drove him was now killing him. The greed, the fear of never getting a call from the police again was now a reality. Greed influenced his approach to the O'Driscoll case as it had done with so many others. It resulted in a lack of attention to detail. It resulted in the inevitable conviction, without an appeal, for O'Driscoll. Rankin started to think for the second time that day of O'Driscoll's mother in tears in his office and the manner of her death. The image of her razor-sliced arms and throat lying in a bath of water, as recorded by her inquest photographs, flashed before him. An inquest that he stumbled into by accident and took no interest in, as he had money to make elsewhere in Derry courthouse that day. No-one would have paid him to represent the only living next of kin: O'Driscoll himself.

The silence in the room with his hostages was broken by Rankin saying: 'She died alone in the bath, wrists cut, the bath water thickened with her blood. I thought her throat was cut, too, just by the photos. How could she do both, really?'

He was about to sit down; tiredness was catching up on him. The Bank of Emerald would bankrupt him now for sure. He stumbled but made sure he did not trigger the device. He was not yet ready to die. Not immediately.

'Those photos haunted me. I never let on. I suppressed it. Not that long ago, suicide was a real no-no. That made her suicide all the more, shall I say, problematic for me. You see, if you have faith, or had faith, like that woman, why would you kill yourself? But then that just makes it worse. She went from a living hell to a dead one. She must have had some courage in the end. That is, if she did kill herself. Well, poor Father Doherty, the last to see her alive and the first to see her dead. What drove her to it? Seems obvious, but was there any shame? Any guilt on her own part? There she was, surrounded by the evidence of her husband's DIY success. A newly plastered bathroom with a bath and walk-in shower and all her family photos left out by her. Then that bloody bomb. To get a couple of Provos, they murdered her husband. All with a papal blessing. Paul O'Driscoll the butcher. Butchered by those bastards.'

O'Driscoll was listening to all of this and watching the reaction of the terrified faces of those left in the bank while also watching Valberg and Commander Ruth Everett at the scene.

'Party time, Sidney. Get going. Time to see what Jon is made of.'

O'Driscoll's icy voice in his ear caused Rankin to shiver. He ordered the emotionally drained bank officials to leave.

Rothschild emerged from the bank first, slowly, with Harper. Rankin and Baxter followed. As he passed through the reception area, Baxter grabbed a small ornamental letter opener from a desk and hid it down by his side.

Outside, Rankin was shouting for Valberg.

'Mr Valberg, where are you?'

Valberg broke away from his safe position behind the police cordon and went straight to Rankin, who moved towards him. Baxter followed Rankin closely. Rankin was holding his hands up to the police marksmen in a plea not to shoot. Without warning, Baxter plunged the letter opener into Rankin's neck. Almost at once, a shot rang out which hit Baxter in the centre of his forehead. Baxter flew backwards while Rankin fell forward, bleeding all over Valberg. He bled over his clothes and his face and the blood soaked into Valberg's beard. Rankin barely managed to stay on his feet but only with the aid of Valberg's outstretched arms. Valberg gently eased him to the snow-covered ground. He could not stop the bleeding. Rankin held on, but as his heart was pumping, the blood was flowing like a shower from his neck.

'Valberg. Jon. I know you and you know me. You look different. Tell Gerry. He's listening and watching anyway. Tell Gerry he was wary of the wrong solicitor. Your da knew all along. Even before the trial, he knew who killed that poor wee child Orla Harkin. What a chance to get picked for jury service. What a mess. He's near. Get away. This might go up. He can trigger it. I'm just another Derryman taking his secrets to the grave. Best fuckin' place for them. Your father knew. He knew who killed Orla. I ... who ... killed Orla Harkin ... I ...'

Rankin pulled the War of Independence medal from his coat and threw it to one side. Valberg heard a click and then a hissing sound, a sound Valberg was familiar with. He looked at Rankin's blood steaming as it gently trickled onto the cold snow, finally not pumping anymore. Valberg scrambled to his feet and ran for cover. The crowd scattered in terror as someone shouted a warning. With that, Rankin combusted in a massive shroud of white-hot flames, obliterating any possible forensic or evidential material on him. Valberg dived to the ground. The light from the ferocious fireball lit up the surrounding area.

A dead solicitor and a dead banker for the next news bulletin.

***

Amid the chaos, no-one was sure yet who had fired the shot that killed Baxter. When it was confirmed over the police radio that there was no PSNI discharge everyone hunkered down, waiting, searching for the shooter. But within a few minutes, Commander Everett advised that the area was clear.

Despite this, Valberg continued to scan the scene and adjacent buildings for O'Driscoll. He used the snow to try and clean himself and his much-loved Canadian Army jacket. Now it was blood-stained forever. The snow, pure as it was, wasn't much use in washing the blood from his beard, either.

Linda and Michael had just arrived to update Valberg on all they could get out of Tommy Thompson. Valberg looked on as Linda went straight to Rothschild and asked him how they got out.

'He was just rambling on and on, staring into space. Then he just told us to leave. He never meant to kill us, did he? Poor wretch. Someone was shouting in his earpiece even as he was rambling. He seemed in control early on, but when he started going on about some woman killing herself, he lost it.'

Valberg continued to search for O'Driscoll, wondering at the same time if he could get his mother's funeral organised for Christmas Eve. After a while he walked up to Commander Everett, shook his head and said, 'I've some things to sort out. I'm leaving.'

Everett looked at Valberg in stunned silence as he walked away, still trying to clean himself. He got into his car and sped off.

'Where does he think he's going?' Everett asked DS Wilson.

'To bury his mother. She was found frozen to death in the cemetery this morning.'

CHAPTER 14

Josephine Mary Valberg's Christmas Eve funeral was a simple affair, the way she would have wanted it. It was confirmed by the pathologist who carried out the examination on her for the coroner that she had actually died on 22 December, the same date as her birthday. Valberg made sure she was buried before Christmas Day.

Many troubled individuals sat in the congregation, none more troubled than her only surviving son. His mother had requested he should read at her funeral – but only if he wanted to. And so Valberg did for his mother what he had done for his father – albeit with a sense of confusion and heartbreak.

'A Reading from The Revelation to John. The Final Judgement.

Then I saw a great white throne and the one who sits on it. Earth and heaven fled from his presence and were seen no more. And I saw the dead, great and small alike, standing before the throne. Books were opened and then another book was opened, the book of the living. The dead were judged according to what they had done, as recorded in the books. Then the sea gave up its dead. Death and the world of the dead also gave up the dead they held. And all were judged according to what they had done. Then death and the world of the dead were thrown into the lake of fire. Whoever did not have his name written in the book of the living was thrown into the lake of fire.'

Valberg could only remember one odd note that struck him about the funeral. It was just outside Long Tower Church when his mother's coffin was being placed in the hearse. He distinctly recalled Ian Haslette, who had been very upset throughout the service, trying to speak to Father Doherty. Father Doherty, clearly agitated, could be heard saying: 'This is neither the time nor the place, Ian. Not now. Later.'

CHAPTER 15

The bottle of Brunello was staring at Valberg. It was tempting him, but he wasn't in the mood for it. Alone in his parents' home, he felt he was in a house of secrets. Just like any other house in Derry. He knew if he started reflecting he would only be conducting an exercise in self-pity, and he wasn't in the mood for that, either. He was angry, agitated, restless, and not in the least interested in the joy of Christmas television. Or anything or anyone to do with Christmas, for that matter.

The Valberg family home still smelled of death. It still felt like a wake house to Valberg, but there was nowhere for him to go. He could recall now with ease all the people who had been at the wake. He could see the indentation the coffin trestles had made on the carpet floor and the remnants of flowers and wreaths not so gently handled and bundled into the back of the hearse by the undertakers. It was just business as usual for them. A few flowers and petals scattered here and there, Valberg thought, meant nothing to them. The hours of the wake were lost and gone forever, like any hour once it passes. Valberg felt he was rationalising a crime scene, putting all the pieces together of the last few days as he lived it. He had been on automatic pilot.

Absolutely determined to fight emotion and sad reflection, he was looking around the room and noticed the mobile phone he had bought his mother. He'd brought it in from her car and had forgotten about it. He lifted it up to check it, but the battery was dead and he threw it down again. He stared at it, feeling guilty that he wanted to check his

51

mother's calls. But it was just something to do. Something to investigate.

He decided to cut and shave his beard and freshen up, but on his way to the bathroom he found his mother's phone charger on the hallway table.

Curiosity got the better of him and it was another excuse not to clean and shave.

There were a number of unanswered calls dated from the fated day his mother had gone to the cemetery. Valberg dialled to retrieve the voicemails. The majority of the calls were from Ian Haslette in an extremely distressed state.

Valberg put the mobile on speakerphone, set it down and looked at it as he listened.

'Josie, Josie. I can't do this anymore. I can't live with it. I had to tell you this morning. I know it was difficult to hear, but I had to tell you. Sorry. I'm so sorry, Josie. Josie, call me. Let me explain about Lily. You never gave me a chance. I'll call round now before this bloody snow starts. I can't live with myself any longer. I just can't live with this. I'm haunted and damned, Josie.'

Four other messages were similar, but Haslette was getting more distressed. He was sobbing and crying and Valberg remembered his phone call to him to tell him his mother was dead and Haslette's peculiar behaviour at his mother's funeral Mass.

It was approaching midnight, almost Christmas Day. Valberg swore quietly to himself. 'Fuck. Fuck. Fuckin' fuck. What the fuck's all this about? *Blodigt hel* fuckin' *vete.*'

His concentration was broken by the sound of his own voice.

'Hey, Mum. Where are you? I'll be finished here at five, and no, just as I am speaking I am signalled away so I won't be finished at five. I'm good tomorrow after court in the morning and I'll be straight down. Okay? Call me or I'll try again later. Cheerio.'

Valberg didn't phone later or call down that night.

He fell onto his knees and hands and started growling like a monster and listened again to the messages from Ian Haslette and himself to his mother continuously. Anything would do to avoid shaving and Christmas, and to keep his mind focused.

This went on until three in the morning when his own mobile rang. Valberg could see it was Father Doherty calling.

'Hello. Hello? Father? Father, is that you?'

All Valberg could hear was heavy breathing.

'Father, Father? Are you okay there, Father?'

Then the line went dead.

Valberg, now glad he hadn't touched the Brunello, got straight into his car and drove to Long Tower Church. He wasn't sure the priest would be there, but it was the obvious first place to look.

In the rush to get out, he left both mobile phones and his personal-protection weapon behind him. Once again, PSNI protocol and procedure were ignored by Valberg.

CHAPTER 16

The season of good cheer was well underway now. The temperature showing in Valberg's car was minus five but it didn't stop two drunk young girls doing their best to show Derry everything they had to offer. Both were barely clothed. One screamed and then vomited onto the Strand Road, just yards from the police station.

Meanwhile, two separate fights were taking place. It had nothing to do with Valberg having to check on Father Doherty; he just ignored it all. What was his duty, he thought? Crimes were being carried out and as a policeman, off duty, should he stop and get out and help, assist and report? Was there a legal obligation on him or a moral one? Valberg thought about it for a few seconds. He didn't care. He drove on, listening to Jimi Hendrix's *All Along The Watchtower*, now realising he had forgotten his phone and gun. Traffic was moving carefully and slowly because of the weather and Christmas shoppers delivering seasonal presents. Valberg thought Derry might wake up to some good news and joy on Christmas Day.

He also searched for more music on the radio. It was reported with dismay that the recent cold snap of weather would change overnight and it was doubtful if it would snow for Christmas Day. However, flooding was a real possibility.

Valberg drove past the courthouse and turned right off Bishop Street down into Charlotte Street. Long Tower Church had cleared of Midnight Mass goers by now and the place was in darkness. He parked his car and walked stealthily down towards it. He knew Father Doherty had been saying Mass that night and would likely still be in the parochial house. He climbed over the gates to get inside the grounds and approached the house. The doors were all locked and everything was in darkness there, too. Valberg thought he was wasting his time, but just to be sure, he went to the front entrance, on the south side of the church, to try and get in from there. One of the doors was open and Valberg went in. It was extremely dark and only the outside lights shining in gave some visibility. He could not believe he was back where he had started his day.

Valberg heard the rumblings of thunder in the distance.

He knew by now that he had dealt with all this completely wrongly. He should have called Strand Road first to say what he was doing. He should have arranged for back-up and above all he should have organised, just to be safe, an ambulance. But it was Christmas and he did not want to cause a fuss. Once again, Valberg's procedurally improper conduct was going to land him in trouble. It would be a great end to a fantastic year, he thought.

Valberg's footsteps were loud and his voice echoed in the darkness. The atmosphere was strange, even in these early hours of Christmas Day.

'Father? Father? Father Doherty? Are you there, Father?'

The church was silent as Valberg walked closer towards the altar. His feet appeared to be sticking – and he suddenly realised he was walking on blood. He caught sight of two figures beside the altar and went to reach for his gun, immediately remembering he'd forgotten it.

'Fuck. Jesus.'

He approached rapidly and picked out Father Doherty collapsing on the ground. He fell facedown with his head to the side, gurgling through the blood that enveloped him.

Valberg got down on one knee to him immediately and took his right hand and held it firmly. Father Doherty had no strength but was trying to speak.

He whispered, 'Jon … trap … he's here.'

'Who's here, Father? I must get help. Let me go.'

Father Doherty took his hand away. He could hardly speak and was breathless but kept trying.

Valberg got down close to the marble floor his mother's

55

coffin had rested on earlier and put his ear close to Father Doherty's mouth. He could barely make out what he thought he was saying. He could make out 'killed' but couldn't understand anything else.

'Killed? Killed who? Who, Father?'

Then Father Doherty tried to speak again, but the words would not come out. He pulled his hand away and managed to sketch out an untidy circle in the blood leaving his body.

'O? Killed O? Father? Killed O? Is it Orla? Orla Harkin?'

Father Doherty moved his head weakly in the affirmative.

'Who killed Orla Harkin?'

Father Doherty tried to speak but could not. All he could do was a straight line in the blood before Valberg was knocked unconscious and fell over him.

Valberg was covered in someone else's blood again, for the second time in the space of a few days.

CHAPTER 17

When Valberg started to regain consciousness, he was still lying partially on top of Father Doherty, saturated in the priest's blood. He went to move, and as he tried to roll over on to his side, his neck felt tight. He put his hands up to his throat and felt a thick rope around his neck. He was staring straight at Father Doherty's clouding open eyes. The thunder was getting closer and the odd flash of lightning, which again still seemed far away, lit up the sky outside. Valberg tried as best he could to draw breath in and heard a familiar voice.

'Did you know he was an exorcist?' the voice asked.

Valberg moved the rope a little and could tell that the figure standing over him had loosened his grip slightly. Behind the figure was a huge cross up on the balcony of the church around which the rope was stretched. Valberg could not make out the face but knew the voice. It was familiar to him. And if it were not for the rope around his neck, he could have vomited in disgust.

'Grimestone. You fuckin' lowlife. What the fuck have you done now?'

'I've got your attention ... cunt.'

'You piece of shite. Go on, fuckin' kill me, too.'

'Listen, boy. You fuckin' listen good so you can think about all this while you burn in hell. The path this dead fucker took brought him face-to-face with evil. Another big Derry fuckin' secret. Our very own papal-appointed exorcist. And if it breaks on Radio Foyle or the *Derry Journal* that he was an exorcist, that's only half the story.'

'So fuckin' what. Big deal. Religion. Load of fuck.'

'If you move, Valberg, this rope will get tighter and you're gonna dangle up there behind me. What a great Christmas present for the dissidents in the morning. Our very own Chief Inspector Valberg of the not-so-great PSNI murders Father Fuckin' Pious Doherty and then hangs himself in shame. Lovely sight first thing on Christmas morning. And me, the last person you see. Couldn't make it up. All the trash cleaned. All those loose ends tied up.'

'Surrender yourself to the dissidents, then, if you're such a big shot, and tell them you raped a sixteen-year-old girl and her mother and see how you get on. Maybe their justice would be more convincing than the circus up the street. You fuckin' wretch.'

'Don't make me laugh, Valberg. Your naivety is, in a way, reassuring, I suppose. Will I tell you who sent me here and why my trial collapsed? I got out on the promise to kill you. Fuck, with friends like yours in the police, who needs enemies? And did he tell you about the confession dear old Mister Upstanding Member of the Legal Community made to him? And him a Prod. He sat in that confession box over there. Blubbering like a child. The child he killed. That paedo.'

'I have no idea what you're slabbering about. That's all you are and ever will be: a fuckin' slabber and a rapist. A coward, a murdering piece of shite and you should be burned alive. I'd pour petrol over you and light the fire. But fuck you and fuck me. Get this man help. Let me call an ambulance. Kill me then. I don't care what you do. Let's save this man. He's bleeding to death, in agony. Why? There's no need. Come on, Grimestone.'

'Ah-ah. Easy on the coward, now, Jon. Jon, Jonny boy. Happy Christmas. By the way, did you know Orla Harkin's little white coffin was just there? And your ma's? Where the exorcist is and you. Just this morning, and you up there telling us about the fires in hell. And which book will you be in? And him? The book of the living or the dead?'

'Go fuck yourself.'

'Up we go, Valberg.'

Grimestone pulled the rope back and the cross pivoting the rope rattled hard while Valberg was pulled up to his feet.

He tried to loosen the rope from around his neck but wasn't quick enough. Then he jumped up on the wooden seats beside him to try to slacken the rope that way, but Grimestone was in control and the more Valberg fought the worse it got for him. The cross was creaking and rattling and Valberg only had eyes for it as he tried to figure a way to escape. He jumped from the wooden seats to the steps leading to the altar. But that still wasn't high enough, so he had to get up on the altar table, gaining some relief. But Grimestone's grip was still too tight and Valberg knew he was just giving him enough slack to move and no more.

'Now, stop moving, Valberg, and listen. It's hopeless. No-one will save you. Or him. No-one. Sad, isn't it?'

Valberg was trying to draw breath again after all the movement. He looked down at Father Doherty's unmoving body and the emotion that he had been holding back was welling up inside him. He had no energy. He looked up at the cross being used for leverage by Grimestone, and it was tight against the balcony. Valberg thought if he could struggle more, perhaps the huge cross would dislodge itself and fall over and give him some chance – or break his neck. The rope seemed to be getting tighter and he was feeling weaker by the second.

'Why don't you just fuckin' shoot me, you bastard?'

'Naw, boy. They need you to get the blame for all this. They need your reputation in tatters. They need you disgraced and they—'

Then another familiar voice interrupted from the darkness in the south side of the church.

'Excuse me. Who's "they"? And please, gentlemen, your language in the house of the holy.'

The voice gave Valberg an adrenaline rush.

O'Driscoll.

Valberg was in familiar territory. The situation was, if it were possible, getting worse.

CHAPTER 18

'I hate rape – and I hate rapists. Especially you, Mister fuckin' Reaper.'

With that, O'Driscoll sprinted at top speed up the aisle of the church towards Grimestone and hurtled straight into him, knocking him out. But the rope was wrapped around the Reaper's right arm so when he was catapulted over rows of wooden seats, Valberg was pulled off the altar table and rendered semi-unconscious.

O'Driscoll tied the other end of the rope around the Reaper's neck and hauled him up with the slack available so that the Reaper's tiptoes were now precariously on the wooden seats. He slapped the Reaper on the face to bring him around. Grimestone and Valberg were now swinging like two pendulums from the cross, choking and gasping for air.

'Look at you two and the Lord Jesus up there on the cross as your only saviour. You might kill each other, if each of you struggles. Or I might save one of you ... and the man upstairs there on the cross? Well, he's moving, as he can't hold the weight of the two of you much longer.'

All dressed in black and with a mask on, O'Driscoll was menacing and now in control. The dark figure was walking towards Valberg. Just before he got close to the altar, O'Driscoll turned his back on Valberg and took off his mask to reveal his shaven head. O'Driscoll rubbed the left side of his face and touched a scar he had there. Then he pulled the mask back down over his face. He turned around and got closer to Valberg. With one leap, he was up on the altar, right at Valberg's face, and whispered, 'Forgive me, Jon. It has to be this way. I need to know what he knows. Sorry. Please find a way to forgive me.'

Valberg by now was as good as dead anyway. He could see the outline of a sharp knife, and suddenly he fell, like a rag doll, landing once again on Father Doherty and all his blood. But the tension was gone and the tightness around his neck vanished. He tried to take in large gasps of air but was certain he had been stabbed in the stomach and that breathing may be a waste of time. Valberg could not understand why he still felt alive.

He started to whisper: 'Who killed Orla? Orla, where are you? What happened? Finbar. Finbar. I remember.'

Valberg looked up at the altar and saw O'Driscoll pulling on the rope still delicately levered around the huge cross on the balcony while the Reaper was now struggling the way Valberg had been. But it was no good. Unconsciousness was looming and inevitable. The rats were coming. He couldn't stop it. They would be eating through his eyes soon. In fact, Valberg was certain a big rat was just waiting for him to pass out so it could come and begin gnawing at him.

A terrible thunderstorm had now settled over Derry. It was as if the seasons were in turmoil as lightning fired from the sky and lit up the inside of the church. The rain was going to wash away all the snow that had fallen; officially it would not be a white Christmas. It was a wet and dangerous one. Valberg knew he was about to slip into dreamland. He could still see O'Driscoll holding the rope and heard him say, 'That's all I need to know.'

Then the rats came in multitudes, running across the church floor and changing direction every time thunder and lightning struck.

The thud of the rain on the roof of the church was angry and loud, the wind now howling as well.

Valberg was convinced he was dying. He had lost all sense of time.

***

As Valberg was regaining consciousness, the sounds he heard were more fitting for a church: lots of talking and

61

some whispering; incessant footsteps. The storm had passed now and the rain had stopped and the wind eased. The first voice he could distinguish and face he recognised was Detective Sergeant Wilson.

'Jon, Jon? Can you hear me? This medic guy here wants to look at you. You have a serious cut on your head and we are just untying you. Jon? Can you hear me?'

'Father Doherty? Father Doherty?'

'Jon? Can you hear me?'

'Well, I smell you, Linda, for sure. Do you want to go out for dinner some night? I've always been meaning to ask you.'

'If you could see the state you're in. Perhaps you might want to shave, clean up, change your clothes and get your head seen to first. And I mean that. Before I take you seriously. I've never seen anything like it.'

'Barney Dunne. Remember him, Linda? Aye. Barney Dunne. I'll never forget him. He totalled five cars and miraculously injured no-one, including himself. That's how he survived. On his way home from shift work going down the Greenhaw Road. Fell asleep at the wheel and woke up when the ambulance crew came. They told him he was so relaxed, with no tension, he didn't injure himself.'

'You definitely banged your head. How on earth do you remember that now, and why?'

'He cut me from a height. I was almost unconscious. It saved me. It must have done. What a drop.'

Then Valberg could hear a police officer saying, 'How could it have happened? The angle. The timing. To get the top of the cross to come off that balcony, land clean on this scumbag's head and then fall back on him. Jesus killed him. What a magnificent achievement. Ace. Dynamite. Perfect. Crushed his head and he deserved it. Is this some sort of divine justice?'

As Valberg was being helped, he realised he had been tied up by O'Driscoll before he left to make it obvious he could not have killed the Reaper.

'How did you know to come here, Linda?'

'Someone used Father Doherty's phone, we presume. He was still alive when we got here.'

Valberg shuddered.

'What? He couldn't have been.'

'One of the ambulance crew spoke to him after seeing his eyes flicker.'

Valberg rose to his feet but collapsed. Linda helped him up again. The medic on the scene said Valberg should be going to hospital and he needed his head stitched.

'What did he say? What did he say? Father Doherty. What did he say?'

'I'll go talk to the ambulance woman later. She had to be taken to hospital. She broke down at the sight here when we all came in. She was down on her knees talking to him. I watched her. Then she went hysterical.'

'Derry hysterics – nothing like it. We have a big fuckin' problem, Linda. A big one, and everyone will ask why he didn't kill me.'

'And why not, Jon? Why didn't he kill you, and who are you talking about?'

'Is Father Doherty alive? Are you sure? I thought I was looking into his dead eyes.'

'Jon, I know you won't listen but you really need to go to the hospital. That's where Father Doherty is off to anyway. Just as you were waking up.'

'You need to get me to Father Doherty. Don't let him talk to anyone. He'll not live. It's not possible.'

'He was alive when he left here a few moments ago. Barely, but alive. Jesus, Jon, I'm only seeing now. Your neck under that awful beard. Look at you. We have to get you to the hospital.'

Valberg did not want to go near any hospital, but it would be a safe passage out and the quickest way to get to Father Doherty. He hated having to leave what he believed to be his crime scene. But things had changed again. All he was here was a witness and a victim. Someone to help police with their enquiries. Perhaps it was better to leave.

Valberg asked if Constable Bell was about. Linda confirmed he was just arriving from his home, having heard the news on the radio.

'Send him to me. I need someone who takes good notes. Some arsehole is going to be looking for a statement. O'Driscoll must have followed me. The Reaper wanted to kill me and tarnish me. But who put him up to it, Linda, and why? Something is rotten here on Christmas-bloody-Day. Anyway, are we still on for dinner?'

'Jon, you really took a bump to your head. Is this the new Jon Valberg? Because I'm not sure if I like you.'

'Well, did you like the old one?'

CHAPTER 19

Crowds had been arriving in their Christmas best for Mass since 7.30am. They were not expecting a fleet of ambulances and police vehicles to be surrounding the church. The bright yellow police tape confirmed the entirety of the Long Tower site was a crime scene with no entry.

Then the Derry rumours started, and quickly on the scene was Amanda Cleary from the *Derry Journal*, camera in hand, photographing everything and everyone. She lived nearby and got there immediately, having arranged in any event to go to early Mass with her daughter and mother.

She wanted Valberg. She knew he had to be here. This sort of situation had to involve him.

Uniformed police fought hard to keep everyone there calm. They had to get help from the bishop and any other priests who would come, many of them ashen faced and terrified on hearing the rumours doing the rounds, a select few in shock at the sight and desecration of a place of worship.

The inside of the church was like a battle zone. It was no longer a place of serenity and prayer. It was a crime scene, but one which Chief Superintendent David Kells allowed the Bishop of Derry, the Most Reverend Deasun Moore, and a handful of senior clergy to enter and pray over. It was a moving experience for all of those there. Everyone stopped what he or she was doing and any police officers that could, joined in the prayers. Everyone ceased moving, and all the forensic teams removed their white masks and hoods and stood either in silence or prayer. Valberg, still refusing to move, spotted the blonde hair of Abigail Burns and was pleased to see her. He took the opportunity to survey the scene and everyone there. He asked Linda to have the entire scene photographed, including all the spectators gathered.

'Get photographs of everyone. I mean everyone. Every priest, police officer, SOCO crew member and the public. I also want photographs of the photographers. Everything and everyone at this scene.'

There was a sense of doom. Word passed to all those outside that prayers were being said inside and all joined in, reciting the rosary. This was all captured for all the news bulletins going around the world. It was the last thing expected on Christmas morning.

Linda helped Valberg to his feet but she needed the medic, who was trying his best to treat Valberg, to hold him as well. There was a huge sense of respect for the bishop, and sympathy for him, as Valberg and most police there realised he was going out to face a bewildered public and a story-hungry media.

***

The bishop said his piece and finished by offering his prayers, and those of everyone, for the police in their work, asking 'God to guide them and protect them'. He asked everyone to pray for Father Doherty, whom he was going to see straight away.

'Not before me,' Valberg said. 'Linda, get me to the ambulance now and get me out of here. Before David Kells comes looking for me. Jesus, look at him. He looks like a rabbit caught in the headlights of an oil tanker.'

Just as Valberg was being helped away, the bishop called him.

'Mr Valberg. God bless you. Your mother loved it here but she is with the Lord now.'

'Thank you, Bishop. I am sorry about all this. I truly am. I, too, want to get to Father Doherty. He was more than a teacher to me. I held his hand, Bishop, but I can't believe he's still alive. He was badly cut. I'm sorry, perhaps I shouldn't have said that.'

'No, Jon. No. He was special to many people, and some were very special to him. You will get there before me, I am sure, as I must deal with our friends and people here. Tell him we are praying for him. He is in the Lord's hands.'

'Indeed, Bishop. I will. Thank you.'

'No, Jon. Thank you and for all that you do for this community. The police need people like you. And, Jon, you have nothing to fear from embracing the Lord Jesus Christ.'

Valberg stared back at Bishop Moore but didn't answer. He didn't know what to say. He was thinking about Father Doherty and his blood.

Linda sat in the ambulance but was saved by the arrival of Michael. On leaving, she said to Valberg, 'So polite, Jon. What bloody happened to you?'

'The Stations. Stations of the Cross. Go, Linda. Over at the altar on the corner. I've just remembered. I was thinking about the whole scene here. There's a camera. Right at the corner, or near it. See if it was working. Maybe we'll have better luck than earlier this year. Check it to make sure I wasn't dreaming. That's why he turned away from me when he took off his mask. Away from the camera. He knew it was there.'

'Right, Jon. Will do. Get to the hospital.'

The crowds were gathering now as word spread about what was supposed to have happened in the church. By now it was claimed Father Doherty was dead but that he had killed the Reaper first. With Valberg spotted being put into the back of an ambulance, covered in blood and obviously in pain, it was rumoured he had killed the Reaper in revenge as a result of the trial that had collapsed.

Valberg's final thought before the ambulance doors shut concerned Felicity White's reaction to all this. He knew she wanted justice, not vengeance. He was sure her daughter Diana would not have wanted this, either. Valberg truly believed that.

67

CHAPTER 20

'**B**loody hate hospitals. Have you ever been in one on Christmas Day, Michael?'

'Naw, never. I don't really like being in the back of an ambulance, either – if I can avoid it – any day.'

'I had to visit my dad one time on Christmas Day, early in the morning. I even got my photo taken with him. It was a strange one. Really strange. In the photo we both look happy and I look well. Fit and healthy. But far from it. I remember feeling particularly awful then. That's the past now.'

'Yes, sir. All gone. What do you want me to do over here? Uniform are already on their way.'

'If we get to Father Doherty and he's still alive, write down everything he says. And check out the paramedic, too, and get her story.'

'You want me to write down everything this time?'

'Yeah.'

'And then the medic? What medic?'

'She was the first to talk to him, then she fainted or went mad or something. Some sort of shock. I'm wondering what he said to her.'

'Okay. But what about you? You need that head stitched or looked at. You must have had some heavy concussion. Were you out long?'

'Long enough. Too long, it seems, to do any good.'

'Sir, I dare not ask. But was it O'Driscoll? Was he there? Is he back?'

'Michael, not now.' Valberg nodded towards the driver and the other medic trying to help in the back of the ambulance.

68

'Yes, I understand. It's just ... Linda was wondering ... understandably so.'

'I know.'

Michael's mobile rang. 'Sorry, sir. Can I take this? Speak of the devil.'

'Aye, go on. It might be important.'

Linda spoke to Michael. He listened intently, then handed his phone to Valberg.

'Hello, Linda. It's a yes, then. Dinner?'

'Jon, I've just had a call from Strand Road. There was a report of a disturbance and possibly a gunshot or gunfire at that solicitor's house in Talbot Park. Well, uniform went down and ... sorry, Jon ... Mr Haslette. I know he was your family solicitor. He's dead. Shot in the head. One bullet. I'll go there now. Jon, can you hear me there, Jon?'

'Sorry, Linda, I think I am dipping again. I can't believe it, but ...'

'What is it?'

All Valberg could hear in his head were the distraught words of Ian Haslette to his mother.

'Nothing. Leave it until later. What a Christmas this is turning into. Definitely shot? Not suicide?'

'Suicide? Why do you ask?'

'Leave it for now. I need to get to Father Doherty, and we're just arriving. Linda, can you leave everything as is until I get there? Once I'm finished at the hospital I'll be straight over.'

'I'll do my best, Jon, but you're not the only one in the police. Kells is on my back, and I think he's calling for help again from headquarters.'

'Do what you can. I'd like to see the place.'

Valberg looked at Michael and handed him back his phone.

'Another dead solicitor. Mr Haslette. Shot in the head. Jesus!'

Valberg rubbed his neck.

'You know what all this is, Michael?'

'What, sir?'

'Something that just can't be understood. It's a mad world getting madder. I wonder if I will live to see a remake of *It's*

69

a Mad, Mad, Mad World with an all-new Hollywood cast?'
'Yes, sir. Sorry about Mr Haslette, now. He was a good solicitor, I hear. A lot of police used him. A good man, I'm told. Sorry. That's terrible. It's been a hellish night.'
'It has. And he was a good friend to my father. They were very close. Like brothers, almost. We need to get to Father Doherty urgently. Time, as lawyers say, is of the essence.'

CHAPTER 21

Casualty was still in lockdown mode but quieter than they expected. A nurse and young doctor wearing a Santa Claus hat, anxious to help, were waiting for Valberg. Valberg decided to ignore the doctor wearing the hat and made eye contact only with the nurse.

Valberg told her he wanted, and needed, to get to Father Doherty first. The nurse looked at him and the state he was in.

'You really need that head seen to. Let us do our job.'

'Nurse, no disrespect, but where is Father Doherty? Please. Please let me do *my* job. This is a matter of life and death. My wellbeing can wait.'

'He's been taken into a room on his own, Inspector, at Intensive Care. The ICU. But he may have gone to theatre already. They worked on him in the ICU first. He was very loud. We had to try and calm him. He was upsetting everyone in Casualty, too. We just thought it would be more dignified. You never know with the media floating about. But what about you? Even if you sat in a wheelchair, I could patch you up on the way or clean your wound more at least. Look at your neck. It needs some treatment.'

'Just show me or take me to where I need to go. And I'm not going in a wheelchair.'

The nurse looked around her and said, 'I've enough witnesses here to prove I tried to treat you, Inspector. Come on. This way. I checked our system here. It's not the first bad bump on the head you've had this year. You were in here in May. I was on duty then, too.'

71

'Comes with the job,' said Valberg, shrugging his shoulders.

They made their way to Father Doherty. Valberg, as he limped along in obvious pain, asked if the priest had said anything on arrival.

'He was incoherent. No-one could understand him. But it was loud and unfortunately he let some bad language slip. Perhaps the trauma of what happened to him. Doctor Vail was here, down from paediatrics, and helped us to remove him. There was another priest, too. He arrived just after Father Doherty and helped get him settled and then left. The uniformed policemen who accompanied the ambulance let the priest go with him. But he arrived on his own.'

'Another priest? What did he look like?'

'Just the usual. All in black with the white collar. Tall. Fit and healthy looking. Very athletic-looking for a priest, if you know what I mean. About your age. Thick, black-rimmed glasses. He was, if I can say, sort of fashionable looking. Completely bald or shaven head. He spoke very softly and politely. He said you would be following on behind and gave me your details. In fact, they corresponded exactly with what Strand Road Police Station said even before the officers arrived with the ambulance. I knew you were a PSNI inspector anyway from all that stuff earlier this year. My sister knows of you as well. She's a trainee barrister. Julie Seymour. She'll be fully qualified soon.'

Valberg took in a deep breath and let it out slowly, looking intently now, almost with concern for the nurse as she continued.

'And that other priest had a scar on his left side. Left side of his face from his ear down. Looked like a bad fight earlier in his life.'

Valberg turned to Michael,

'Michael, get all the video footage you can from here after you're finished with the paramedic.'

'Here it is, Inspector. In here. I see Doctor Vail in there,' the nurse said.

Valberg recognised him but he didn't personally know him nor had he spoken to him in his life.

'Con Vail. Constantine Vail. It's you. But you were a

72

languages man. A year or two above me. You won all those prizes and scholarships. A doctor?'

'It's a long story. My wife is French, and a doctor. Met her in Paris and ended up back here. I work in paediatrics up above. But that's for later. Look at your head, man. You don't look well at all.'

'Don't worry about me, I'll be okay.'

'You need that seen to. Jon Valberg? You were in that big case earlier this year. I've been reading all about you lately.'

Everyone gathered around Father Doherty. Michael had his notebook at the ready.

'Look, how is he? Will he survive?' Valberg asked.

'He's lost a lot of blood but he's calm now. Anaesthetised. There's not much chance of him regaining consciousness until after the operation, if there is any point. He's out of here any second. The team is nearly ready. He's for the operating table for sure. It's strange. His bowel is lacerated, but I don't think the knife went into his organs. Definitely missed his liver. Even from my look at him there briefly. But whoever drove the knife in, twisted it and moved it, and really his stomach and intestines, I think, well ... it will be a miracle. It's a miracle that he has made it this long. And just one more thing. I'm only here because they thought he was speaking in French down below. I got a bit of what he was saying when I first got to Casualty. But also Arabic, Spanish, Italian, Latin and Hebrew. Perhaps some German, too. It was a mixture. I got the odd phrase or two. He never taught languages. It was just English, wasn't it? I have no memory of him teaching other languages.'

This made Valberg recall Grimestone's allegation that Father Doherty was an exorcist.

'What odd phrases, Con? Can you give me anything? Anything? This is important.'

Valberg turned to Michael.

'Write this all down, Michael. Everything.'

'Look, you probably need to know as well that perhaps the reason he is still alive is that he had some powdered morphine put over his wounds and adrenaline injected into him,' said Doctor Vail.

'You mean the ambulance crew saved him?'

73

'No. They told me at Casualty that that's the way the crew found him. Someone else treated him at the scene before the ambulance crew arrived. Whoever that was may have saved him, for a while anyway. But a huge amount of blood has been lost.'

'What did you get from him?'

'It didn't make any sense to me but I recognised Baudelaire, believe it or not,' said Doctor Vail.

'Beauda what?' Bell asked.

'French poet. I read all his stuff. My wife is fanatical about him,' Doctor Vail politely explained.

'What did he say?' asked Valberg.

'Well, only because I know the stuff so well – and I know this sounds bizarre in the extreme – but in clear and very well-spoken French, he quoted directly from *Destruction*.'

'*Les Fleurs du Mal*,' said Valberg.

'Then you know it. It was just a wee bit, but I knew it anyway, and my wife wouldn't forgive me if I forgot. He spoke the first verse just before he went unconscious. "Ceaselessly beside me the Demon writhes/He swarms around me like impalpable air/I swallow him and feel him burning my lungs/And filling them with an everlasting guilty desire." That was it. That's what he quoted. In the best French I've heard since my wife's.'

Valberg was stunned.

'Jesus! Baudelaire. That's one from left field for sure. A priest in Derry quoting Baudelaire.'

'The other priest left but I didn't really get talking to him. But, Jon, I thought I recognised him. Was he at our school, too? What's his name? Do you know? Nurse Seymour had a good look at him, too. I know within our years a lot joined the priesthood, but most of them dropped out – as far as I know. It was just strange seeing him. Who is he?'

Bell stopped writing and looked at Valberg, patiently waiting on his response so he could record it as he was ordered to do.

Valberg was saved by Father Doherty, who started to move and try to speak.

Doctor Vail moved towards him, absolutely astonished, and said, 'This is impossible. I've never seen anything like

74

it. He should be unconscious. Nurse Seymour, get the operating team. I think they're on their way anyway. But get them down and get him to theatre.'

Valberg was agitated. He didn't think he'd see Father Doherty again once he left the room.

'Father? Father? Father Doherty? Can you hear me, Father? Did he say anything? Father, can you hear me? Help me, Father. Help me.'

'Sorry, Jon, that's a waste of time. He doesn't hear a thing.'

Valberg knew it was now or never. He got down close to Father Doherty, avoiding everything plugged into him.

'Help me, Father.'

Father Doherty was trying to pull Valberg closer. Valberg looked at everyone else in the room and put his ear to the priest's mouth so only he could hear. Father Doherty whispered something in Valberg's ear but Michael could not pick it up. Whatever it was that Father Doherty said, it was just in time, as he was whisked out of the room to the operating theatre by a team of masked medical staff.

'What did he say, sir? What was it? What did he say?' Bell asked.

Valberg did not dare repeat what he had just heard. He knew that Father Doherty's reference to 'my son' wasn't a religious reference or phrase.

'My son saved me. Save him, Jon,' Father Doherty had whispered.

Doctor Vail was leaving to go back to the paediatric ward and said to Valberg, 'You really need to get your head and neck seen to, Jon. Let me examine you here now or we can get you to Casualty again. You're in an awful-looking state. I hope you got what you wanted from him.'

Valberg was staring at the wall.

Doctor Vail continued. 'Jon, I've got to get back to the kids' ward. Are you okay?'

Valberg snapped out of it.

'Sorry, Con. Thank you for your help. I'll not keep you back from the children. Not today. Thanks again. I really appreciate it. I'll go to Casualty if Nurse Seymour could take me down.'

'Sure. No problem. Take care of yourself.'

With that, Valberg shook the doctor's hand and got ready to leave.

'All these years, Con. Where do they go? I can see you in your school uniform in the distance. A black figure that I never knew until now. This is what introduces us to each other. Take care of yourself and, really, thank you so much.'

Valberg asked Nurse Seymour if there was a wheelchair about and said Michael could push it. He was feeling weak again and needed a rest and some Disprin.

'It's the only headache tablet I like,' Valberg explained to the nurse. 'My mother always gave it to me as a kid and, believe it or not, I liked the taste of it. Still do.'

CHAPTER 22

Valberg was patched up as best as possible and allowed Nurse Seymour to cut or shave most of his beard away. He needed time to gather his thoughts and reluctantly had allowed the nurse to do her job. He was bandaged around a large part of his neck, all cleaned now, and had to get a number of paper stitches on the side of his head. Thankfully, the wound did not go beyond his hairline, so none of his hair needed shaved. He had promised to return for a review and possible head scan just to be sure no other damage was done.

The stitching and bandaging finished, Valberg wasted no time and had uniformed officers take him straight to Talbot Park.

'Don't move anything,' he insisted. He walked in to see Ian Haslette's body sitting back on his chair with a bullet hole right in the centre of his forehead.

Valberg had left Michael at the hospital to take a statement from the paramedic who first treated Father Doherty. He sent him to do it while he was being treated at Casualty and that way, too, he wouldn't have to talk to Michael.

Linda Wilson and other senior PSNI officers, and the SOCO team who wanted to take charge of the scene, had waited long enough and had done what they could in the meantime.

Valberg had all sorts of questions. He met Abigail Burns busy at work as ever but now anxious to leave. He remembered a discussion they had when she complained about the myths perpetuated by the media and television dramas suggesting that a pathologist or scenes-of-crime officer could say with absolute certainty that a murder was caused by such-and-such and death definitely occurred at such-and-such a time. Abigail hadn't been certain but believed Valberg's mother had survived until her birthday on 22 December. The pathologist had confirmed it. But this time there was no doubt. A bullet to the head. It was obvious.

Haslette was positioned with his right hand on his desk and the other by his side. He was lying back on his chair as if he were just relaxing and staring at the ceiling. Valberg even thought that, although he was dead with a bullet through his brain, he looked strangely content. The blood which had dripped down the front of his face was dry now. Brain matter had exited the back of his head and onto the floor. He was in his office at the side of his house where he did all his legal work. By now, everything was photographed and filmed so the body could be removed. The white-suited forensic team were still checking what they could.

Valberg stood behind the body and looked around the room. He examined everything closely.

'Shot by someone at close enough range. Someone who knew him, it seems. Probably from where you're standing there, Linda. What do you think?' asked Valberg.

'It's too early to say, Jon, surely?'

'Well, surely if there had been an intruder he'd have been up on his feet? He was relaxed here. Look, he's got his house slippers on. And it's not a suicide.'

'No, Jon, not a suicide. But we got what was left of the bullet in the carpet and the casing was by the bin.'

'Sloppy, then. Not a pro. Opportunist, perhaps. What is it? No plastic bag around the gun to save the casing. It just falls here. Strange.'

'It looks like a bullet from a handgun for sure from what I've seen. Something small but deadly. We'll know later.'

'What was he reading or doing? What's on his desk?'

'More like, what's in this room and in his cabinets?' Linda replied. 'Are we not in danger of infringing some sort of client privilege? It belongs to the client, not the solicitor. It's legal professional privilege, isn't it?'

'No, Linda, it belongs to me now and I'm going to look at what I want before the Law Society weighs in. I had this before in a case. Yes, you're right, but no, I don't give a fuck.'

'Jon, we can't go poking through all his stuff now. Would we not need some sort of court order?'

'Do you think I'm waiting on that? No chance. I'm starting with his desk. Has anything been removed or touched?'

'Nothing, as far as I can see at the moment, Jon,' said Linda nervously.

Valberg looked at the desk while the body still looked at the ceiling, eyes wide open. Valberg noticed and gently shut the eyes. He wondered why no-one else had done this.

He asked for gloves and as he put them on he spotted his mother's will in a brown envelope with her name on the front. He did not feel guilty about removing the will from its envelope or reading it. He knew he was the main beneficiary – Haslette had already told him – but he was startled by his mother's reference to a secret trust. He didn't let his concern show but he did wonder if anyone else in the room had examined it. He carefully replaced the documents and continued his examination of Haslette's desk and the room in general.

'Jon, are you looking for anything in particular?' asked Linda.

Valberg would have preferred to be on his own. He looked through Linda and didn't answer her.

She tried to distract him again.

'Did you get anything from Father Doherty? I hear they're going to operate, but he has no chance.'

'Later, Linda. We'll talk all about it later. Look. His dominant hand is down. He was left-handed. And without a pen or a pencil in his hand or nearby. At his desk, working. Something is odd here, or something is missing. He's carefully put my mother's will to one side. Do you know if you damage or even stain a will it could invalidate it? Even a small tear on it can cause problems. This man would never make that blunder. He couldn't have been sitting at a blank desk. He's either put the will away or was just about to look at it. And no forced entry?'

'None, Jon. A neighbour heard the shot – and light footsteps, she claims.'

'Light footsteps?'

'That's what she said.'

'Someone nimble on their feet. And this was last night, too. Christmas Eve or early Christmas morning?'

'In the early hours, before we got you at the church.'

'Sitting up working or meeting someone at that time. Mad, isn't it?'

'What's not mad at the moment? I'm sick of all this, too, Jon. Fed up with it. Standing here on Christmas Day and it's nearly lunchtime.'

'Linda, a solicitor doesn't sit at his desk with nothing in front of him. Something has been taken. And check all his calls this evening or later today at least. A load of law books and Robert Bolt's *A Man For All Seasons*, that's all I see. No files. No paper, and my mother's will to one side. Carefully placed to avoid disaster.'

'He threw some letters and stuff in the bin. Some leaflets and a small ticket for something. There was a leaflet, too, about the National Trust. It's all bagged and tagged. We got it all sealed as well in case of any legal problems. Some letters were in there from another solicitor. Will we annoy him today?'

'You know what, Linda?'

'What? Tell me.'

'You're right. I've changed my mind. Let's annoy the Law Society and that other solicitor, too, on Christmas Day. The body can go. But before we start going through his office, let's see what the Chief Superintendent has to say and the Law Society. I'll touch nothing. Seal it all and nothing moves out of here except the body. He's got no children. His wife's family disowned him after she, ah, died, and his elderly brother, in his nineties I think, died in South Africa a few years back as well. He's got no relatives I know of.'

'I think the Chief Con knows someone very senior in the Law Society personally.'

'That's right, Linda. And she was on to him, if I am right, about Sidney Rankin as well and his office. What's his name? Let's have his Christmas dinner fucked. I'll phone the Chief Con. Leave that with me.'

'Jon, I dunno how many times I've asked you this, especially this last year, but are you okay?'

Valberg paused and rubbed his neck and head. He let out a sigh.

'Linda, I must confess.'

'Confess what?'

Valberg paused again and looked intently around the room, then said, 'The darker it gets, the brighter my mood becomes. I need to keep busy and my mind active. I'll go home now, as I've left everything there. I shouldn't say it, but what a happy Christmas. At least you have some life away from all this crap.'

'Jon, headquarters are going to insist on police protection for you. You can't stop it. It's inevitable. You know this, don't you? Don't ignore the reality of this, Jon.'

'Well, sure we can have that dinner surrounded by other policemen and women.'

'They'd only be doing their job.'

'Well, it is what it is. Whatever. I'll worry about it later, and someone here can take me home. You go home to your family, Linda.'

Haslette's next-door neighbour Veronica Cassidy called Valberg as he made his way to the police car.

'Mr Valberg. You came here as a boy with your father.'

'Mrs Cassidy. I remember you.'

'Look at you, son. Are you all right? That Mr Haslette was a good man. A real civil gentleman. Very private and quiet. He was lovely and he never really got over Lily, did he? Poor man. Who's doing this? What's going on? Can you tell me? Everyone is terrified again. And it's Christmas Day.'

Mrs Cassidy pointed up the street and said to Valberg, 'I told that wee girl in there, but I think the car was parked up there when she left.'

'She?' Valberg looked at Linda, who was talking to other police officers and taking off her protective gloves, getting ready to leave.

'Aw, aye, son. I only heard a woman go in and out. Definitely a woman. A man doesn't walk that way. Sure I told her. I rang nine-nine-nine right away. I was lying in my bed. I heard it all. Well, just the footsteps, the shot, and then the footsteps again, then the car leaving. She parked it facing the Culmore Road. Definitely.'

'How much time between the footsteps and the shot, Mrs Cassidy?'

'Twenty or thirty minutes, perhaps. I was awake all night. My son called and got all the presents for the grandchildren, then I went to bed. But I just lay there. My son cleaned the entire footpath outside from any slush still about and that's why I heard the footsteps. He was scared I'd slip. You know, there's a lot of to and fro with Mr Haslette. His clients call at all sorts of strange times. I'd know a police officer a mile away. Even without their uniform. Not like you, son. They look different. Or you look different. You don't look like a policeman. Anyway, all the to and fro, I got used to it. And poor Father Doherty. Is it true what I've heard on the news? Will he survive?'

'I hope so, Mrs Cassidy. Perhaps pray for him.'

'You know what, son? That's a lovely thing to say. And I will. And for you.'

CHAPTER 23

When Valberg got back to his parents' house, the mobile phones and his hand gun were still on the kitchen table. He lifted his mother's phone and listened again, over and over, to the messages left by Ian Haslette. Valberg was utterly confused.

He needed to change into some new clothes but all he could find was an old South Park T-shirt with the motif 'Hey, dude, this is pretty fucked up right here'. But he put it on anyway. Then he found an old dressing gown that had belonged to his father and put that on, too. He could smell his father from the gown.

Valberg looked at a picture of his father with his fishing gear on and spoke to him.

'What did you know, Dad? Tell me. What secrets are buried with you?'

Looking around his family home, Valberg caught sight of his father's copy of Seamus Heaney's *Human Chain*. The hardback edition fell open at page thirty-five; little surprise, as Valberg had been reading *A Herbal* for months.

He had read it so much he hardly needed to look at the book but did so for comfort, as he would always spot a new word or phrase that he hadn't picked up on before. He sat in his father's armchair and let Heaney's voice read to him calmly. He hadn't done this for ages. He had been reading all the new poems in his own voice in his head and sometimes out loud. It took almost six months to start to feel relaxed with this new wave of poetry. He placed no personal interpretation on any of it yet but took the odd phrase from his present favourite poem and had Heaney emphasise the bits he liked best.

Valberg read the poem, imagining Haslette's body being carefully removed for autopsy and on its way to the morgue before the practicalities of yet another funeral: 'Everywhere plants/Flourish among graves/Sinking their roots/In all the dynasties/Of the dead.'

Valberg knew he was going to have to provide his colleagues with the phone messages from Haslette to his mother. As he pondered over the messages again, he began to crave a drink. The bottle of Brunello red wine he had bought for his parents years ago was sitting unopened on the side cabinet. He locked all the doors in the house and began drinking directly from the bottle. He also found a cigar all the way from Puerto Vallarta in west Mexico, which his father had been keeping for a special occasion. It was huge. Valberg took it out of the wooden case it had rested in for years. He thought the scent from the cigar was just beautiful as he sniffed it with great pleasure.

As he drank and inhaled the delight of the cigar, perhaps his life, he thought, like O'Driscoll's and Father Doherty's, was a sham. Just a life of lies and subterfuge. All he did was bluff his way. He could only hold his stomach in for so long. Valberg felt Father Doherty's dying breath on his face. Worse than that, Valberg knew he was going to have to reveal how Father Doherty had confessed he was O'Driscoll's father. Valberg was physically and mentally at home – believe nothing, trust no-one.

He stared at the picture of his father and raised the bottle to him. He slugged some more red wine in a crude fashion, directly from the bottle, and smoked the cigar.

'How the fuck will he take this news? His mother had an affair with a priest; his real father wasn't blown up; his real father was a priest – and, it seems, a fucking exorcist. It all makes sense now, doesn't it? Sure it does. Happy fuckin' Christmas. No wonder Gerry can't shift that anger living inside of him.'

Before long, Valberg was sinking. Falling. Dropping to the bottom of a poisoned well. Headfirst into the dark mire. Down forever and ever. No return. Never into the light.

Never to see the day. Gone. Falling down into that bottomless, stinking pit. Unable, because of gravity, to turn around. Everything was downwards. It was like travelling headfirst to the centre of the earth or down into hell. Always falling down. Valberg wasn't sure if he was dreaming, hallucinating or just remembering.

Then Valberg heard a young Spanish female voice – the voice of a child.

'*Izquierda, derecha.* You see? You look. Hand. Look. *Izquierda, derecha.* It easy. *Entiendes?*'

Maria was laughing. She was teaching Valberg his right and left in Spanish. Valberg understood but pretended to get mixed up. Maria was laughing so hard.

'No. No. No. Look, see? *Izquierda, derecha.*'

But there was a monster coming and Maria was lost.

'My dream world, Maria,' said Valberg.

'It's a very scary place. Picasso's Minotaur is coming. Run to your mother. Maria. Maria. Minotaur is coming. It's alive.'

'No. Is okay. *Izquierda, derecha. Pistola.*'

'*Lo siento.* Always saying that. No. *Pistola?* Acts of the Apostles? You mean the Apostles?'

'No. *Pistola. Izquierda, derecha. Mesa.*'

'*Mesa?* Table?'

Valberg dipped again. This time he was burning. It was usually a sign his spiral was coming to an end. He still felt he was falling, though. He had difficulty breathing.

'*Si. Si. Izquierda, derecha. Pistola. Mesa.*'

But Valberg couldn't stop the tight downward spin. Whirling and turning. Down, down, deeper and down. Getting hotter. The only way to stop burning was to walk to the water.

He was walking into the sea and waiting for the seventh wave to take him out and down further. Someone told him the seventh wave was the biggest. He intended to test the theory. He wasn't going to fight. He wanted to get inside a diving bell. Straight to hell where he belonged. His life was worthless. He felt blinded. He felt ashamed. He was going to try and relax, just like Barney Dunne, and let the current take him. It was so relaxing and comfortable. Not a worry in the world now. Minotaur was going to kill and eat Maria. But there was nothing Valberg could do. Carolina had to save her own daughter. Carolina looked as if she could not save herself.

'Where's Pablo? Pablo, Pablo, stop the Minotaur. She's only a child.'

'*Izquierda, derecha. Pistola.* You check. *Asi. Izquierda, derecha. Adios.*'

Nothingness enveloped him.

CHAPTER 24

'Sir! Sir! Inspector! Sir! It's Michael. Are you in? Is everything okay?'

Valberg was lying unconscious behind the television in the main living room of his family home while Constable Bell was banging on the window trying to awaken him.

Valberg began to come around and took his time getting his bearings and steadying himself. He got to his feet and to the front door. All in slow motion. Years of experience of awakening after drinking and sleeping for a long time taught him to take his time. If he moved too fast he knew he would get light-headed and fall over. He would contribute further to the many physical injuries he already had. Valberg opened the front door and said to Michael, '*Izquierda, derecha.*'

He left the door open and Michael standing at it. He turned away and went straight to the kitchen table. He looked at his pistol. It had been moved. When he'd left it there on Christmas Eve, the firing direction had been towards the cream Aga cooker. Someone had lifted it and replaced it towards the back garden window. It had been pointing left and now it was pointing right. He hadn't noticed until now.

Valberg stared at it intently.

Michael held up a copy of the *Derry Journal* with a front-page article by Amanda Cleary entitled 'Return of the Saturn Killer'.

'Look at this, sir.'

Valberg did what he often did with Michael: he ignored him. He got down even closer to look at his pistol without touching it in front of Michael and began sniffing at it with his hands behind his back. The smell of his father was now replaced with the odour of a recently discharged weapon. As he did this, and without looking at him, Valberg asked Michael what day it was.

'Tuesday, sir, the twenty-seventh. This is the Tuesday edition. You're in it. Want to read it?'

'Surely Linda told you ages ago, Michael? No media, no press, no news, no TV, no radio, no comment. You know that, don't you?'

'Aye, she did, sir. But you better look at this.'

To allow one part of his mind to think about the movement of his recently fired weapon, and in an attempt not to be rude to Michael for a change, Valberg took the *Derry Journal* from him.

'Jesus, fuck, shite,' he said and shook his head.

Valberg read parts of Amanda Cleary's 'exclusive' out loud to demonstrate to Michael he really was reading it and not bluffing. Valberg had his vision steadied now and again focused on his pistol.

'Resurrection of the Saturn Killer ... The Public Inquiry no-one wants or will talk about ... Shocking scenes at Long Tower Church ... The Saturn Killer has returned like the snow ... Something is gripping and paralysing the city ... Calls mount for the police to confirm or deny that Gerard O'Driscoll is dead ... Who was taken from the River Foyle at Boom Hall last May ... The policeman at the centre of the investigation hailed as a hero ...'

'Well, what do you think, sir?'

Valberg paused. He looked at Michael and at the pistol again to get him to do the same.

When Michael finally looked, Valberg answered.

'Indian suttee or Japanese hari-kari. That's what I think, Michael.'

'Suicide, sir?'

'She may just have signed her death warrant. He'll not like this and all the details here. I don't think so anyway.'

'He, sir? It's him again, isn't it?'

'Do you know who Johnny Fean is, Michael?'

Michael sighed and shook his head.

'Sorry, sir. No.'

'I am hearing in my head the new acoustic version of *Trouble* by Horslips. It's simply brilliant, I can tell you. The song entered my thoughts the moment I walked into the kitchen and had a look at my pistol there. Anyway, Johnny Fean. Master guitarist. Unbelievable and modest. Just fantastic. Great singer, too, with Horslips. I must get you one of their CDs.'

'Okay, sir. I'm working through all those others. I like that *Moving Pictures* one. One of those Rush ones.'

'Yeah.' Valberg smiled wryly. 'One of those Rush ones.'

Back staring at the pistol but still now and again glancing at the *Derry Journal* in his hands, Valberg said, 'He won't stop. Everyone must die.'

'It's been quiet enough since Christmas Day, sir, but I assume you will want to go to Mr Haslette's funeral. They only had that other solicitor's funeral yesterday. Or buried what was left of him. Even his bones turned to ... the only thing that survived was some old medal.'

'Poor Sidney Rankin, and now poor Ian. I'm sick of funerals. I can't take any more. Just sick of them. It seems you reach a certain age when all you do is go to them.'

Valberg was drifting again but came back.

'I need to clean this house, or arrange to get it cleaned, and myself, and get back to some sort of normality. Is there anything else?'

'No, sir. I'm on my way to the station, but I thought I'd just call in and see how you are.'

Valberg glared hard at Michael.

'Well, sir, I can't lie. Linda asked me to call in. She knew you'd be here and not at your own place. The Chief wants to do a general talk or something about where we are at legally with everything and, I think, who is to do what. But it's all very stressful, this stuff, isn't it? I thought I'd be dealing with domestic disputes and petty crime. I think Linda has had enough. I hear she's put in for a transfer to the Historical Enquiries Team.'

'The what? The fucking HET?'

'Ah. Just heard one of the boys mention it. I'd never say. Only to you, sir. I didn't mean to ...'

Valberg shook his head. 'The HET? Linda? It's not happening. I need her. I don't think I could function without her. She's a fantastic officer. Over my dead fucking body before she goes to the HET. The HET. Fuck. Traffic Branch wouldn't have been as outrageous.'

Valberg was getting agitated.

'Sir, would this stuff in the *Journal* be prejudicial to any court case? I know you looked over some of it, but it's very detailed. Photographs of all the victims, diagrams, statements and plenty of opinion. Everything in real detail following on from her report in May with your dad's stuff. Them defence solicitor guys might complain. You know what they're like in court.'

'Michael, let me ask you a question.'

'Aye, sir, go ahead.'

'Do you really think Gerard O'Driscoll will let himself become the subject of another mockery of justice?'

'A trial?'

'Yes, Michael. Do you think he is going to surrender himself to the justice system – our justice system – or will we catch him?'

'I have to believe, sir. I don't have a choice. What if I don't believe? Where does that take me? I have to believe. I have to work to that end.'

'You mask your insight well, Michael. You sound like a modern-day Sir Thomas More. I used to believe. I was brought up with the same belief as you. Everything has a purpose. I used to believe in a lot of things. The search for truth and justice, the rule of law and equity. Sometimes it comes. It does. The walls come tumbling down and the truth comes marching out. But for me the damage is done. I accept you believe. Perhaps you should hold on to that as long as you can.'

'Aye. Jenny said something like that, too.'

'Jenny?'

'Jenny Hastings, sir.'

'Yes, oh, aye, I know now. Lovely-looking girl, Michael. Don't get too close to a policewoman, though. I see her about. Keep your distance. Sorry, Michael, that's none of my business. She is a lovely-looking girl and carries herself well as far as I can see. Very well.'

'Aye, she does that, sir. Aye, she's on another team.'

'But the truth, Michael.'

'Aye, sir, the truth. What about it?'

Valberg shook his head and raised his voice.

'Fuck the truth. Fuck it.'

Valberg had talked enough for one day. He wanted Michael to leave now and said he would see him at the station. He asked him to let everyone know he would be in.

On leaving, Michael asked, 'Where's this all going? Will he kill the tea ladies and anyone who brought sandwiches in for the jury?'

Valberg was staring at his pistol and the *Derry Journal* again and replied, 'Do you want me to answer that?'

Michael cleared his throat. 'Fair enough. See you in a while for the big chinwag at Strand Road.'

CHAPTER 25

Four-year-old Maya Sarah Cleary got everything she wanted from Santa Claus for Christmas. Peppa Pig stuff galore. Her home was steeped in it. Books, DVDs, toys and a costume. She loved nothing better than to live in the world of Peppa Pig, and it was safe and good. When Maya wasn't in the world of Peppa Pig, she was in the world of Angelina Ballerina.

Her mother adored and worshipped Maya. She would die for her, even kill for her. Maya was her universe. No-one would harm her. Amanda's life worked around her daughter's life. The way she worked for the *Derry Journal*, almost freelance, suited her. Today, she had some Derry celebrity status after being invited on Radio Foyle to talk about her investigative work on the Gerard O'Driscoll case. Then BBC Belfast picked it up and she was on there speaking as an authority on the case and the pending public inquiry, the terms of reference of which were still not agreed.

But every second Amanda spoke, she thought of Maya. She could see her as an angel singing '*Hallelujah, hallelujah, sing hallelujah, Christ is born today*' with her friends in Primary One.

Amanda was annoyed her iPhone didn't have enough battery life the day of the school Christmas play to record it all on the morning of 21 December. But she was sure one of the other parents would get a copy of their recording for her. The music and the words of the song were in Amanda's head together with the dance routine the children had confidently put on. Amanda thought it was beautiful and just thinking about it reduced her to tears. She loved Maya so very much.

Today, she promised Maya she would get her a Curious George DVD as soon as she was finished on the radio and even take her up to Foyleside shopping centre to buy it. She wasn't going out of her way to spoil Maya, it was just that Maya got a Curious George toy monkey from her grandmother for Christmas and Amanda thought it would be a good idea to get her a DVD. It would also have the added benefit of stopping the Peppa Pig theme tune being played a million times a day at home.

Amanda was in a rush and flustered. Unlike Gerard O'Driscoll, who was patiently waiting outside her house, watching Maya playing with her grandmother through the living-room window.

Amanda steered through the usual domestic commotion with polished ease: what Maya should wear, what toy to take in the car, if Maya needed to go to the toilet before she left, and remembering to kiss Nana bye-bye. O'Driscoll watched it all.

In the shop, Maya picked *A Night at the Zoo* for her first Curious George DVD. She couldn't wait to see the monkey on the television.

Amanda tried to rush through the shopping centre to make her way home. She had parked her car in a remote spot, the only space she could find. But before she got out, there was the public duty to sort out.

Plenty of friends, and people wishing Amanda well, met her and an overexcited Maya. The child was protection for Amanda. She stopped those they met talking about what was going on in Derry in any great detail. But the comments came.

'It's dreadful. Are we safe in our beds?'

'Heard you on the radio. Terrible stuff. Awful business. What next?'

'That was a great article. God bless, now. Take care.'

'Any word on Father Doherty?'

Amanda politely dealt with it all as best she could in the presence of her daughter, whose hand she held in a tyre-fitter's grip.

The exit door at last. Pressure off.

Hurrying back to the car park, Amanda felt a slight presence behind her. Nothing that gave her great concern, as there were plenty of other people about. But just something that left her a little uncomfortable. She wanted Maya safely strapped in her car and out of Foyleside.

She went to pay her parking ticket, which meant letting Maya's hand go. Again Amanda felt uncomfortable, almost nervous. The sense of foreboding was irrational but it was disturbing her.

Her car was in a really remote location on the top floor, all on its own. The walk to it seemed to take forever. But she eventually got there. With Maya safely strapped in – Peppa Pig in one hand and her new Curious George DVD in the other – Amanda was relieved. She hastily walked around to the driver's side and was about to open the door when a voice behind her said, 'Don't turn around. Don't move and don't make a sound. Look at the ground and stay calm.'

'Jesus. Jesus. Don't hurt her. I'm begging you. Maya. Maya. Don't hurt her. I'm not looking. I can't see you. She's only four. Don't hurt her. Her name is Maya, Maya.'

'That's great, Amanda. I know her name. No need to personalise. Well done. So, do you think I would harm a child? Do you?'

Amanda thought hard before she answered that question.

In the window of her car she could see the outline of the reflection of a tall, athletic man, wearing a black hoodie, standing only about eight feet behind her. This was a man whose presence induced fear. Amanda felt she was a different person. She felt a change come over her. The fear changed her. She thought she was feeling the fear all O'Driscoll's victims had before their demise. It was the end of her life. The east wing of the Foyleside car park seemed a peculiar place to die. She was sure she was going to face a horrible death in front of her daughter. The speculation she had written in the paper was one thing, but now she had insulted the man who was wrongly convicted for killing a child. Nothing she could say now could correct that insult. Life stopped for her in the presence of O'Driscoll. After all her research, all the gossip and rumours and media and police reports, this was it, the real deal. She wasn't safely in her study at home, with Maya fast asleep, writing comfortably and trawling the internet. She hadn't the safety of Seamus Heaney's poetry in her head or Gustav Valberg's pristine notes to look over and, with joy, decipher. This was death. Blackness. Nothing. Bleak and desolate. Lonely and violent.

The tears and the sobbing began – as if it mattered. She began shaking her head and talking into the ground.

'Sorry. No. Sorry.'

She felt her body go weak and her legs were starting to give way. But if she fainted or started screaming, her daughter was certain to die as well.

Amanda looked in on her daughter, who hadn't a care in the world as she sang away to herself.

Amanda started shaking, particularly her hands. She had never experienced fear like it. Any objectivity she had tried to convey about O'Driscoll was gone. In the eye of her own personal storm, she was a wreck. She was about to go under.

She waited for a gunshot to the back of her head, preparing herself for the thud. The strike and the darkness. All the normal sounds associated with a busy shopping-centre car park vanished. Everything stopped.

Then there was silence. She looked in again at her daughter, who was still singing. Amanda could no longer see O'Driscoll's reflection. Terrified, she slowly looked around. He was gone.

She immediately opened the back door of her car and hugged Maya tightly, cried into her, told her she loved her so much. Shaking and tearful and anxious to get away, Amanda could see an envelope and what looked like a memory pen in a clear packet on the ground where O'Driscoll had stood. Looking back again at Maya, she walked quickly to pick it up, realising as she grabbed it she had probably just contaminated important evidence.

She ran back to her car and sped out of Foyleside. Amanda frantically searched for her paid parking ticket and was going to crash through the barrier if she couldn't find it. But there it was, safely in her purse. With her hands shaking, she almost pushed the ticket into the console and roared at the barrier to open. It did. She pulled in immediately, right outside the tourist office, up on the pavement to call Valberg on his mobile. But her call went to message and Amanda knew that Valberg never listened to messages left for him. Nonetheless, she cried into the phone: 'He's alive. He's alive. He really is. He knows my daughter and me. Knows her name. What am I going to do? I've got to get her home to safety. Call me. Call me.'

Amanda couldn't stop crying now but started up her car again and rushed for home. As she drove, she opened O'Driscoll's envelope and pulled out a sheet with typescript. The top of the page read: 'Dedicated to the Pope and all those who think they can hide from me.'

Underneath that was written something that made no sense to her – 'Heautontimoroumenos'.

'What the fuck is that? A poem? Jesus Christ!'

Amanda tried to pronounce it as she read it but it was no good. She couldn't understand it. She was in danger of killing herself and her daughter as a result of her dangerous driving.

Then she spotted a message on her own phone, now sitting in the Bluetooth cradle. It was from Valberg, so she put it on speaker.

'Amanda, wherever you are, I hope all is well. Call me. Look, there's no easy way to say this, but your article has caused a bit of a stir here and some arseholes in here may be looking for you. But look, one more thing. Or a few more things I need to talk to you about in person. Not on the phone. Look, call me as soon as you get this message and I'll explain.'

Amanda just kept crying while Maya went on singing as usual, the theme tune from her favourite show.

'La la la la! La la la la la! Peppa Pig! Peppa Pig!'

CHAPTER 26

Valberg asked Linda to confirm who was still alive from O'Driscoll's trial. Michael was listening in.

'All the jurors are dead,' she told him. 'Including, we've just learned, Eoin McFlynn, the Sinn Féin councillor. He was the last one. He's been found dead outside Malaga Cathedral with a knife in his head and an arm missing. Still unaccounted for – the arm, that is.'

'Malaga? The Cathedral? *La Manquita*. The one-armed one?'

'We're just hearing about it, Jon.'

'Seriously? Malaga? A knife in the head in Malaga?'

'Yes, Jon, Malaga. I've spoken to the officer dealing with it, and the story is about to break. His family know. One less problem for us to deal with. But let's get ready for this meeting with the Chief Superintendent. We're about to be sacked, I fear. The Serious Crime Unit will be replacing us.'

'The Cathedral in Malaga? I know that city well.'

Linda continued. 'So, most of the witnesses are dead or missing and all the jurors are dead.'

Valberg turned away and was rubbing his head with his hands, lost in thought.

'Missing? What do you mean?'

Linda kept talking.

'Just let me recap and, Michael, tell me if I have anything wrong. Mickey Houston's wife said her husband read the *Derry Journal* article and got up in the middle of the night and just vanished. He was the poacher who contacted the police about Orla Harkin on the riverbank. The two fishermen from the boat who restrained O'Driscoll at the scene are dead. One from natural causes, we are told. The other man committed suicide recently. I'm getting it all checked out.'

'The councillor was dead before he died – if you know what I mean. We would have abandoned him anyway. No use anymore,' said Valberg.

'I've heard rumours he was going for a sex change,' said Michael.

Valberg looked at Michael dismissively. 'Was that a Derry rumour, a police rumour or evidence? What was it, Michael? Which one?'

'Jon, leave it,' said Linda.

'No, Michael, tell us. Where the fuck did you hear that and what use is it to us?'

'Sir, I just heard—'

Valberg wouldn't let Michael finish and talked over him.

'Go on, Linda, give us the facts. Let's stick to police investigation – not gossip.'

Linda continued, 'That leaves us with whoever is still alive from the trial. Most of the witnesses are dead. And all the jurors now, of course, with McFlynn the last in Malaga.'

'Well, who *is* alive from the trial now?' asked Valberg.

'We'll double-check today. But not many and, if so, they would be quite elderly.'

'No-one wants to die at the hands of O'Driscoll.'

'That's for sure,' said Linda.

'And you are sure about the recent deaths? You're checking everything? No stone left unturned and all that?'

'We're doing all we can, Jon,' confirmed Linda.

'Right. Something is going to give. I have a sense we are on the verge of something. The *Derry Journal* article is good and bad. It could be in contempt of court, or potentially.'

'More potentially, Jon, we've nothing before the court ... yet.'

'I think O'Driscoll will be annoyed. I really do. It's the calm before the storm.'

'This is the calm?'

'I know. I know. I know. Something is brewing against us.'

'Against us or you?'

'You've had enough, Linda, have you?'

'We're under-resourced, underpaid and about to have all this taken away from us. We can't handle it. And you know full well the Serious Crime Unit are all over this. You think a little CID unit operating out of Strand Road in Derry can run this? We're pawns here. Witnesses almost. Nothing. We need O'Driscoll to hand himself in. We're never going to get him. And just one other thing before I forget. The bullet that killed Baxter, the bank manager. Turns out it wasn't one of ours. It was from a different weapon. I mean, it wasn't a PSNI marksman's bullet. So, if it was O'Driscoll, we can add that on.'

'He might get an award for that one. Fucking bankers. Bastards.'

Linda laughed. 'You're back to your old self, then?'

But Valberg just sighed. 'I live here but I don't feel part of here. I'm not part of here ... am I? I am cut away. Almost living in a diving bell I dream a lot about, in some sort of trance. I can't explain it. It's strange, I know. My mood is up and down. Too many bumps on the head, Linda.'

'Jon, wake up. This is all Antrim- and Belfast-bound. The whole thing. We will be back to petty crime and thefts. Nickel-and-dime law as you always call it.'

'Or worse.'

Linda walked out of the room, leaving Valberg on his own looking at what was left of their notice boards and pictures, diagrams and photographs. But his mind was drifting to Malaga and the thought of the dead councillor with a knife in his head and a missing arm. Then he drifted to Carolina and her daughter Maria. He called her and just got her answering message. Perhaps she was with another client. He wanted to talk to her. He felt the need to hear her voice. He wouldn't leave a message but took solace in hearing her voice.

The Operations Room was strangely quiet. Valberg locked the door, knowing that he was in another now-or-never moment. Something had to give. Strand Road could not deal with all the deaths and murders. It was all so personal to Valberg. He didn't want to let anything go. He needed time. He was portrayed as some sort of hero in the *Derry Journal*, much to his embarrassment, but bore the paper or Amanda Cleary no ill will. She was the one journalist he respected as a result of the way she had sympathetically reported on the suicide and inquest of a poor homeless teenager Valberg had been trying to help.

Valberg could see the girl, Janice Sloan, sitting in the room now, swinging around on a chair with her arms visible and cut to pieces. She wouldn't look directly at Valberg. He closed his eyes and put his head back and was convinced Janice was examining all the documents, trying to help him while he thought of Carolina.

Valberg's thoughts drifted towards a policeman he felt sorry for – Francis Steen, better known to all as Frank N Steen. Francis had a nervous breakdown in what Valberg called 'the furnace'. This was the witness box in any courtroom. Francis stood up under cross-examination and started accusing everyone in the courtroom of being characters from a *Star Wars* movie, even the judge. This was a typical Valberg moment wherein something peculiar or strange and totally unconnected with what he was doing entered his thought processes. Valberg had a sudden urge that he wanted to speak with Francis. He had trusted him and helped him through his illness and early retirement from duty.

The Strand Road Station remained more quiet and peaceful than usual. Valberg, or Hans Solo as Francis called him that day of his meltdown, tried to call Carolina again. But there was no answer. Valberg listened to her voice message and hung up. He could still see in his mind's eye the spectacle of Francis losing it in court and Valberg trying to help him from the witness box while Francis was yelling at the trial judge, 'Master Fucking Yoda ...'

100

CHAPTER 27

At the newly refurbished front desk of the Strand Road PSNI Station, Norman Nesbitt was waiting on a cup of tea. His last 'bailer' for the day had just signed his sheet and left. No-one else was due. It was all calm now and he could relax for five or ten minutes before anyone else arrived at the public desk, usually bewildered at the new layout and the absence of any actual police officers. Today, it was civilian personnel who dealt with the public from behind a protective glass screen. It still involved shouting through it to any visitors, loud enough for everyone to hear the visitors' personal business.

Nesbitt sat there thinking about his indoor bowling club and how much he was looking forward to his match at the weekend when Constable Jenny Hastings, who was on her way out on duty, popped in to get the mobile phone she had left behind.

'Ah, Jenny, love. How are you? You left that here and I kept it for you. You're looking great as ever. You keeping well?'

'Aye, Norman, just on my way out – my sister's expecting.'

'That's great news, Jenny.'

'Aye. We're all over the moon. God, nothing like the news of a birth to cheer everyone up. I just got the call there now. I expect my phone will have a zillion texts and calls. I squealed out of me upstairs.'

'Great, Jenny. Give her my best wishes.'

'Ah, I will, Norman. I see you have a customer coming.'

'Aye. All my bailers are signed in for tonight, so no doubt

someone has had their cat stolen. You'd better go before you get caught.'

'Right, Norman. Thanks again for looking after my phone. Bye.'

'No problem, Jenny. Take care out there. Cheerio, love.'

Jenny switched her phone back on and sure enough all the text messages and phone calls from her sister and parents came flashing up and Jenny smiled. She was just about to turn around to say goodbye again to Nesbitt when she heard a calm, measured voice from the other side of the glass screen.

'My name is Gerard O'Driscoll. I would like to speak with Detective Chief Inspector Jon Valberg. I apologise in that I have no appointment. But I understand he is on duty and I would be obliged if you would call or page him for me.'

Jenny turned around and could see that Nesbitt was stunned and shaking. She noticed he had wet himself. His whole body was shaking. Jenny walked over to him and touched his arm.

'Norman, have the internal doors locked. Don't let anyone else in. Relax. Move away from the desk and go outside and get help. Do not sound any alarms. Get the station tight. And get someone to get Inspector Valberg and his team. Now go. Please, Norman.'

Nesbitt was petrified and speechless. He backed away from the figure on the other side of the glass screen who was all dressed in black. He could see that O'Driscoll's stare was now fixed on Jenny.

Jenny let Nesbitt out and moved forward. She could see her own reflection in the glass as it merged with O'Driscoll's body.

'Mr O'Driscoll, I will not ask for ID, but if you are Gerard O'Driscoll, and even if you are not, please step away from the glass window. Please move back and get on your knees and put your hands behind your head. Please, sir. Will you do that for me?'

O'Driscoll stared at Jenny, and both could hear all that was coming. There seemed to be a stampede outside and shouting and roaring.

'For you, Jenny, of course. You have nothing to fear. You are perfectly safe. I wouldn't harm you. If you want to, come through the side door there with your cuffs. When I'm on my knees, I will lower my hands and you can cuff me. That would be nice. I would like that.'

O'Driscoll stepped back and got on his knees in the middle of the room. Jenny entered the public area and cuffed him just as a horde of police officers rushed through the door. All the while Jenny was focused on O'Driscoll and he on her.

Jenny, who was the most junior officer present, assumed command: 'He must not be harmed in any way. He is on his knees now with his hands cuffed. He is not to be harmed.'

Valberg heard all the commotion and his first reaction was that there was a car bomb abandoned outside the station. He didn't care. When the banging on the door started, he thought he was just going to be told to evacuate. Then he thought that if Abba reformed with the original line-up, no-one would be able to afford the price of a ticket for the world tour. But he would get one somehow.

By now, Constable Bell was screaming for Valberg to open the door.

'Jesus, Jesus. Okay. Okay. Don't get hysterical. It's only a bomb. Jesus.'

Humming Abba's *Dancing Queen*, Valberg opened the door.

The young constable was breathless and terrified.

'Sir, he's here. O'Driscoll. At the public office. He's here, sir.'

Valberg pushed past Michael and rushed over to the public office. Every police officer was out and armed, and the police station was in lockdown. Sirens were sounding and officers were shouting.

Valberg arrived at the same time as a fully armed Tactical Support Unit. They would take over. Valberg knew that the public outside would have been unaware of the commotion inside the police station.

Jenny was still in the public waiting room ensuring no-one harmed O'Driscoll. Valberg thought Jenny had the look of someone hypnotised, not with fear, but with bewilderment.

Valberg, despite the huge armed police presence, drew his own weapon.

Here he was. The man Valberg had been chasing, kneeling on the ground now looking up at him.

Valberg could see that O'Driscoll appeared to have no concerns at all about the armed officers with all their weapons trained on him. This was all being filmed and recorded anyway. Valberg could see that, with the amount of weaponry trained on O'Driscoll, if everyone fired at once, O'Driscoll's body would be torn apart. Valberg had never experienced a situation like it in all his career. There should not be the slightest procedural hiccup here at all. Everything had to withstand anxious scrutiny, and O'Driscoll must not be harmed.

Valberg motioned to Constable Jenny Hastings to move back with him as he lowered his weapon. They watched as two helmeted officers entered the waiting area and secured O'Driscoll, who put up no resistance. He was completely compliant.

Valberg watched it all with Constable Hastings, then signalled Michael over to give her some assistance and take her away. Without looking at her, Valberg said, 'Well done, Constable. You acted with great courage there and didn't panic. Well done.'

He witnessed O'Driscoll being led away, surrounded by at least ten PSNI officers in an internal circle and twice as many more in another formation around them. There was no escape for O'Driscoll. He was marched to the custody suite through the courtyard in full view of all the other police officers watching as well. Valberg knew somebody would tip off the press and thought it would just be what O'Driscoll wanted.

Linda arrived on the scene, also stunned in disbelief.

'He'll have to be charged,' Linda said, almost reluctantly it seemed to Valberg. 'Now – so we can have some control.'

'Charge him with what and on what evidence? We don't have any. Arrest him, aye, but we need evidence. I'm fucking shocked and confused. We actually have him. He's about to be processed and in our custody. What happened? Come on, Linda, let's get organised. Time is, as ever, of the essence.'

Now Valberg had another problem. He knew there would be an attempt by senior command to have O'Driscoll moved to Antrim or Belfast. It was time to call the Chief Constable.

CHAPTER 28

O'Driscoll had to be processed properly and Valberg realised that it needed done quickly before the politics of this new era intervened. He knew that if he could get O'Driscoll started on a PACE interview then it would be more difficult to move him to Antrim or Belfast. If an issue over national security arose, or was created, O'Driscoll was definitely gone. He would be driven to Antrim and flown out to a secure location somewhere. Perhaps even to the same place the 'Pope' – as the disgraced former Chief Constable Seán Carlin was known – was secured. The thought of losing O'Driscoll was realistic and probable. But O'Driscoll had provided the best thing Valberg could have wished for – himself. Too good to be true, perhaps, but too good to miss.

Valberg said, 'Yasser Arafat, Linda. He never failed to fail to miss an opportunity. Let's not fuck this up. Make sure he is processed right. You do it – arrest him. You do it and do it right. But don't mention Detectives Montgomery and Dickey for the moment. Or even Avril Gibson. Keep it to the ordinary murders for the moment.'

'Sure. They're very ordinary indeed, Jon.'

'And when we get to interviews, he will try and split us, undermine us, ridicule us and lie to us. We won't know the truth from fantasy and you must not react. Maybe he doesn't either. I trust only you to do this right.'

'What about you, Jon? Will you be cool? If we get there, will you be cool? Don't you lose it.'

'I've lost enough this last while. I've nothing else to let go. He'll be dangerous, Linda. We do this really formally. By the book. Don't answer any of his questions. Stay in control. There will be no real structure to the way the interviews go. We will have to let him ramble if he talks at all. But stay calm, Linda. Don't react. This will be like no other PACE interview you have done before.'

'Jon, I get it, I think you've made your point. You go and get ready and see what you can do so we can hold him. I'll head for the custody suite and get everything ready, arrest him and get all the crap out of the way. Don't worry. Leave that with me. I hate procedure as much as you.'

'Make sure you over-emphasise the solicitor bit and make a good record of it. Make sure he studies the list of the local great and good. Let him take his time or mention someone else. We're going to get into trouble for starting the interviews at all, but I'll take the rap for that. I think I can throw back all the security issues, making the case it is safer to keep him here first of all, and the Chief Con will back me.'

'I'm sure she will.'

'We'll have him for a while. Charge him with something. Even just one of the murders and the rest later. But remember, leave Montgomery and Dickey and Gibson out of it for now. We need more than O'Driscoll himself.'

'You mean a confession? What about what he said on the bridge, if it was him, last May?'

'It's not enough. We need more. I fucking hate doing a verbal on anyone – even him. I hate the "he said, she said, in my presence" stories. We need more.'

'Jon, he won't confess. You don't think that, do you?'

'I want you or the custody sergeant to call me up in the Operations Room when he's all processed and ready for interview. Leave the fixing of everything else to me. You tell the custody sergeant me and you will be interviewing him, and you will be arresting him for all the murders we know of. He's hardly a real voluntary attender, free to leave at any time.'

'I've got that, too, Jon. Jesus. Anything else?'

'Don't talk to him during the processing. Keep your guard up. He'll sense fear. You might even feel like strangling him yourself, but don't.'

'Right, Jon, got it. You go make your calls and we'll buzz you when ready. I'll ask him, too, if he wants any medical treatment. Look, I may have to agree with the custody sergeant that he is fit for interview. That could take time. What if someone asks me if he's insane? I'll not go there. I hear you. Leave it. Did you notice the scar on the left of his face, just below his ear towards his mouth?'

'Aye, I did. It looks nasty. He's shaved his head. Not bald. Easy for disguise and moving about. Aye, the scar. Perhaps I'll ask him about it. Look, one other thing. We'll have security around us like nothing before. I'll try and negotiate the clear-out of the custody suite to leave nothing but an armed Tactical Support Team. Armed to the fucking teeth. Strand Road will have to go into shutdown. We'll get away with that for a day. Or two at the most. So we need to move fast but carefully at interview. Just don't lose it, Linda.'

'If you say that to me one more time, Jon, I'm cancelling our dinner date. I get it. I'm off now. Go and make your calls.'

'Look. Also don't wait for the tapes to stop. I mean we are in the Stone Age here with analogue tape-recorded interviews. Don't wait on that noise all the time. Mix it up. Do some at forty-five minutes but don't be afraid to go shorter and try to break up his thinking.'

'Right. Okay.'

'Sorry. One last thing. Very last, I promise. I want you to watch and tell me what he gives, if anything, of his personal possessions to the custody sergeant. Anything at all, even a pen or paper. Tell me – and where it goes as well.'

'Okay, I will. I better go now.'

Valberg was still stunned and confused but he liked this state of being. There was nothing like a dark drama to cheer him up. As soon as the word was out O'Driscoll was in captivity the media would go wild. The families of O'Driscoll's victims would be getting their make-up on, ready to be interviewed by television, the printed press and radio demanding justice. Valberg could see social-network sites starting their own illegal process, which was impossible to control. O'Driscoll had to be protected. Valberg could see the spectacle of a court appearance in Bishop Street. The glorious public now demanding that contrary thing – the truth. For Valberg, the truth was too good to be true. Yes, thought Valberg, believe nothing, trust no-one. Fuck the truth.

CHAPTER 29

'This is being tape-recorded. It is being conducted in an interview room, er, ah, interview room number one, at Strand Road Police Station. Ah, Strand Road, Derry. I am Detective Sergeant Linda Wilson from CID and the other officer present is ...'

Valberg paused. This could all be a colossal waste of time. The silence in the small, cramped room was eerie. Valberg thought O'Driscoll was out of place. Especially in his white suit, courtesy of the PSNI, as all his clothes and belongings had been taken from him. What was the point in all of this? Where was it going? Valberg looked at the two armed officers in the room, neither of whom he recognised. O'Driscoll wasn't going to help. He was here to tease and fool everyone. He was in from the cold and back in the interview room in which he previously had said nothing but 'no comment' for days. On the advice of his solicitor in 1982.

With reluctance, Valberg spoke for the purposes of the tape.

'My name is Jon Valberg. I am a Detective Chief Inspector, also from CID.'

Valberg and O'Driscoll stared at each other.

'Okay,' continued Linda. 'The date is the twenty-eighth day of December, two thousand and eleven, and the time from the interview room clock here is twenty-one twelve.'

O'Driscoll smirked and looked at Valberg. The armed officers momentarily shifted their positions.

'Sorry. And the other person in the room here is ... State your name and your age, please, just for the tape.'

'Gerard O'Driscoll. That's my birth name anyway. I'm definitely over twenty-one as well.'

'Okay, Mr O'Driscoll. And sorry, just for the purposes of the tape, we also have in the room, with your consent, Mr O'Driscoll, two male officers from our Tactical Support Unit who are armed, and you do not object to this?'

'Oh, not at all. They are very welcome, Linda. Just like the dozens, at least, outside this room. And for that matter all the police and army now descending on Derry. I may have brought the British Army back to Derry. It's nineteen sixty-nine all over again. Anyway, everyone is very welcome. I would not object in the slightest. Very welcome. And I do not need any medical treatment, nor am I medicated. I declined examination by a doctor but if you want me examined, I will not object.'

'Right, then. And, Mr O'Driscoll, at the moment there's no-one else with you? You're unaccompanied at the present time?'

'Well, you're here, Linda. And Jon. And, of course, welcome to everyone listening in. This room is bugged, isn't it?'

'In compliance with procedure, this interview is recorded. Just for the purposes of the tape, am I correct in saying that at this time you do not wish to have a solicitor?'

'That's right, Linda. A solicitor? We'll not go into all that again. Not for now anyway. The last time I was in this room my experience with my solicitor was not pleasant. So don't worry, everyone. I waive my human right to have a solicitor present. I looked at the list of the solicitors available to me – very kindly provided by the custody sergeant – and no. The answer is a definite no.'

'Right, well then, you voluntarily attended the police station here earlier this evening at around seven o'clock and, in summary, you were then arrested by myself for the offence of murder. Well, a number of murders. The murders of William Bolton Black, Patrick James Sharkey, Majella Ann McLaughlin, and Samuel Hamilton Carson. You were cautioned at that time when I arrested you. I'll just remind you of that caution. "You do not have to say anything, but I must caution that if you do not mention when questioned something which you later rely on in court it may harm your

109

defence. If you do say anything it may be given in evidence."
Do you understand that okay?'

'I do, Linda. Well done. And we don't have to worry about
the Terrorism Act even. Well done. Hopefully, you can
keep me here in sweet old Derry for a while, then. Or as
long as Jon keeps his cool and sorts it with Anna professionally. I hope the man at the desk is okay, as he looked
somewhat perturbed. I apologise for any inconvenience to
him. Or embarrassment. And I want to commend the young
officer, Miss Hastings, for her grace under pressure, especially since the Chief Constable is not far away either and
is hearing all this. Excellent work. Miss Hastings is about
to become another Derry celebrity. Just like you, Jon. Now
the hard part is over. We have all that tedious processing
over. Nice one, Jon. You ducked out of that. Well done. The
rest is easy now. Relax, Linda. I'm sure your father would
be very proud of you. Do you miss him? Another botched
investigation. And him a policeman, too. There wasn't even
an inquest or a trial. The guys who did that. Jeez. Amateurs
dot com. Idiots. Terrible.'

Linda did what Valberg told her. She ignored O'Driscoll's
attempts to engage with him.

The tape machine squeaked a little. Valberg looked intently at the man who gave him the run-around. Now that
he was in captivity, Valberg felt deflated. The chase was better than the catch or in this case, voluntary surrender.

'Anything for me, Jon? Anything at all?'

Valberg looked down, sighed and said 'Tell me about prison. Tell me about custody. What happened, Gerard? Nineteen eighty-two. What happened to you?'

'That's three. Three questions. Smart one. We'll be all
holding hands next around the table here and talking about
truth and reconciliation. Well, if I could be released from
these cuffs. Is that possible, Jon? I promise I'll behave. What
if some smart-arsed, low-life solicitor challenges the basis
of this interview? Well, if I need one that is. Me cuffed with
guns to my head wearing a white all-in-one suit here. Not
very stylish, is it?'

Linda interjected. 'Just for the purposes of the tape, the
guards that are here, with your consent, Mr O'Driscoll, are

indeed armed but they are not pointing any guns to the head of Mr O'Driscoll. Their weapons remain in their holsters ...'

O'Driscoll laughed. 'Holsters? That sounds like something from the Wild West. Or I suppose the Wild North West. Pouch might be a more neutral term. Yes, I agree with that assessment – for the purposes of the tape. I was speaking metaphorically, of course. Well, looks like a "no" to the cuffs, then?'

Valberg knew to let O'Driscoll ramble on. He was going nowhere. Eventually, some psychiatrist would be listening to the entirety of all the taped interviews and weighing up O'Driscoll from a prosecution and defence point of view. Or, thought Valberg, MI5 and MI6 would also be listening in.

The decision by Valberg to ask about O'Driscoll's first captivity was just a gamble to see if O'Driscoll would talk. Valberg believed he could go back even further with O'Driscoll, if O'Driscoll would let him. O'Driscoll could easily refuse to answer any of this. Of all the people in the room, Valberg was of the view that it was O'Driscoll who understood and knew the most about the Police and Criminal Evidence Act and even more about the procedures to be adopted at any PACE interview. But the gamble paid off. O'Driscoll relaxed himself as best he could and stared at Valberg.

'Let me tell you about my first night in prison, in a holding cell with Raymond Grimestone. The "Reaper" as you knew him. Raymond the Reaper. The mad sheep eater. Yes, my first night on remand.'

'Go on, tell us everything, Gerard,' Valberg replied as he nodded his head in encouragement.

Linda interrupted. 'Just for the purposes of the tape. Sorry about this. It's, er, ah, five murders. Raymond Grimestone. I cautioned you in relation to his murder also. Otherwise known as Raymond the Reaper.'

Silence descended again. The tape machine squeaked again. O'Driscoll stretched his neck and shoulders. Linda looked at the panic button in the cramped interview room. Valberg stared intently at O'Driscoll and waited for him to talk again.

O'Driscoll closed his eyes and put his head slightly back.

'I've thought about this a lot. But not talked about it. Us

Irish are beyond therapy. You're a sort of Swede in Ireland, Jon. Beyond therapy mumbo jumbo, too, I bet. Anyway, let's talk. I told him I was mad. Grimestone, that is. Thinking that I would scare him. I was put in this holding cell on purpose with him. I know that now. I had been crying and whimpering. Calling for my mother. Calling "Daddy". But no-one came. I sensed someone in the dimly lit cell. It hadn't any windows. I thought my best defence was to play mad. Easy enough. His eyes were black. Dead eyes. No life, compassion, soul or feeling. He came close enough for me to see them. Not dark brown – black. And he had this horrible smell. The smell of evil. That's the first thought I had. It was the devil. I was in a locked cell with the devil. Definitely. Well, he told me that if I thought I was mad, then he was madder than mad. Then he moved away. All he said was, "You think you're mad?" Then he pulled his trousers down and started groaning. I'd no idea what he was doing. He sounded in pain and I thought he was pleasuring himself. I couldn't see. And if I am honest, I was terrified. Absolutely petrified. Real fear. Not just being scared. Fear. I was sweating it. And, Linda, do you know what he was doing and what he did?'

'No, Mr O'Driscoll, I don't. Tell us.'

Valberg kept his stare on O'Driscoll just before he lowered his head and sighed. O'Driscoll looked straight at Linda.

'He was extracting a screwdriver from his back passage. It was up his ass and he was forcing it out. And he was pleasuring himself at the same time. One hand doing one thing and the other doing another thing. I think you have the image. I backed away. Rolled myself up into a ball. I did that childish thing. I closed my eyes and covered my head in the hope it would all go away. Then I could smell him again. I could smell his sperm and the disgusting odour of his screwdriver now on the side of my neck, resting on my jugular vein. And you know what he said? He told me he ate sheep. Ate them raw. He backed away. Aye, for some reason he almost seemed to jerk backwards away from me. I thought I scared him. He seemed relaxed now after what he had just done. But I could still smell him. Then I remembered there had been stories of a fox or stray dog on the loose in County Derry around that time attacking sheep. But naw, it was him. He cut them open and drank their blood and ate their intestines. You know he used to collect their blood and spray it about? He was totally mad and I began to feel sorry for him. He told me he would escape. And he did. Eventually. He told me what would happen to me in prison. As I was a kiddie-fiddler and a child rapist and murderer. All nonsense as we now know, Jon, don't we?'

'We can deal with that later, if you wish. So, I suppose the question is, if *you* didn't kill Orla Harkin, who did?' asked Valberg.

'I would rather leave that for now. I'm not dodging the bullet. I'm just not taking it now.'

O'Driscoll directed that answer at Linda then asked for a cup of tea.

'And, please, no truth syrup in it. I don't need it. I tell the truth for free now. And on my guess, that tape machine is about to make a noise and switch itself off soon.'

'No, I think we're okay for a wee while yet, Gerard,' said Valberg. 'Do you mind if we continue? We'll leave Orla for now. So that was your first night in prison as a convicted killer. No, sorry, Gerard. On remand. Just as a remand prisoner.'

'A remand prisoner like poor Janice Sloan and so many other poor souls. Your father, Jon. Jon, look at me. Your father, Jon. Are you looking at me or through me? Has your training allowed you to switch off? Or perhaps you are looking through me at someone else. Do you imagine seeing other people? The dead, perhaps? Is there someone on the chair in the corner behind me, Jon?'

'Okay. My father. What about him?'

'Do you miss him?'

'Gerard, *we're* asking the questions. Will you please kindly answer them. Help us. Now, what about my father?'

'Well, it's complicated and evidentially not much use.'

'What's not much use?'

'Hearsay.'

'Well, there are exceptions to the hearsay rule. Just tell us. Let us worry about the evidential weight later.'

'I've jumped the gun. Run away a bit, Jon. Sorry. It's just that I always remembered the look on your father's face. Gustav Valberg. What a man. Good old Gustav. The look on your father's face when Billy Black read out the verdict. Of course, he knew it was coming. All the other jurors looked at me on the way to their seats. Your father was ashamed. He didn't look at me. He was very upset. But his shame was deep. Really deep. It was as if he knew who killed that poor little girl. Not just that he didn't agree with the verdict. It was obvious to everyone he was the dissenter. Why, Jon? Why? Did you think about all that over the last while? What do you think, Linda?'

'I think we will pause now and turn off the tape and get you a cup of tea. The time is twenty-two ... oh, sorry, 10.00pm exactly,' said Linda.

With that, Linda turned around and switched off the recorder and pulled the tapes out of the machine.

Linda put the two tapes down on the table and said, 'Pick one. Left or right.'

'What do you think, Jon? *Derecha* or *izquierda*? Or you, Linda? Pointing left or pointing right?'

'It's your choice, Mr O'Driscoll. One will be the master tape.'

'I'm leaning left. Towards Jon. The left one.'

Valberg said he would sort out all the paperwork with the first tape and Linda left to fetch some tea for O'Driscoll.

All the while Linda was gone O'Driscoll did not speak. Valberg continued as if O'Driscoll wasn't in the room with the two armed guards. He meticulously completed all the paperwork in relation to the tapes and ignored everyone. Valberg knew this was usually the job of the more junior officer and not something he would normally do. But he carried out his task deliberately and in silence. He ignored O'Driscoll, who was staring at him, and now and then also glanced at the two armed officers and their weapons. Then he asked O'Driscoll if he needed anything.

'Well, I was thinking of asking the custody sergeant for a small mat, a copy of the Koran, a metal bowl, some water and confirmation of an easterly direction. But don't worry, I didn't want to cause a fuss. Tea will be fine.'

'East is behind you. In this room your back is to the Waterside. If you want a Koran I will get you one. And the mat and the bowl – if you want.'

'Praise Allah.'

Linda came back with tea and a new set of tapes. Valberg seized the chance to speak to O'Driscoll before the tape machine could be switched on again: 'You're fucking me about, aren't you?'

'Are you ready, Jon? Ready to hear about your father? My father, too? There's a mystery I only just found out about. Ready? Sure? This will be difficult. For you and me. That's why I'm really here. That *Derry Journal* article intrigued me. All this stuff I've recently found out. Are you ready to hear about Orla? Is justice and truth really worth waiting on? Is it, Jon? The truth. Is it worth all the bother? Why are we so fucking obsessed with it? I'll tell you what happened as far as I can work it out now. But perhaps you might have a question for me in relation to what I was arrested for instead of the stink of cover-up and distortion. Hey-ho, here we go. It's nineteen eighty-two and you are looking out of your bedroom window in the lashing rain. Your dad's buddy has something in the boot of his car and he and your dad are staring at it. You probably went back to your homework.'

Linda placed two tapes into the recorder, started it going, and reminded O'Driscoll he was still under caution.

'So no tea for the interviewee, Linda?' O'Driscoll smirked.

Linda ignored O'Driscoll apart from to say: 'Hear you are, then. No sugar and a little milk.'

After he had taken a few sips, she reminded him of the wording of the caution and asked him to continue.

CHAPTER 30

'Jon, this is going to be difficult and littered with hearsay. But I'm presenting to you all I know now from speaking with everyone. And I mean everyone. Even my so-called legal representative from nineteen eighty-two. So I am asking you again: are you ready? And this jury thing. Is it conjecture? Or worse than that, just the gossip of lawyers? Jesus, lawyers do some gossiping. They love to talk about their own big cases and gloat. Is it true that the jury usually give you a good look and maybe a small grin or smile when they come to acquit you? Or is that a Derry rumour or urban legend? But not my jury, anyway. Your dad was the only one to show any real shame.'

'Look, Gerard, enough of the questions, it's answers we want. So speak freely and don't worry about the rules of evidence. Tell us what you know. Then we will evaluate it and see if it helps us – legally or evidentially.'

O'Driscoll leaned over and sipped some more tea.

'Have you ever heard *Lacrimosa*? Derry's theme tune. Weeping. When I came here last I merely planted the seeds of the flowers of evil. All pleasure lies in evil, Jon. I would have saved her for you. Your mother. I am so sorry. I was otherwise engaged in consultation with my old legal advisor that evening. He was very helpful. I couldn't help you. At least you got to her funeral. I, sadly, did not get to the funeral of my own beloved mother.'

'Gerard, we have to get on. Speak freely. We won't interrupt you. In another life, perhaps, we could drink wine and talk about dead French poets into the wee hours of the

116

morning. But not now, Gerard. Can we move on? Please?'

'Sure, Jon. We seldom get to talk. Not just you and me. Everyone. There's always an idiot with a cell phone in a rush. Always rushing and diving to try and beat the brutal dictator. Time dictates all.'

'Nineteen eighty-two, Gerard. What do you want to tell us? Just what you know, without any comment.'

O'Driscoll leaned over and sipped more tea while the tape machine squeaked again. He loosened up his shoulders and his neck as best he could while his hands remained cuffed and his chair chained to the floor of the room.

'Big storm on the way and a bit of high pressure. I remember the storm building up. In fact, I even went and checked meteorological records – can you believe that? Well, anyway, Reilly's shop there on Bishop Street, around the corner from Lecky Road. Gone now, of course. But Orla was sent for a pint of milk. By her mother. And guess whose Jag is parked outside as he pops in for a few Panatelas? Your dad's buddy, Ian Haslette. The wonderful solicitor. No CCTV footage in those days. Just a wee shop anyway. And on noticing Orla on her own, and the thunder and lightning just starting, he got into his Jag and followed her. Altruism? I don't know. Jesus, wouldn't happen today. But Mr Wonderful pulls up alongside her and offers her a lift home. She refused, for sure. All that stuff about not talking to strangers. But then she dropped the pint of milk, as her hands were wet. Those old glass bottles. Smash. Everyone was gone. They had dived for cover from the rain. Rightly so. But poor Orla was now in trouble. She had no more money, and our charity worker offered her fifty pence from sitting in his car to help her. He told her he would take her back to the shop and on home. Then Orla put out her innocent hand and tried to lean in and take the money, and here's where the evidence gets hazy. This is where the doubt comes in.'

'What doubt, Gerard?'

'Well, on one view she slipped, and on another, he grabbed her hand and pulled her in. Was it, in that slip and fall, or pull, that her neck was broken? Was it deliberate? Was it an accident? What happened? Because she's dead now in Haslette's car. He has the body of a child in his car and panic

117

sets in. Or the beginning of the cover-up? He told your mother all this, Jon. I'm sure of it. This fucking truth thing again. For some insane reason he feels unburdening his guilt onto your frail mother would be okay. For what? Especially since he confessed everything anyway in a bizarre confession to Father Doherty. Yes, Father Doherty. What's the legal position there, Jon? If he survives? Sanctity of confession and all that – but Haslette, a Presbyterian? You'll have young Michael getting the canon-law books out. But smelling of cigars and wine, his odour unforgettable I'm sure in those old confessional boxes in Long Tower, he cried like a baby. All to Father Doherty.'

'Can we stick with Mr Haslette and Orla for the moment? What do you say Mr Haslette did next?'

'It's not so much what I say, Jon. Yes, I am saying it, but I am not making it up. Anyway, the rain was thundering down. The roads were flooded and the sham of a lifelong lie begins. He would have hoped for better things. The distortion begins. In this case, is the subterfuge worse than the act? Or does it just make it worse? Well, for certain, even if he didn't mean to kill Orla, he certainly set about covering it up. With your dad's help, Jon. Your father. And now a sticky situation gets worse. And you witnessed it. Remember? All those years ago. The rain. The storm. The car. Your father and Haslette looking into the boot of the car. Remember, Jon? Haslette caught you looking down. It's a wonder he didn't do you in later. Pity you didn't hear the conversation. And just as well your mother never knew. But I am going to tell you now. And my own personal dark storm begins. And physically, emotionally and spiritually you can be—'

'Can be what?' asked Linda.

'Oh, Linda. Ask Jon. You can be dead before dying. He is. Look at him.'

Linda interjected.

'Perhaps we should take another break. The time on the clock is 11.15pm and I am about to turn off the tape machine. Before I do, I confirm, as agreed in advance, the guards here will change as well for interview number three.'

118

CHAPTER 31

At 11.30pm, with O'Driscoll confirming he did not need to use the bathroom, the third interview of the evening commenced.

'Jon, when you layer a lie on lies the truth is gone forever. It's gone into an irreversible coma. In fact, the Glasgow Coma Scale doesn't even come into the equation. But I'll come back to that later. So, Prehen Wood or as far away as Gortin Glen; he was going to bury her in a shallow grave. That's the first thought he had. So he said. Or dump her in the Foyle. Now, long before any ceasefire, there he was, driving about with a dead body. The dead body of a child. All over Derry and beyond. In a daze himself. You know, part of me thinks he wanted to be caught. Even in the middle of a huge thunderstorm you might still run into an RUC checkpoint – or the Brits. That's why he was driving about. He stopped out the Victoria Road, in a lay-by there, and managed to get Orla's dead body into the boot of his car without being caught. Simply amazing. And very lucky. Then he drove to your house, Jon.'

'Really? Are you making this up, Gerard? Seriously? Are you for real?' asked Valberg.

'Haslette becomes the way you and me are now, Jon. A tormented individual. Another one. He's got a bad dose of Shaken Solicitor Syndrome now. Even if he didn't mean to harm Orla, who would believe him? You see, his wife, Lily, never believed him. Not from then, of course. She found Orla's pendant in her husband's study. Her poor mother had all Orla's details in a note stuffed in the back of the pendant in case she was ever … well, in case something happened to her. Something else the wonderful solicitor kept. Snapped it from her neck and held on to it. Deliberately? Not sure. Hapless Lily presented this to him. Unfortunately for her, the presentation was on the landing at the top of their staircase at home, and she slipped backwards down the stairs. Now there's a shock. Another broken neck. There's another unfortunate episode for this solicitor. Jesus, how many people are dead now? Anyway, murder or accident, she is dead. Poor Lily. And poor Ian sobbing down the phone and tormenting your mother there just before Christmas. Spilling the beans on everything to her. What a shame and pity. More shame, really. No wonder your mother headed for the cemetery. It makes sense now. What do you think, Jon? Linda?'

Linda asked O'Driscoll to continue.

Valberg was getting agitated and was trying to remember the advice he had given Linda to be calm and let O'Driscoll say what he wanted. It was easy to give the advice. Hard to abide by it. Valberg wanted a drink of any alcoholic substance he could get his hands on. His mouth was dry. He was starting to think he was in the presence of a malign force. Something was stirring inside him. There was evil in the room. O'Driscoll was needling him. The personal comments were grating. They were working, much to Valberg's own surprise. He was starting to believe that what O'Driscoll was saying was true. His whole life perception of his father was diminishing. What was most heartbreaking was that he actually could remember Haslette, in the teeming rain, opening the boot of his car in the Valberg family driveway. He had been listening to his Rush *Hemispheres* album and recalled lifting the needle from his record to listen to the commotion outside his bedroom. He could see his father standing, staring into the boot, ignoring the rain and ignoring Haslette as he spoke to him. Valberg recalled his father's stare but couldn't make out what was being said. He remembered the slam of the boot lid and Haslette driving away and his father still standing in the rain.

Valberg was snapped out of his reflection as O'Driscoll started chanting and moving back and forth in his chair as best as his restraints would allow. 'I smell fear in this room. *Mea culpa, mea culpa, mea maxima culpa.* "Mournful that day/When from the ashes shall rise/A guilty man to be judged/Lord, show mercy on him/Gentle Lord Jesus/Grant them eternal rest/Amen." Jon. Jon. Are you with us? Getting to the truth is like a bloody tap. Do you know what a bloody tap is?'

Valberg ignored him, clenching his own hands.

'Go on,' said Linda. Her voice was breaking slightly.

'A bloody tap. The nick of a vein. So getting the truth out of someone is like a bloody tap. If you are taking spinal fluid out of an individual, or extracting the truth as in our situation here, you see, some blood might come out and into the syringe. You have to be careful. You can imagine it. You lying there unconscious, hopefully. And this needle going into your spinal cord and it sucking your life out of you; then – nick, the vein is hit. The hand shook. Blood is mixed in with the spinal fluid and extracted from you. But the blood is all consuming. The clear spinal fluid vanishes. All you see is this blood. You tried to get the clean and clear fluid, the truth, but now it is imperfect. Full of doubt. A world of doubts and fears. Then that mixed-up fluid, if you drink it, alters your perception. The fountain is sealed. You might suffer an emotional or spiritual trauma that results in a permanent alteration of your character. Paranoid delusions. Most unfortunate.'

'Mr O'Driscoll. Please continue with telling us what you say happened after Mr Haslette left the lay-by on the Victoria Road.'

'He drove straight to Jon's house with the *corpus delicti.*'

Valberg remembered hearing the crunch of the wheels of Haslette's car braking sharply as it slid to a halt on the gravel driveway. It broke him away from him singing along with Geddy Lee's lament about people divided and that every soul was a battlefield. Valberg was breaking. He was crumbling. He was welling up with emotion and anger. All this would now be on the record and public knowledge. His enemies, and there were many, within the PSNI and beyond, would revel in this. It was everything they wanted. Valberg was annoyed that O'Driscoll had got to him so quickly and decisively.

'Did you touch her? Did you touch her?'

'What do you mean, Mr O'Driscoll?' asked Linda.

'That's what Jon's father asked Haslette. When the boot was opened. Not: what happened? Or: is she dead or alive? But if he had touched her. And we all know what he meant there, Jon, don't we? Touch her. You see, Haslette called good old Gustav before he came. "Not that way, Gustav," said Haslette. Yeah. What way was that, Jon? Your father must have been remembering this when on the jury and he didn't let on. Protected him like he protected you. Eh, Jon? Little Patrick. Did you let his hand go? Daddy protected his friend at my expense and you at his own expense.'

'What are you saying, Mr O'Driscoll? Are you making more allegations or do you have any facts?' asked Linda.

Valberg boiled.

'Jon, your dad sent him to a place out the Letterkenny Road, towards Milltown House. To a stretch of open ground he used to fish at. You used to fish at with him. I used to sit there, too, in the sun. No-one would have been there in the storm that night. Haslette followed his instructions exactly. He laid Orla's little innocent body down on the grass. On her back. It was as if she were sleeping. His anguish and tears were insignificant in the heavy rain. The grass was just long enough to hide Orla. Then Haslette followed your dad's instructions again. He went home and cleaned his car thoroughly. Especially the boot. You know, on his way to the Letterkenny Road, one of your colleagues unwittingly even stopped him. Flagged him down and had a chat with him, then waved him on.

'Brilliant. Simple. Valbergishness at its deceptive best. The great man. A cheat. A liar. He could have squealed on his mate, but no. Knew I was innocent all right. The look on his face when that fucking judge started to tell the jury what the case was about. And he did nothing.'

Valberg snapped. He launched himself with a roar across the table and grabbed O'Driscoll's neck. The back of O'Driscoll's chair broke in two while the rest remained chained to the floor. Linda started screaming and pushed the panic button while the two guards in the room jumped to get Valberg off O'Driscoll. By now, more armed guards were storming into the room as O'Driscoll began bleeding quite badly from the scar he had on the left hand side of his face which got re-opened in the melee. But suddenly O'Driscoll managed with his strength to turn himself around and wrapped his handcuffs around Valberg's neck.

'One snap. One pull,' O'Driscoll roared, with blood pouring from his open wound onto his white suit, 'and I will break his neck.'

He tugged on the chain and Valberg grunted.

'You decide.'

CHAPTER 32

O'Driscoll held Valberg tight to him and whispered in his ear: 'Sorry, Jon. Daddy a big let-down to you? Not the daddy you thought he was and you not the son you think you are? Something else we have in common.'

Valberg couldn't move as he was choked so tightly by O'Driscoll. He could feel the steel of the handcuffs cutting into his neck. He was already in pain from the injuries inflicted upon him at Long Tower Church. He knew he had no escape.

The cramped interview room was crowded and the custody sergeant could not get in, despite roaring and demanding entry. O'Driscoll was completely covered with Valberg's body lying on the floor with his back slightly raised against the wall. The custody sergeant eventually clambered through the thick collection of armed officers, all now with their weapons trained on Valberg and O'Driscoll.

Valberg tried to speak and O'Driscoll loosened his grip to allow him to. 'Gerard, let me go. There's nothing more than these guys would like than to shoot you. Please. They won't harm you if you let me go. I promise. I'm sorry. It's my fault. Now, please, let me up so we can get you some treatment for that cut. I am sorry, Gerard. Please do this. I'm … I'm begging you. Please. Let's stop this.'

O'Driscoll let his grip go and released Valberg. Both remained lying on the floor and rolled over in pain.

Valberg shouted, 'Get him a doctor! Get the bleeding stopped!'

The custody sergeant had acquired a first-aid kit and was

about to get down to help O'Driscoll when Valberg intervened. 'Here, let me do that.'

Valberg cleaned O'Driscoll's wound as best he could without the aid of any protective gloves. He and O'Driscoll were
both out of breath. But Valberg more so. The armed guards
and police were still pointing all their weapons on O'Driscoll.

'How did you get that scar, Gerard?'

'It's a long story, Jon. If you have time. The bleeding will
stop. Don't worry, I've always been very careful with it.
Would you get me my Dead Sea salt for cleaning up and
sterilising the wound? I carry a little batch of it everywhere
I go. It cleanses me. Would you do that for me? It will make
the custody sergeant feel better. It's the only thing I came
with and the only request I make. I don't need a doctor.
Don't worry. Make sure that's recorded. Then I'd like some
rest. I am allowed eight hours.'

'You can make a complaint about this now to the custody
sergeant in the presence of everyone here.'

'No, Jon, I'm not a snitch. The other officers can complain
about you and so can Linda there when she gets her breath.
We're just about getting ours here.'

Valberg continued cleaning O'Driscoll's wound.

'Thank you, Jon. Thank you for staying and ensuring no
maltreatment here. Thank you. Can I use the bathroom and
have a little sleep?'

'Of course you can. And sorry again.'

With that, the tape machine made a high-pitch noise signalling it was coming to the end of recording and snapped
to a stop.

With everyone looking on, and several weapons still
trained on O'Driscoll, the custody sergeant allowed Valberg
to help O'Driscoll to his feet to use the bathroom for cleaning.

With the tape machine off, the atmosphere relaxed slightly. Both men were on their feet now.

Valberg washed O'Driscoll's hands for him in the ablution
room across from the interview room.

'Can you use the salt, Jon? Ever been to the Rift Valley in
Jordan?'

'No.'

'It is one of the most beautiful places on earth. A place to rejuvenate both body and soul. Then go to Saint Antimo, just outside Siena in Italy. You know there for sure?'

'Yeah. It's beautiful.'

'Meet me in Saint Antimo when this is all over, Jon?'

'Not sure about that, Gerard.'

'Is Derry the lowest point on earth?'

'Geographically, surely not.'

'Well, maybe not. The Dead Sea is. Can you clean my face and my wound again, Jon. Don't worry about the sting of the salt. I've had a lot more pain. Not complaining, though.'

Valberg continued cleaning O'Driscoll with copious amounts of Dead Sea salt. He rubbed it in as everyone looked on.

'That's nice, Jon. Feels good. Cleopatra's Choice. Nothing like a bit of potassium and bromide. It's a unique batch I get. Can't get it here at all. There's a little market I get it from in Jordan. This particular salt can't be bought anywhere else. Look, you're nearly finished. Wash your hands now before you dry me. Look at your nails and hands. Look at your skin. Look at how clean they are. Works every time.'

'Okay. I'll give it a go.'

Valberg washed his hands with O'Driscoll looking on.

'Jesus. You're right there, Gerard. Look at that. Clean as a whistle. I've a load over my clothes here.'

'Don't wipe it away. Save it for later.'

Valberg dried O'Driscoll and checked his wound again. 'You're right, Gerard, the bleeding has stopped. I have to walk you to your cell now.'

'Okay, Jon, do that. I understand. Do what you have to. A few hours' sleep will be enough.'

'I can't sleep, I never do.'

'You know, Jon, I asked our dear old friend Raymond if he agreed with Thomas Jefferson. Jefferson didn't like rapists. It's one thing I have in common with him. Try killing in the Balkans for a living and watching rape after rape after rape. I had to take care of one particularly nasty individual from there. Or in the Congo. Jesus, what a place. The rape capital of the world. The blood line there is fucked up forever. It made me very anti-rape. Well, Jefferson was all for castration for the likes of Grimestone.'

'Okay, Gerard. Perhaps we can talk about that another time.'

'Perhaps, Jon. Before you go. I am no longer the hunted now – Anna is.'

'Well, we can talk about that later, too.'

'George Orwell was right about the Brits, wasn't he? And there was me recruited into the good old British Army at the tender age of eighteen.'

'What was he right about? Orwell?'

'Well, that the Brits only see the writing on the wall when their backs are up against it. Think about it, Jon, and I'll see you in a few hours.'

Valberg then arranged for the cuffs to be removed just before O'Driscoll was locked up and got a cup of water for him as well. Linda stood in the hallway of the custody suite. She stared at Valberg and shook her head.

'Jon. You've just fucked this whole thing up. You do realise that, don't you?'

'Let's speak with Superintendent Kells now. And tell the custody sergeant to write up his notes and wait for a call. See you upstairs.'

Linda shook her head again, put her right hand over her eyes and sighed.

CHAPTER 33

When O'Driscoll finally got relaxed in the cell his mind drifted back to Angola: 22 February 2002. He was touching his scar now and checking if the bleeding had definitely stopped.

O'Driscoll had a clear photographic memory of the events of that evening and the days thereafter. It seemed to him as if it had all just happened that very day. He could hear screams, shouting, gunfire, hysteria and the rotor blades of a Stealth helicopter. It was shortly after the MPLA regime had come to terms with the USA. Jonas Savimbi, the leader of the UNITA, had just been killed in combat with Angolan government troops.

'I can't accept rape, Karl. She's just a kid. Couldn't be ten,' said O'Driscoll.

'If you go back, all the men will, too. Savimbi is gone. We need to stop his men getting the diamonds.'

'Karl, I hear her screaming.'

'But those so-called independence fuckers will get enough diamonds to keep their dirty war going for another lifetime.'

'I'll end it now. I'm going back.'

'You can't save that girl.'

'Don't say that, Karl. I can save her. Distribute my cut with the men and go.'

'You go, we all go. The men won't leave you.'

'The men don't know me.'

'We got the bonus plan. One Navy SEAL rescue team and a Stealth out with a load of the sparkly stuff. This dump will never be independent. It's fucked up. Just like that Irish

128

shithole you come from. You think saving one kid will mean anything? Come on, Gerry. Let's go.'

O'Driscoll pulled away from Karl and looked straight at him.

'Baudelaire was right. The devil pulls my strings. I'm going.'

'Sweet fuck,' said Karl, shaking his head.

With that, Gerard O'Driscoll vanished.

He disappeared into the jungle of the Moxico province to try to save a child from rape and almost certain death. The sight and screams of the little girl cut through O'Driscoll like razor wire. He had to go back. He knew the area well and in any event the CIA would be content now if he were killed in action. Unofficially.

O'Driscoll moved swiftly and decisively. He knew Karl and the team would follow. He knew he was putting lives at risk but he had confidence in the men surrounding him. One by one, O'Driscoll picked off the futile resistance in front of him. Young men and boys in battledress dropped like flies. Cries of 'Savimbi, Savimbi, Savimbi' filled the air.

All the Angolan forces were heading towards the Luvuei River. It was littered with hacked limbs and blood and dead bodies. Amid the chaos, O'Driscoll arrived back at a hut in a small area he had left just hours before. The discovery of Savimbi's body had taken most of the Angolan forces away from the area and towards the riverbank in the wild frenzy.

O'Driscoll lost heart for a moment. He couldn't hear the child screaming anymore. But when he peeked through a hole in the hut he could see her unconscious. She was stripped and face down on the red-dirt floor. The older of two soldiers was starting to pull down his trousers. He, like his partner, had discarded his weapon. O'Driscoll could easily have shot both in the head from his hidey-hole and it would be safely over. But no. In what was remaining of the thirty minutes O'Driscoll knew he had, he decided to go in and confront them.

Outside, the Luvuei River was thick with the blood of every single person in the small village who had tried to protect Savimbi. The girl was the only survivor. The noise was intensifying as the battle drew nearer.

O'Driscoll kicked open the door of the hut and fired one shot to the head of the younger boy soldier, who died instantly. O'Driscoll kicked the older soldier, prone over the girl, with such ferocity that he was knocked to the corner of the hut and out through it. The hut collapsed around O'Driscoll and he was obliged to shelter the girl from the debris falling.

O'Driscoll lifted the girl and what he could of her clothes and put them around her. Karl and the rest of the team now moved forward and took the girl to shelter.

O'Driscoll knelt down over the soldier who was writhing in agony. He pulled out his knife and held the soldier down, keeping his left hand and knee on his chest. O'Driscoll then disembowelled and castrated him in less than fifteen seconds. As he wiped the blood from his knife over the soldier's face, he realised he was looking at the corpse of a teenager in the uniform of a man. No more than nineteen.

O'Driscoll got up, looked around him and moved to Karl.

'We're taking her with us. Give her to me.'

***

O'Driscoll and his team had ten minutes to get to their pick-up location, twenty minutes away. Karl took from O'Driscoll what he could so he could move faster with the child. As they ran, they took a call from the helicopter.

'Balor 1. This is Cygnus 1. What is your location? ETA five minutes. Come in, Balor 1.'

Karl responded. 'Cygnus 1. This is Balor 1. We're on our way. All safe and full team for transport. Over.'

The noise of an American Stealth helicopter could be heard faintly.

'Come in, Balor 1. What is your location? Enemy forces closing in on pick up at Sector 5. Over.'

'Red Sector A, Cygnus 1. We are nearly there. We are at Red Sector A and hear you. Over.'

The Angolan forces knew the sound of the Stealth, and O'Driscoll was well aware that they would love to capture a group of CIA-led mercenaries and torture them as their own bonus prize.

'Cygnus 1. This is Balor 1. We're nearly there. Permission to move out. Over.'

'Balor 1. Secure your location. Your perimeter is about to be breached. Enemy fire closing in. It's now or never, Balor 1. Move forward. Move. Move. Move.'

'Karl. You take her now,' O'Driscoll said. 'And hold her tight. Get all the men out. I will follow up. That's an order.'

Karl took the child and signalled to all to move. Then the shooting came at them from all angles. O'Driscoll pushed everyone out, and then drew fire away from them to allow them to get to the safety of the Stealth. It, too, provided enormous fire cover, unmatched by the firearms of the Angolans. But O'Driscoll was not going to make it. Harry 'the Hurricane', the Navy SEAL pilot, was not going to wait. For the second time in his life, O'Driscoll was about to enter involuntary captivity.

Karl was screaming at the pilot.

'Don't you fucking leave him. Don't go.'

O'Driscoll pointed hard at the sky ordering the Balor 1 team to take off without him. The girl covered her ears and crawled into a corner of the helicopter, terrorised, but on her way to safety.

O'Driscoll was surrounded. He laid down his weapons. He got on to his knees with his hands behind his head. Immediately the butt end of a SLR rifle knocked him unconscious. The rifle had been captured a few days previously from a headless corpse that was floating down the Luvuei River. The corpse added to a human dam of limbs, dead bodies and blood that nature would eventually rot away. Rodents of all types got a bonus plan, too.

***

The Angolan government were quick off the mark. They got photographs and film footage of the dead Savimbi out around the world. He lay in his olive fatigues surrounded by soldiers and flies. His body was riddled with bullets, but especially so around the neck. This was shown in an intense effort by the Angolan government to prove that the CIA-sponsored rebel leader, and their nemesis, was dead.

131

Savimbi's eyes were half open.

The CIA later denied all knowledge of Balor 1, while the Angolan government claimed they had captured a CIA operative.

***

Bentiaba Detention Centre in Luanda made the Crumlin Road prison look like the Ritz Hotel in Paris.

Luanda was a world away from Derry and Belfast and all the training O'Driscoll had taken part in for the Force Research Unit. However, O'Driscoll knew he had to close down to survive, to become frozen. He was battered unconscious while prison guards and soldiers poured Atracurium into him via a dirty syringe. The muscle relaxant paralysed him while a young soldier took great delight in dropping maggots into his left ear.

In his more lucid moments, O'Driscoll realised that if he wasn't rescued or hadn't managed to escape within a few days he was dead. He lay listless on the floor and, when he awoke, experienced the worst itch he had ever had. He was so weak he could barely scratch the area below his left ear that was driving him wild.

He sized up the military prison guards hoping he could get one of them on his own who would be tall enough with a uniform to fit him. He felt as if he were about to pass out again when at last the bigger guard came in, knelt down over him and pulled out his knife. The guard was just about to scoop up some more maggots to drop into O'Driscoll's ear when O'Driscoll swivelled around, grabbed his hand and twisted the knife up in between his neck and chin. O'Driscoll then pulled the knife out immediately and punched the guard so hard in the face that his septum ended up in his frontal lobe. He fell back silent and dead.

That double move exhausted O'Driscoll. If anyone were to come into the room now O'Driscoll would be done for. It was now or never to get rid of what was moving below his left ear. But a sharp knife in the hands of a weak man was dangerous. One cut the wrong way could be fatal. O'Driscoll wiped the blood off the knife and held the blade up to his shaven head. He could see in the faint reflection something moving for sure at the side of his head. The maggots had laid eggs and they were hatching. He had to get everything out now. But then what?

It took the point of the knife steadying on the side of his face to stop his right hand shaking. He felt one last time along his left side with his right hand, then gently penetrated the side of his face, just below his left ear. He just went deep enough to cut out whatever was moving inside him. It felt like he was relieving himself from the worst toothache ever, with no anaesthetic. He did not attempt to stop the blood pouring. It would flush out what had grown within.

Through all of this he had to keep silent.

O'Driscoll knew he was in Bentiaba – he'd heard so much about it. He got changed into the dead guard's clothes and used an old rag to stem the flow of blood once he was satisfied the maggots were all gone. But just as he was getting himself together he heard the other guards starting to return. He stumbled over to the corner of the room and cocked the guard's SLR ready for automatic fire. He sat down opposite the door, bleeding profusely but sensing he was getting stronger. He held the rifle close to himself and waited.

The first guard to enter was shot straight on by O'Driscoll in the head and simultaneously from the back by Karl.

They'd come back for him.

Karl rushed in to O'Driscoll as shooting continued.

'Jesus, Gerry, you're looking well. Cut yourself shaving, or are you on a Wolfe Tone trip?'

'What took you so long?'

'Ah, don't talk. Now get your sorry ass up and hold on to me until we get out of this pigsty. We couldn't land in the yard. We have a ways to go, *amigo*. But no going back this time – for no-one.'

When O'Driscoll stood up he got light-headed and fell into Karl's arms. But he held on to the SLR and would not let it go. He was losing a lot of blood. This was a very unofficial rescue but O'Driscoll knew from experience that his team would have medical help on hand.

As soon as O'Driscoll heard the sound of rotor blades he knew safety was within range. The battle to get him out was a blur to him. He tried to identify the type of gunfire and the direction – all the things that his training had taught him. But it was no good. He was getting weaker, struggling to keep his breathing and heart rate down. He knew the more anxious he became the faster his heart would beat and the more blood would be lost.

O'Driscoll couldn't work out if he was on the Falls Road in Belfast or William Street in Derry. He was disorientated and confused and starting to vomit as well. He began getting flashbacks of everything they had put into his body. He found himself shouting: 'Every one of them. Every last fucking one of them. That bastard laughing. I'm gonna get every last fucking one of them. I'm tracking them down. Every one of them before I die. I swear to you, Karl. Every last one except ...'

'Nearly there now, Gerry. And, fuck, no. We've got everyone here, and you are not going back. No way. Nearly there. Hold on.'

With that O'Driscoll passed out again, but he was safely out of Bentiaba Detention Centre.

***

When O'Driscoll regained consciousness he was in a clean hospital bed and the pain had gone.

'Is she safe?'

'Well, the Americans got their bonus plan, too. She's safe for sure. Paraded by our brothers as a symbol of freedom. The PR coup will more than cover the cost of the rescue! Fuck me. She'll be on the *Oprah* show next. She'll be adopted. American citizenship. The whole works. Celebrity status. The American Dream. Miss World in a few years.'

'Okay, Karl. I get it. She's safe. That's the main thing. And the men? Did everyone make it?'

'Oh, for sure. Happy as pigs in shit now and rich as kings after we grabbed the diamonds. The CIA paid up, too. Allah praises them.'

O'Driscoll looked at Karl and they both began laughing.

'For fuck's sake, Gerry. Don't die laughing on me now after all we've gone through. And get that head of yours shaved again. You look too normal and boring with hair.'

CHAPTER 34

The mood in the office of Chief Superintendent Kells was low and depressing. Linda Wilson was still shaking her head and Valberg was silent.

'Will one of you tell me what happened? He's killed, murdered and butchered and he will be the one filing a complaint, not only with the Police Ombudsman's office, but with us for the PPS, alleging an assault. He'll get a lawyer, or maybe he doesn't even need one. Anything he said or says will be dumped as a result of his unjust treatment and the cruelty towards him. I'm told, Jon, you leapt over the table, tried to strangle him and in the process burst open a wound he had, and there was blood everywhere. Then there's a smashed chair that was chained to the floor. It's all being photographed and filmed now. Look at you. You have blood all over you. To say that there has been some impropriety on the part of the interrogator – well, that is an understatement. The Human Rights Act is about to knock us out and he walked in here voluntarily. We didn't even catch him. He has effectively been tortured and subjected to cruel and degrading treatment. And to make it worse, it's all on tape, Jon. Including you apologising to him. His solicitor is going to have a field day. And even before we gain it, we have lost the support of the public, not forgetting the families of all his victims. Jesus Christ. Have I missed anything?'

'You are well informed, then, sir,' said Valberg, looking at Linda.

'And that journalist woman is calling here saying it's a

matter of life and death that she speaks with you. The word is out that O'Driscoll is held here and in the morning we will be under siege. You knew the deal here, Jon. Get him on anything. Something to get him kept in custody. Anything. But no, you couldn't do that. Instead you attack him. Jesus. How are we going to sort this out?'

'We're doing what he wants us to do. Fight, split and disintegrate. That's all he wants.'

'And you bloody well delivered part one of his plan to him. On a plate. Every officer in there will be a witness. The custody officer will be writing statements forever. The Chief Constable's office are looking for answers and an explanation. I don't need this.'

'Just charge him, then. Charge him with all of the murders,' said Valberg.

Linda asked, 'How can we do that in accordance with PACE? We kept this "non-terrorist" to keep him here. We'll be a laughing stock. A joke with our colleagues. What evidence do we have? We have nothing. What if someone asks how we connect him to any charges we bring?'

'Let him rest. I'll tell him what we're doing and see if he'll appoint a solicitor,' said Valberg.

'Jon,' said Chief Superintendent Kells, 'that's where the fun and ridicule will really begin. You think you can wander into his cell down there and just tell him? Are you on Planet Reality?'

'But we just need something to keep him under our control,' said Valberg.

Linda looked worried. 'Jon, you sound like those RUC men you always complain about. The ones you very openly and vocally criticise about abusing the legal system. Now what have you become? What do you think will happen here?'

Kells, however, shook his head. 'I agree with Jon. Let's charge him. He'll never be released by the courts. We have to do it. For all the wrong reasons. And I really mean it. Get him charged before anything else goes wrong. We have no choice – unfortunately.'

Linda still wasn't happy. 'We are making a bad situation worse. That's between us in this room. I don't want it repeated, but I want my objection noted between us. We're losing this case to Belfast anyway. That's what I think – if either of you care.'

'Jon,' said Kells, 'Linda is right. When this is done, you're out. It's too personal now. I can't be subtle. Do what you have to for now between tonight and tomorrow. But that's it. I'll agree it with the Chief Constable's office. You are out.'

'Nobody asked if I was okay in there. He had me in a neck lock. I think the ideal outcome would have been me dead with a broken neck and O'Driscoll shot to pieces. The two of us out of the way.'

Valberg got up out of his seat and left the room.

Superintendent Kells got up out of his seat and followed Valberg.

'Jon, that journalist who wrote the article for the *Derry Journal* – I think you need to speak to her.'

'Why? Sure I'm out of this after tomorrow. You all got what you wanted. Or you're getting what you wanted.'

'It's not what I want. But look at this from my point of view. I'd defend you forever if I could. That journalist is in a bad way. She said she's left messages on your phone and texts.'

'Never turned the thing on so I don't know.'

'Well, look call her now. Please. Call her back. She mentioned something to me about a memory pen and meeting O'Driscoll in Foyleside. I have Constable Bell sorting all the CCTV now. Call her.'

'Okay, David, I've her number on my phone.'

'Sorry, Jon, there is something else a bit more delicate.'

'What's that, then?'

'Have you fired your personal protection weapon recently? There's no log or record. But is it fully loaded?'

'What sort of fucking question is that? I haven't fired a gun in years.'

'Right, okay. Well, that's that, then.'

'Look here, David, I'm a Detective Inspector, not the office idiot. Why the fuck are you asking me this?'

'We can get back to this tomorrow. If we get to court and we get over everything. Go and ring that girl from the *Derry Journal*.'

'Right. Okay.'

'Just one more thing.'

'What is it now?'

'You need to know. The barrister, Bostridge. He's made a statement of complaint. About what happened in court. I have to have someone investigate it from somewhere else.'

'You do that, David.'

'It's not a complaint from the Bar Council or Law Society this time. It's a real statement of complaint. He says he believes you were trying to kill him and he thought he was going to die.'

'Well, that's something else for tomorrow I have to look forward to. *Mañana. Mañana.*'

Valberg walked away in disgust, knowing full well his gun had been moved from its position he left it on the kitchen table on Christmas Eve night and one bullet had been fired. He was content in saying he hadn't fired any gun. But he had no explanation for what had happened – yet.

CHAPTER 35

'Amanda, it's Jon here. Are you okay? You were looking for me?'

'I've been calling you constantly. I spoke to Mr Kells. He was as helpful as he could be but asked me more questions than anything. O'Driscoll was at my daughter's school play. He videoed it and gave me a recording on a memory pen along with a bloody poem. There is something else on the memory pen but it needs a password. There is a question for you, too. Can you come and meet me? I'm petrified. Absolutely petrified, and I'm not leaving my daughter.'

'Okay, I'll come to you now. What's the question?'

'What ladder did Rush climb in nineteen seventy-nine?'

'That's easy. We'll be down now in few minutes.'

'Jon, is it true? Have you got him? Are the rumours true? I'd like to know. For my own safety.'

'We have him, Amanda. But nothing is ever straightforward. Say nothing. See you in a few moments. Leaving now. But, Amanda ...'

'What is it?'

'We'll have to take the memory pen from you and view it here. And anything it was in. You mentioned a poem.'

'Aye. Some French poet I'd never heard of. I have it here. He tore it out of a book. And it's dedicated to the Pope, for God's sake.'

'Aye, my old friend Seán Carlin. Look, I want to get everything myself. We can get a statement from you later.'

'Great. Can't wait to give a statement for the prosecution. Don't worry, I understand. I would only give the memory pen personally to you. See you soon.'

'Okay. Bye, Amanda.'

Valberg had Constable Bell drive him to Amanda Cleary's house. He arranged with Linda to keep a close eye on all that was going on at the custody suite when he was away. Valberg could sense Linda was very unhappy with him – more so than usual. He knew to press on and go and get the memory pen. He thought that Linda always trusted him and that he trusted her. But he was doubting that now. Even doubting Linda.

Amanda Cleary was more than glad to see him. He could see the relief on her face on hearing that O'Driscoll was indeed behind locked doors. He apologised for not getting back to her sooner but explained that he never picked up phone messages and had his phone turned off most of the time recently.

Amanda handed over everything O'Driscoll had left for her, sealed in a clear plastic bag. Valberg got to hear about the encounter she had with O'Driscoll. He told her that Constable Bell, who was waiting in the car, was already chasing down all CCTV footage from Foyleside for the day she was there.

'Perhaps no more articles for a while, Amanda. I'm not telling you how to do your job, but maybe just report what happens.'

'Well, what will happen, Jon?'

'I expect he will be charged.'

'Doesn't matter now, I suppose, but it won't be long before every hack in the town and beyond will know he's in Strand Road. There's even a bloody Facebook page about him – and you.'

'What crap. What utter nonsense.'

'It's hard to control that stuff.'

'Aye. Some prat tells us what she's watching on TV – as if any one gives a fuck – then she will be adding a comment about O'Driscoll. Arseholes.'

'Do you use it at all?'

'Only for investigations, I can assure you. It's mind-numbing. Well, anyway, I'm off. See you up at court some time tomorrow.'

'Oh, is that a tip-off?'

'You know I'll need a formal statement from you? You do understand that? I'm in a rush now. I'll have to write all this up myself for whoever comes behind me.'

'What does that mean?'

'Right, Amanda, thanks again. Lock your doors and stay safe for now, and we'll speak again soon. I'll send someone down with a formal receipt and arrange for your statement.'

'It was Jacob, wasn't it? The code word. Easy enough, even for me when I thought about it. "Jacob's Ladder". Checked it on the net.'

'You know what, Amanda? If only Rush would play it live again. What a song. See you.'

'Bye, Jon.'

As Valberg walked to the car he was certain that Amanda had made a copy of the memory pen or downloaded it all onto her computer. He was also confident that she made a copy of the poem she gave to him. He had visions of her starting to watch the rest of the material on the memory pen, typing in Jacob's Ladder to get beyond her daughter's Christmas play.

CHAPTER 36

Valberg, DS Wilson, Constable Bell and Constable Hastings all found themselves in Chief Superintendent Kells's room to watch the material on the memory pen Valberg obtained from Amanda Cleary. The Chief Superintendent let Bell sit in his seat to get the device playing on his large computer monitor and position it for all to see. Valberg was amused at the sight of Bell sitting at the desk of the most senior policeman in Derry while the Chief Superintendent had to stand and watch. It was a peculiar scene and amid the chaos, Valberg enjoyed the moment. Bell handled the memory pen delicately with gloves so that it could be fingerprinted and forensically analysed later.

Valberg shook his head in horror at the thought of O'Driscoll walking totally unchallenged into a school and filming a children's Christmas play.

After watching the school play, Bell asked Valberg for the code so he could type it in.

'Jacob's Ladder, Michael.'

'There we go. That's it. Can you all see and hear?'

Superintendent Kells immediately said, 'I recognise that music. Beethoven or Mozart? *Lacrimosa*. I know that. I can hear it in the background.'

Valberg knew what was coming.

'He's filmed the killings. He's got a camera strapped to his shoulder or chest. And, yes, it's *Lacrimosa* by Mozart. I've just realised. He quoted the words at interview.'

Valberg asked Bell to pause the footage. He looked intently at Constable Hastings and advised her that she did not

142

have to stay to watch the recording if she didn't want to.

'This will be horrific, Jenny. Are you sure you want to stay?'

'It's okay, sir. I want to help if I can.'

Valberg looked at the Chief Superintendent who nodded his head to proceed. The recording commenced with the voice of a grown man weeping like a child and calling, 'Mammy ... I want my mammy.'

A voice was whispering.

'Say it again, William. What do you want? Inspector Valberg needs to know.'

'I want my mammy. Don't cut me again. Mammy. Mammy. I want my mammy.'

'Don't be crying, son. Let's get you swinging.'

A hand wearing a clear forensic glove began to push William Black's body, which hung upside down from the ceiling of his own funeral parlour. He was positioned so his head avoided hitting the coffins in the large room. He was being sliced with precision and bleeding down onto a huge plastic sheet. The lights in the room were off, but one spotlight kept catching Black as he swung in and out of the beam into the centre of the room. The terror on his face could be seen as he tried, pointlessly, to plead for mercy. He was sobbing and crying loudly. He squealed as the hand rose up again and cut him. The shine of a large blade, with a very pointed tip, was also caught in the beam of the spot lamp. After one of the slices, some blood squirted over the assailant and the small camera lens. The lens was cleaned. This gave Black some rest but he soon began pleading again for mercy.

Valberg was doing his best to ignore her, but he could see that Black's dying pleas were disturbing Hastings. Black stopped swinging and was squinting into the bright spotlight. Rivers of blood flowed down his face, into his eyes and onto the plastic sheet. His thick white hair was turning red.

'Whatever I've done, I'm sorry. Let me go. I'm begging. For God's sake, man, let me go.'

The gloved hand revealed itself again. Black was swung once more, and the crying and the cutting started again.

Valberg knew this was going to be a long process and the filming would continue until meaningful life left William Bolton Black.

It was obvious that no mercy would be shown. The killer didn't reveal his identity. The whispering tones were unrecognisable. With the camera placed on the shoulder or chest of the killer, it was impossible to make any identification. Valberg wanted it to be O'Driscoll; he was sure it was him.

Valberg asked Constable Bell to pause the footage. 'Michael, how long is the recording? Perhaps I should have asked at the start.'

'It's just over four hours, sir.'

'Perhaps we should stop, sir?' said Valberg to Chief Superintendent Kells. 'Perhaps we should pause, or is everyone content to proceed?'

'I think we go on, Jon,' said the Chief Superintendent.

Bell pressed play again and the bloodletting continued until Black fell unconscious. His arms dropped over his head, nearly touching the floor where Valberg had catnapped during his investigation of the murder several months before. There was no more movement. The blood continued to drip and the assailant clearly walked close to the body. The camera focused on Black's bloated and blood-soaked face and head.

Valberg said, 'He must have cleaned him. I remember he was totally clean when hanging over the bridge. I remember cuts and a very clean body, and the sash around his neck. All the photographs will confirm this.'

Constable Bell nodded in agreement. The recording switched suddenly to DS Wilson and Constable Bell arriving by car outside the Memorial Hall in Society Street.

Bell gasped. 'Sir, he was there. Right beside us. He's moved back and taken shelter on the Walls from the way he's walking. He's hunkering down and still recording.'

A loud explosion could be heard and debris began falling everywhere. Bell and Wilson could then be seen running in the direction of the explosion, filmed from behind. The full chaos of the bomb and its aftermath were captured in the recording.

Then, after some white noise, there was the sound of a door creaking and being closed gently. The next voice that could be heard was Majella McLaughlin praying behind another door. 'I confess to almighty God, and to you, my brothers and sisters, that I have sinned through my own faults, in my thoughts ...'

The second door opened slowly and, from a kneeling position, McLaughlin looked around in the direction of the camera. The draught from the door opening blew out two candles burning in front of her. Then there was darkness.

'Have you come for me, son? Are you really the devil? Do what you want. I am in your hands and commend my spirit to the Lord Jesus Christ. I'm not going to scream.'

The same type of knife that was used to slice open William Black appeared again, with the blade on the old woman's throat, ready to cut her jugular vein. But then the microphone attached to the camera picked up the sound of *Teenage Kicks* by The Undertones being played loudly in what seemed to be a car outside or by the next-door neighbour. The introduction of the drums was clearly audible, and everything just stopped.

The next visual showed a man's hands being washed at a sink. They were being scrubbed gently. Valberg was certain it was O'Driscoll and he was using his Dead Sea salt to clean himself.

Valberg was now certain that the camera lens was positioned on the assailant's chest and not his shoulder. 'Michael, can you pause that again?'

'No problem, sir.'

'Michael, is that it all, or is there editing going on do you think?'

'I think he's cut it up. Sorry. I mean he's cut up the filming, and I also think he was broadcasting it, or recording it over the internet. You can see the odd dip. It looks like an effect, but it's the signal transmitted dipping in and out. We'll get it all examined. I'm certain, sir, from an evidential point of view, we can get a lot.'

'Constable Bell is right,' said the Chief Superintendent. 'We're getting a general impression now, but I'm sure as well this will all be forensically analysed in detail for all sorts of things.'

'Okay, Michael. Go on. Start it again,' said Valberg.

Majella McLaughlin was suspended from the ceiling upside down and seemed to be trying to reach her Rosary beads on the floor as she swung. But it was a futile exercise. Her whole body seemed to seize and she died in a spasm, eyes wide open. The room blurred.

The screen went dark momentarily. Then the knife appeared again and Paddy Doherty was gurgling. The sound of him being decapitated was more terrifying than the visual image. The angle of the cameraman-assailant showed Doherty's body and his heels digging into the top of a grave slab.

Then there was a sound Valberg was very familiar with and recognised immediately. It was the sound of the rod, reel and line of a fly fisherman. It was a beautiful sound to Valberg and one that roused so many fond memories instantly. But not for Sammy Carson. He was soon also pleading for mercy and squealing in pain as his hands and feet were chopped from him. Carson's screams were echoing around Boom Hall on the banks of the River Foyle at Culmore, but no-one heard him. He was wailing hysterically as the camera moved away and his cries got fainter.

Valberg told Michael to stop the footage.

The Chief Superintendent's room was in complete silence. Valberg looked at the stunned faces of all there. He broke the silence by saying, 'Do you think there is an encore? Anybody?'

No-one answered. Valberg left, saying, 'I think I need a break. I'll watch the rest later.'

As he went out, everyone else remained quiet.

146

CHAPTER 37

It was time, thought Valberg, to look in on O'Driscoll again and perhaps even read a bit of poetry. Since he collected the package from Amanda Cleary and noted the title of the poem, *Heautontimoroumenos* by Baudelaire, he had been trying to fathom any significance to all that was happening. Valberg was intrigued by any potential connection with what Father Doherty had been saying in French at Altnagelvin Hospital.

Valberg was also reflecting on what he believed to be yet another particularly sinister development – the filming of Maya and the school play. Valberg recalled that O'Driscoll, no doubt in disguise, panned around the small school hall filming all the parents and other children as well. Valberg had seen the faces of joy and expectation of proud parents, some of whom were themselves filming the proceedings. What would this turn to when the PSNI demanded their filmed footage and the reason for it? That was going to be horrific, but something that definitely would have to be done. Valberg realised that, as ever, a police investigation had to go where the evidence took it.

Then there would be the outcry over O'Driscoll being able to walk into a school unnoticed and film the children, parents and teachers.

Valberg had a look at his mobile phone and could see very little battery life and a lot of missed calls. He recognised 0034 coming up as the international code for Spain on a substantial number of calls. It got his attention straight away. He immediately assumed it was Carolina, then realised it

147

wasn't her number at all which he had stored on his phone. He pressed the number for redial, but his phone immediately lost power and cut out. On searching for the spare charger he kept at the police station in his desk drawer, he found the old plastic evidence bag dated 14 May 2011 in which Chief Superintendent Kells had placed Heaney's *Death of a Naturalist*. This was the signed copy O'Driscoll had left for him at the Peace Bridge that originally had been intended as a present for Valberg's father.

Valberg had disregarded the poetry book as having no evidential value at all. But he had kept the unsealed and dated plastic bag. He recalled Kells had told him that it had not been formally registered as evidence.

Then he stopped what he was doing and muttered to himself: '*Teenage Kicks*. He heard it and spared Majella's throat.' He recalled the halt of the blade at Majella's windpipe immediately upon the sound of the song being loudly played elsewhere.

Valberg started singing *Teenage Kicks* to himself as he further paused for a moment of reflection and decided to Google Charles Baudelaire. He had noticed the name of the poem O'Driscoll had left for Amanda Cleary – *Heautontimoroumenos* – and realised he hadn't read it in years. He found the poem on the internet and printed it out.

Valberg put the evidence bag in his inside pocket and found the charger for his phone. He left his phone on silent, and charging, as there wasn't even enough juice to make a call on it. Valberg then made his way back to the custody suite downstairs to check on O'Driscoll. On his way there he read the poem with O'Driscoll's voice in his head: '*Like a butcher I will strike you/Without anger and without hate/As Moses struck the rock!/And from your eyelid I will cause//In order to irrigate my Sahara/The waters of suffering to gush forth/My desire swollen with hope/Will float on your salty tears//Like a vessel moving out from shore/And in my heart which they will intoxicate/Your dear sobs will resound/Like a drum beating the charge.*'

The police station was a fortress now. It was difficult to move and get past all the armed officers. But they all recognised Valberg and let him through. Valberg had never witnessed a scene like it in Strand Road Station. He wondered how all this security would work at court and on the drive up to Bishop Street courthouse.

The custody sergeant said there wasn't a sound from O'Driscoll. He had been continuously monitored and everything was recorded. Valberg noticed the sergeant making a note of his visit and timing it at 4.00am. Valberg looked in through the cell spyhole at O'Driscoll, flat on his back, seemingly fast asleep.

'Would you like a chat, Jon?' asked O'Driscoll. 'I know it's you. I can smell you. That Fahrenheit aftershave follows you. Well, it actually sends out a scent you are coming. Linda is very fond of Coco Chanel. You know my father always told me he had no sense of smell and that I inherited his as well. As well as the perfume and the aftershave, I smell fear and apprehension. Some tension as well. Tension between you and Linda. And I smell a sense of confusion. All too good to be true this. Don't you think, Jon Valberg? Ever heard of the Alexander Technique?'

With that, O'Driscoll sat up.

'It's a great relaxant. Great for the body and especially your posture. Did you notice how I got up there? Perhaps looked a bit mechanical to you. A bit awkward. But it's good. I've a book at home on it.'

'Where's that, Gerard? Home?'

'Clarendon Street, number one-o-seven, just round the corner. Top apartment there. I was fed up staying in hotels. I already told those people in the suits who came here after you left me. I expect it's being torn apart now. But there's nothing there. Maybe they'll clean it all out for me. What do you think? Nice place. And your dad's old buddy Mr Haslette helped me with the lease. Hmm. That's how I got to know him recently. Merely a peccadillo for him. But the naughty, naughty custody sergeant. Slipped him a few bob did they? To make no note of their visit. Those guys in suits here earlier? Go ask him. Or perhaps a higher authority than you gave him an order? I dunno. I'm wide awake now. Just like you. The Alexander Technique. Try it. Do a bit of research on it. As I said, it will help your posture. It will help your breathing as well. Very relaxing, once you get into the vibe.'

'Gerard, I'd prefer not to talk about anything unless it's formal.'

'Oh, I see. Our relationship is such that we can only communicate when it's being recorded. Is this being recorded, Jon? I'm sure it is. No secrets here, Jon. *No secretos a voces.*'

'Well, Gerard, is there anything formal you want to tell me?'

'A "Letter to Coroticus", is that what you want? My *confessio*? Tut tut, Jon, don't disappoint me – again. Come on in here. Sit down. Let's have a chat. Then you won't have to talk into a metal door. So how is he anyway?'

'How's who?'

'Come on, Jon. Dear old Father.'

'Oh, Father Doherty?'

'You haven't even checked, have you?'

'That's right. I'll check now, though, and let you know.'

'That would be nice, Jon. Would you? Anything else, then?'

'Well, we might do another interview before—'

'Before what, Jon? Before you charge me? Charge me with what and on what evidential basis? Oh, sorry. I forgot to tell you. Just when you were away there, I gave the custody sergeant the phone number for my solicitor.'

'Someone local?'

'Well, yes and no. More no now. Miss Christina Maguire. And a real hot item she is. Remember that name, Jon? She left this beautiful place and moved on to brighter and better things in London and beyond. But kept her practising certificate for here and all. Ring a bell, does it, that name? She's on her way. Will be here on that awful flight into Eglinton in the morning. You remember her, Jon, don't you?'

'Yes, I remember her.'

'She did her own investigation because the RUC one was a joke. Another whitewash. Another inept investigation. They must have done all these investigations so awfully on purpose. They couldn't have been that stupid.'

'I haven't heard her name in a while. She—'

'Jon, why don't you come in here and we can talk about it? Just the two of us. Come on. I won't bite.'

'Okay, Gerard, stay back.'

Four armed officers accompanied Valberg who entered

150

first. They stood at the door of the cell while O'Driscoll sat on the bed – a blue mattress with a plastic cover.

Valberg sat down beside O'Driscoll.

'He's still alive, Gerard. Father Doherty's still alive.'

'Do you speak the truth? I don't want you to lie to me.'

'I speak the truth.'

'Do you think less of my mother now, Jon? Or should I? Since you know, don't you?'

'No, Gerard. She most obviously loved you so much and was hurting so much. Her pain and anguish was unimaginable.'

'And her guilt?'

'Let's not judge anyone, Gerard. What's done is done.'

'Did she die for me? Did she die for me or die in shame? Her own private shame.'

'She had nothing to be ashamed of, Gerard. Nothing. She had a son she loved very much and lost her husband in terrible circumstances.'

'You do know that we had two major coincidences on my jury. Your father and the dead councillor McFlynn. Did you know that? Do you know McFlynn's code name? Still the same to this day. Although he'll not be setting any more timers now.'

'Tell me what you know. Go on, I'm listening.'

'It was Carcan. Named after the events of July nineteen seventy-two. Operation Motorman, that is. But sure Derry had its own operation. It was 'Operation Carcan'. Aye, a blunt instrument of torture. A Belgian word, I understand. Trotsky gets a pickaxe in the back of the head in Mexico City and Carcan gets a knife in the front of the head in Malaga. Although I don't think Trotsky was a traitor – was he?'

'Not to my knowledge. No. History's not my best subject, though. How did you know that about McFlynn and the detail about the knife?'

'Well, imagine the glee for him as a juror on my case. There he was. Mister Double Agent. Set the bloody timer early. That arm and hand of his a bit jittery. More than once. He was delighted and glad to get me out of the way then. But you knew all about him. Still friendly enough with him, I assume, in recent times. You know how rotten things are, Jon.

151

Peace process and all that. Or processed peace? Not just one or two bad apples in the barrel. The whole thing stinks.'

'Nothing is ever straightforward, is it, Gerard?'

'No, Jon. And think about it. A Sinn Féiner convicting someone on the word of the RUC. That was never believable. No wonder Derry became a laughing stock. Every operation a fiasco. Carcan in the middle of it all, ramming his Irishness down everyone's throat. Never shut up about his "Four Green Fields" and "The Rifles of the IRA". Worse than a born-again Christian. In fact, I'd rather have those who think they are saved.'

'So, Gerard. Would you like to do another interview? Will I start asking you the questions everyone wants to know the answers to?'

Valberg stood up.

'Gerard, you will be charged with murder. You know that. We only need one for now. Then we will lose you to whoever, whatever. Then I'm gone. My temper tantrum confirmed that. I'm out. Finished with this.'

'Well, Jon, the Serious Crime Unit will certainly weigh in and stamp on you. But who else and then what? And for what?'

'The rule of law? Justice? Isn't that enough? The truth. Isn't that meaningful?'

'Don't go there. Don't get all proper with me. Don't bore me, Jon. Sometimes the truth offends ...'

'Gerard. Come on. The truth. Did you kill those people? All those people? Mr Black and the others? And why? Come on, give me a scrap. Anything.'

'The truth has consequences. Think about it. Then there's that other thing.'

'What other thing, Gerard?'

'I feel guilt, Jon. All the time. Every child I see, they remind me of something I didn't do.'

'How can you feel guilty about something you didn't do, Gerard?'

'You explain it, I can't. There's some psychobabble term for it, I'm sure. I get really depressed with it. It affects everything I do. I've heard so much about Orla Harkin. I've read so much about her. I've thought so much about her I began to feel I'd killed her. And that guilt made me angrier and angrier and angrier until I exploded with rage. I felt ashamed over nothing. Can you explain it for me? Do you feel ashamed when you sleep with a prostitute? Or do you think Carolina ever feels guilty after performing acts of pleasure on you? And she did that, didn't she? And you liked it. Then there's Anna. You lit her fire. And it needed lit. She's surrounded by bores all the time. Rough and dangerous sex with you is a tonic for sure. But you both love losing control. You see, she is always in control but then is very submissive for you. But I think you are getting bored with her. It's becoming a bit mechanical. Maybe let her be more dominant, Jon? So, any guilt there with Carolina or Anna? But Anna. The first by your side all night in the hospital. The first there after Finbar's bomb, holding your hand and comforting you. She stayed all night. Did you know that? So ... guilt. Do you feel any?'

'It's not the same is it? Hardly the same now, Gerard. Come on. Look. What about the killings here earlier this year. Do you feel any guilt about those?'

'Cheap even for you, Jon, to weave that in. Not too clever, either. You've let me down again.'

'When did I let you down before?'

'I felt like a dog: weak. I felt dirty. When people I knew died, I felt they would find out I was guilty of what happened to Orla – instead of innocent. Even now, sometimes I get a twinge of guilt. I thought of my mother lying in her own blood bath and wondered: did she believe I was really innocent? Or did she just want to believe that? It's like a disease growing and moving all around your body. Then the anger comes again and I can't control it. The urge rises. It takes over. I'm not in control like I used to be when I killed for money. Acting on orders.'

'So every time you get this twinge of anger, do you have to kill someone? Is that it? You have to cut someone to pieces? You have to hack a pensioner's head off? You have to vaporise another and cut the hands and feet off a fly fisherman? And what about Majella McLaughlin? Why didn't you cut her throat? Did your anger shift? What happened?'

'Have you ever felt that way, Jon? You must have got the

urge to kill someone. Come on. Give me that at least, Jon.'
O'Driscoll paused for a few seconds. 'Well, anyway. There
it is. The truth and what it does. And now misplaced and
undeserving guilt. I think we are themed out.'

'Come on, Gerard, give me something.'

'You already got it. I hear and smell trouble coming. It's
Chief Superintendent Kells.'

'Come on, Gerard.'

O'Driscoll stood up and the armed police officers moved
closer. Valberg didn't flinch.

'Did you kill them, Gerard?'

'Inspector Valberg. What are you doing? Get out of there,'
ordered Chief Superintendent Kells.

'Did you kill them, Gerard? Come on.'

'I'm all legal now. All processed and formalised. In from
the outside. I'm more trouble now in here than out on the
streets.'

Valberg roared at O'Driscoll. 'Did you kill them?'

'Inspector Valberg. Stop it and leave. Everyone out of
here. Now!'

O'Driscoll began to shout back as Valberg was being led
away. 'Anna, Jon. She's in great danger. I am the hunted no
more. She is. And what's worse, you have a rat close by. A
rat in your sinking, stinking ship. A real nasty one. But sure
I told you already, and it's all recorded. Watch your back,
Jon. Anyone who has a false father is usually deranged.'

Valberg was forcibly removed and the Chief Superintendent ordered the cell door locked.

'Get away from here, Jon. Now,' commanded the Chief Superintendent.

O'Driscoll could be heard shouting.

'A rat trap. Evil, Jonny. A big fucking rat. It's coming.
All the way down. Valberg for Chief Con. Meet me at Saint
Antimo. After the Palio. I'll see you there. Valberg for Chief
Con.'

Valberg could hear O'Driscoll laughing then roaring wild-
ly and incoherently in his cell.

CHAPTER 38

By the time Valberg got back to the Chief Superintendent's room, Linda was seething: 'What have you done
now? Did you get your confession?'

'You mean you weren't all listening? Look at you all. Have
you all seen a ghost?'

'No, Jon,' replied Kells as he slammed his office door behind him. 'We've been watching a montage of you on the
memory pen. It includes footage of you at crime scenes, at
the Bank of Emerald, as well as clips of you with several
ladies in various European countries. All friends of yours,
no doubt. We also had some great footage of you at the Taj
Mahal in Las Vegas. Simply breathtaking. And there is a
threat that it will all go on the internet in the next forty-
eight hours.'

Constable Bell looked at Valberg.

'Sir, I think I know what he's been doing. It's obvious
he has been following us. He's walked straight into every
crime scene suited up. I got his reflection once and could
see. I can make a still of the image and get it enhanced,
I'm sure. There's not much technical wizardry in doing
that now with a good laptop. We don't have to be CSI to
do that. Probably suited up at every murder. Even his face
and mouth. I'll show you later. Technically, he's been using
different miniature cameras and what I think is a pair of
Hawkeye digital recording glasses. They must have been
adapted by him. He was always wearing those big glasses
with the thick rims. I even got a close-up of me searching
him at Altnagelvin. I never noticed. They can record and

155

hold up to two hours of footage at a time. You can operate them with a small keychain in your pocket. My wee brother wanted a pair last Christmas, but I wouldn't let my dad get them. No-one would notice. It's a complete trail of evidence. If we can use it.'

'If we show him the footage he'll just laugh at us and talk babble again. It will be a waste of time,' said Valberg.

'Then what do we do?' asked Linda.

'Charge him,' said Valberg.

'There's another delicate matter, Jon,' said Kells.

Everyone in the room dropped their heads.

'He's filmed you and the Chief Constable. It's not exactly family viewing. Did you suspect anything at all, man? Jesus Christ.'

'Two mature adults having consensual sex. So fucking what?' snapped Valberg.

'Easy for you to say. But what about the Chief Constable? This whole thing is turning into a farce,' replied Kells.

'I want to see it. Put it on.'

Linda said she wanted to use the bathroom and left.

The Chief Superintendent asked Constable Bell to lower the volume and play the footage through from when Valberg had left the room earlier.

Valberg looked at Jenny Hastings and he thought about the night she had experienced and what she might be going through. He realised she was about to endure for the second time the sight of the Chief Constable having sex with him. Valberg thought her innocence had just been lost.

'Perhaps Constable Hastings might want a break,' suggested Valberg.

'I think that's a good idea,' confirmed the Chief Superintendent.

'And maybe, sir, I could get some tea and coffee organised and we could all come back in thirty minutes or so,' said Constable Bell.

'That's an even better idea, Michael,' replied the Chief Superintendent who then took his seat back.

When Bell left the room the Chief Superintendent shook his head and glared at Valberg.

'Jon, this will all be all over the internet in no time. The

Chief Con will be devastated. And she has a teenage daughter and son.'

'Will she? Really? I think she cares even less than me. So what? Are we going to respond and react to threats again from him? Look at where we are. At least we have him in custody. It could be a lot worse. Surely this begs the question for our upcoming fantastic public inquiry into his activities, and others, as to how and why he could even do this. What have we got to fear from the truth? I think I've a lot more coming to me with all this stuff about my father and what he knew about the murder of Orla Harkin. If what O'Driscoll has said is true, I've a lorry load of shite about to fall on me. However he managed to film me and Anna, that is the least of my worries at the moment. And think about it. What's one sure way to scupper a public inquiry? Have a criminal trial. Now, who benefits from that?'

'It will be a major scandal.'

'Good God, David, are you really worried about the reputation of the RUC and the PSNI? Get some blonde-haired, blue-eyed woman in to do your PR and speak to the press instead of some half-educated moron who looks like he has a poker up his arse.'

'Thanks, Jon. That's part of my job. I usually do all that here in Derry. Fuck you.'

'You're not under attack, David.'

Both men then went silent.

'David, this is all bullshit. I just played my own game with him. I fucked about deliberately. You know that. It would have been a waste of time any other way. If we had declared him mad or unfit for interview, then what? I know you have protected me all these years. You have put up with me and been patient. I know that and appreciate it, I can assure you. But look, trust me. I can place him at the scene of one of the murders. Trust me. You always have.'

The Chief Superintendent put his head on his hands and shook his head again.

'Jon, how do we deal with this recording and Anna? I was never so bloody embarrassed in all my life. That young female constable was mortified. I know her father. O'Driscoll filmed you at Anna's sister's apartment in Eglinton, the Savoy in

London and the Alfonso Hotel in Seville. The things you were doing to the Chief Constable and the things she was ...'

'David, don't torture yourself.'

'He was everywhere. He filmed everything. Including you watching a porn movie on your own in one of the hotels. I said to myself that you wouldn't do what you ended up doing. And there's me standing in my own room with Linda and that young constable mortified, watching you watching a porn movie pleasuring yourself, having to endure the whole thing. Had you no suspicion at all? And so bloody dangerous from a security point of view. This is very worrying.'

'Charge him with Majella McLaughlin's murder for now. Then he will be someone else's problem. Or a problem for some other organisation, even foreign. Bloody MI5 or MI6, the CIA, the FBI or the Mossad. Take your pick.'

'Well, what about an organisation a little closer to us, the PPS for instance?'

'Forgot about them. Again, he's their problem then in the short term. We and the PPS will just want him remanded in custody. They don't even have to think. The court will be in uproar, but we have to just get it all over with and let the hysteria run its course. Linda can link up with them now and get all the paperwork sorted with the court.'

'Jon, it's your call really when it comes down to it. A bit like O'Driscoll's position for you.'

'What do you mean?'

'It's your last act of control that I, or those above me, will allow. After he's charged and in custody our influence is gone. I know you have been through hell with this but it's way too personal now. You must realise that. And if it's a criminal trial he wants or gets, or a public inquiry, you certainly will feature in it. So Majella McLaughlin, then?'

'Aye. Majella. Charge him with that one, I think.'

There was a knock on the door. It was Linda returning.

'Sir, it's Father Doherty. Starting to look like he might survive. Apparently he's conscious now. It's unbelievable.'

'Come on in, Linda,' said the Chief. 'Father Doherty has a lot to answer for.'

'What?' asked Linda.

The Chief Superintendent sat back and waited. 'What now?'

'Father Doherty. He's O'Driscoll's natural father,' said Valberg.

'Well, I suppose we have enough blood now from both of them to check that theory,' replied the Chief Superintendent, suppressing his disbelief.

'It's no theory, David, and it makes sense. Father Doherty told me. He must have thought he was going to die. At the hospital. He told me there. They even look alike. Look at the old photos of Father Doherty. He had an affair with O'Driscoll's mother. He must have had.'

'Or raped her,' said Linda. 'I was checking him out with the Care Unit. I checked everyone out in this sordid mess. He was a bit of a ladies' man in his day. Nothing about children, though.'

'That's a bit of a loaded comment, Linda. Why the fuck were you doing that?' asked Valberg.

'I couldn't rule anyone out when I was researching that whole Orla Harkin thing.'

'Well, his mother is dead now and rape is out of the question. Whatever the circumstances, and Father Doherty doesn't have to tell us, he's O'Driscoll's natural father and we must face up to it. No-one outside this room should repeat that for now.'

'It was O'Driscoll then who saved his father at the church, was it?' asked the Chief Superintendent.

'It had to be,' replied Valberg. 'It wasn't me anyway.'

Linda said, 'I think we should unearth the inquest papers in relation to his mother's suicide – if it was suicide. As I recall, Father Doherty was the last to see her alive.'

Valberg ignored Linda's comment. He thought his revelation about Father Doherty was lost a bit on her. She seemed more interested in demonising Father Doherty than anything.

'There's another thing,' said Valberg. 'I have a recording that may or may not be relevant.'

'What is it?' asked Linda.

'Ian Haslette. He phoned my mother a number of times on the day of ... well, the day she went to the cemetery.

159

He clearly had been talking to her at length. But then he left quite a number of disturbing messages on my mother's phone later that day. Very disturbing for anyone to have to listen to. It ties in with what O'Driscoll said at interview to us. In a strange way, it makes sense.'

'What makes sense?' asked the Chief.

'That Haslette killed Orla Harkin and O'Driscoll was totally innocent. Haslette confessed to my mother, I think. And the death of his wife was, as O'Driscoll has intimated, no mistake, either. She stumbled onto something in relation to it and then fell down the stairs.'

'Jon, you don't think that drove your poor mother to the cemetery, do you?'

Valberg turned away and looked out of the window while the Chief and Linda looked at each other.

'Yes, David, I think it did. Knowing that my father could have helped to cover up a killing, a murder, whatever, was the last straw for her. It was information she didn't really need at her stage of life.'

'Bloody awful. Terrible. I can't imagine how she must have felt,' said the Chief.

'Then Haslette confessed all to Father Doherty. Totally oblivious to the fact, like the rest of us, that he is O'Driscoll's natural father.'

'This nightmare just gets worse,' said the Chief Superintendent.

'I think we need to look at the police report in more detail about the death of Lily Haslette,' said Linda.

Valberg turned back to face them. 'Anyway. Turn on the recording, David. I want to see it all.'

'Don't worry, Jon. Just you sit there and relax. We'll not disturb you for a few moments while I have Linda sort out the paperwork.'

The Chief and Linda left Valberg in peace. He began to watch the footage he had missed but he intended to skip through large parts of it. Despite the video evidence, Valberg was of the view there was no point in formally interviewing O'Driscoll again. Valberg would say, if asked, that the material is being forensically analysed as part of a larger investigation.

It was six in the morning and Valberg believed O'Driscoll would soon be charged with murder, then he would appear in the local Magistrates' Court and be remanded in custody. Valberg was also aware of the huge media presence outside the police station and no doubt gathering outside the courthouse in Bishop Street as well. He also realised the court, inside and out, would be teeming with the families of O'Driscoll's recent victims. He used the occasion of watching himself having sex with Anna as a way to shut down and compose his thoughts in respect of what he was about to do.

He couldn't remember the title of the porn movie he was filmed watching as he had seen so many in so many hotels over the years. Nothing was unusual about that.

CHAPTER 39

Valberg was aware that O'Driscoll's solicitor was on her way to Derry but purposely chose to ignore it.

He remembered Christina Maguire well. As a young solicitor herself she had represented Janice Sloan when she was charged with attempted murder almost twenty years ago, a charge Valberg believed should never have been brought. Valberg's belief turned out to be correct.

After Janice hanged herself on her first night as a remand prisoner, Maguire, sickened and disgusted with the lack of care and investigation by the Prison Service and the RUC, decided to do her own investigation and report it to the coroner. Valberg greatly admired her courage in doing this and his respect for the legal profession increased dramatically, although briefly, as a result.

But then Maguire vanished and Valberg never heard of her again until O'Driscoll mentioned her name. Valberg was intrigued as to how she had come to represent O'Driscoll. He wanted to get O'Driscoll charged before Maguire arrived and would worry about her reaction to it later. He was not going to enter into a debate about procedure with her.

Valberg was staring at the flatscreen computer watching himself tying Anna up and simulating strangling her. He knew he was watching footage from the Alfonso Hotel in Seville, even though it was of poor quality. It then clicked for him that he did indeed watch a number of Spanish porn movies there one afternoon while the Chief Constable used the facilities at the hotel to do some work. Although he was watching himself and the Chief Constable, he felt again the presence of Janice Sloan in the room watching him. She was trying to show him all the cuts on her arms as she always did.

After around thirty minutes, Chief Superintendent Kells and Wilson came back.

'Have you seen enough, Jon?' asked the Chief.

'Enough for now. I'm trying to work out how he got the camera in the room of each hotel. The quality isn't great. But audio-wise it's good enough. The real problem, of course, isn't the sex.'

'Well, what is it?' asked Linda.

'It's all the stuff we talked about that he must have recorded as well. The sex is only a teaser. Fuck knows what we said about who and what.'

The Chief shook his head, unconcerned. 'That's another problem for another day. Linda has the paperwork and all sorted with the PPS, so off you both go and charge him. His solicitor will be here between nine and ten. Get it over with now.'

Valberg said to Linda that O'Driscoll would not speak a word to them once charged.

'He's been giving us the run-around until now anyway. We can't get a straight answer out of him about anything. I wouldn't even ask him what colour the sky is.'

'Well, Jon, do as you will. I think it's a waste of time and resources but I am not debating it any further. You know my view. We have no real hard evidence. Not even anything that has credibility from a circumstantial point of view. I've said enough. Let's do this.'

'I'm not so sure about that, Linda – I am surprised at your reticence.'

O'Driscoll was brought from his cell under armed guard. He was cuffed again as well. In the presence of an exhausted custody sergeant, and after Valberg explained to O'Driscoll what was going to happen, he read him the caution.

'You are to be charged with the offence of murder. You do not have to say anything, but I must caution you that if you do not mention now something which you rely on in court, it may harm your defence. If you do say anything, it may be given in evidence.'

O'Driscoll didn't flinch.

Valberg proceeded to charge him.

'That you, on the fourteenth day of May, two thousand and eleven, in the County Court Division of Derry, murdered Majella McLaughlin, contrary to Common Law.'

O'Driscoll didn't make any reply – as predicted by Valberg. The silence of O'Driscoll was broken by the phone in the custody suite ringing. The custody sergeant answered it. He put the call on hold and told Valberg it was O'Driscoll's solicitor, who had just arrived in Derry and wanted to know the up-to-date position.

Valberg asked O'Driscoll if he wanted to speak with her, but O'Driscoll declined and said he would speak to her up at court only, in person.

Valberg said to the custody sergeant: 'Tell the solicitor her client has been charged with the murder of a Majella Ann McLaughlin and he will be taken to the local court for a remand hearing as soon as possible and she can consult with him up there.'

The custody sergeant did so.

'What did she say?' asked Linda.

'Just that that was fine, no problem, and she wouldn't consult with her client in here anyway. And she sent her regards to Inspector Valberg.'

O'Driscoll smiled. 'Can I go back to my cell now before I have to go to court and the circus begins? Did you know it's TV licensing and rates day up there? My goodness, it will be busy.'

O'Driscoll was led back to his cell under armed guard, still cuffed. He refused to sign any documentation acknowledging receipt of the charge sheet outlining the offence of murder.

On their way back upstairs to the Chief's room, Valberg asked Linda, 'What magistrate or district judge is sitting this morning? Whatever it is they're called now.'

'Herbert Bailey. He's a fair age and ready for retirement. I remember his name even from my father's day. Seen it all, that guy,' said Linda.

'So, O'Driscoll is before Old Bailey? He goes back a while alright.'

'Yes. Now, all we have to do is get up to court and leave it to the powers-that-be to bring him up there. We're a fortress at the moment and so is the courthouse. The streets are lined with protesters, but there's a huge police presence. They intend to take him directly up Shipquay Street. They're blocking off roads as we speak. Now, you might have to face a few questions in the witness box. But as the investigating officer, as you well know, you just have to confirm you can link O'Driscoll with the offence. There's enough information in the public domain to achieve that anyway. It should be straightforward, but you have no concrete evidence. I know I'm stating the obvious. Sorry. I'm nervous. I shouldn't be instructing you like this. Sorry.'

'Right. Okay. Not my department.'

'What do you mean? Don't start drifting now.'

'Traffic and security. I'll leave that to others to clear the road to justice. I assume the Prison Service have advised their staff who's coming? He'll go straight into their custody after the remand. And I assume someone will have the sense to get some sort of screen up, even on O'Driscoll's way into the court building?'

'Aye. That's covered, too'

'Just in case someone has a pop at him. We wouldn't want that, now, would we?'

'Everything is organised, Jon. The Chief Superintendent was more than helpful in getting it all sorted. He just wants us up there and O'Driscoll will be brought up.'

'Right. Okay.'

'Look, he wants you flanked as well.'

'You're joking.'

'Jon, open your bloody eyes. Since this all started you're under watch anyway. Just go with it. Michael and Jenny are supposed to be off duty but were asked to stay on and help, so we'll have them take us up. It's a bit of history for them, I suppose.'

'For us all. Okay. Page them now and we'll go. No doubt followed by my security dream team. Some angels to watch over me.'

***

165

On their way to court the four police officers didn't talk much. There was a sense of disbelief at all that had happened and an accompanying sense of doom as well.

Linda checked with the court office and O'Driscoll was correct. Multitudes of people were being brought before the court for non-payment of their rates or TV licence. That plunged Valberg into a black mood, even for him. He had visions of sitting in the court, waiting for his moment, and having to listen to a string of unfortunate individuals being shamed publicly.

Although the court office had advised Linda that normal proceedings would stop at midday to allow the 'O'Driscoll matter' to be dealt with, Valberg had been on the receiving end of such assurances for years, which only resulted in his will to live being sucked out of him.

The city-centre streets were lined with white police Land Rovers and police personnel. A helicopter hovered overhead as well, adding to the claustrophobic atmosphere. Valberg thought O'Driscoll was right about the British Army, too. Officially, they were not on the streets of Derry. Unofficially, Valberg believed, it would be inconceivable if members of the security services were not mingling with the crowds lining the streets all the way to the courthouse.

Valberg, as a backseat passenger, could clearly see about three different sets of protesters at the courthouse. He asked Michael to slow down and be careful, as he wanted to be left off so he could walk in the front door of the court with Linda.

The first group of protesters were the self-righteous angry mob. Within the group, and quite unashamedly, thought Valberg, were a significant number of convicted criminals. Also included were a gang of characters well-known in Derry for their professed hatred of the PSNI.

'I'll not say it, Linda, but look at that crew and the casting of stones there. Throw them a few bibles to read. Fucking arseholes.'

Another group were staging a candlelight vigil for the victims of the killings and sporadically broke into prayer and solemn singing. Valberg could sense this dignified gathering, as opposed to a protest, would soon be unheard once O'Driscoll got closer to the courthouse.

The third and smallest group was the group that brought home to Valberg the magnitude of what he was about to do.

Dominica McLaughlin stood with a large photograph of her mother Majella in a wheelchair at Lourdes. It was blown up to placard size, focusing on her smiling face. Valberg remembered the original, smaller version of the photograph in Majella's china cabinet when he discovered her hanging upside down, dead, in her Bogside living room. He recalled putting his gun away and closing Majella's eyes. He also recalled the comfort of sitting on her sofa and O'Driscoll's father joining him as they talked about what may have happened. Valberg distinctly remembered how upset Father Doherty was then. All this came flooding back to Valberg as he was getting out of the car to go into court.

'Where are the TV licence and rates protesters?' quipped Valberg as he held the car door open for Linda to get out as well.

Valberg knew to get through the security area at the front of the court quickly so as to avoid the press and the throngs of cameramen and photographers. In the middle of all of them he could see Amanda Cleary. Cameras were flashing and clicking, as social websites and blogs were updated by the second.

Valberg let Linda go on into the court building. He stood at the front steps, taking in the chaotic and unprecedented scene, thinking about the last time he stood there during a break in the trial of the late Raymond Grimestone. His vantage point enabled him to watch the crowds swelling outside. It was obvious to Valberg not everyone would get into the courthouse by midday.

Valberg recalled the collapse of the Grimestone trial and leaving the courthouse to go and see his mother's frozen body at the cemetery. He recalled Linda saying she was nervous as they left the station. He was starting to feel nervous, too.

CHAPTER 40

The last image Valberg had, just before he was about to turn and enter the front door of the courthouse, was of a female cleaner, pointlessly cleaning the steps of the court of cigarette butts, ash and discarded rubbish. The steps were also covered with chewing gum, well-trodden into the concrete. It was disgusting and dirty, filled with the remnants and rubbish of those presenting themselves for justice.

But Valberg's thought wasn't so much of the rubbish itself, but that, amid the high drama and historical events of the day, the cleaning lady just continued on with her work, diligently and purposely with no complaint. Life carried on and would continue to do so whatever happened in court.

Valberg turned around one more time and looked at the scene and the self-righteous crowd, free from all sin and criminality, waiting and baying for the blood of Gerard O'Driscoll.

On looking into the court foyer, he could immediately see Christina Maguire waiting for him at the public desk. He recognised her at once, even though it was nearly twenty years since he'd laid eyes on her. She looked absolutely stunning, thought Valberg. And totally out of place.

'Christina, you're looking well. My God, life has been good to you.'

'Jon, Jon. It is so good to see you. Goodness. All these years. My, my.'

'What years? Time has stood still for you.'

'Ah, now. It's just a life of no stress. Plenty of sun, well away from the climate here. That's all. But the no-stress thing is very important. I made that decision the last day of Janice's inquest and I've never looked back. But anyway, have you something for me?'

Valberg had a small file with him that contained a copy of the murder-charge sheet. He gave it to Christina who quickly looked over it.

'God, Jon, it's so short. Murder. The simple common-law offence of murder. There you have it. That's it. Well, you'll want a remand?'

'Of course. There's no choice. He's not scheduled up yet.'

'Fair enough. I see what you are at. Schedule him and he's gone. He's gone anyway. He's such a sweet guy really, once you get to know him. He's been to hell and back.'

'Sweet! You are kidding me. That's not a word I see in the same sentence as Gerard O'Driscoll's name. Sweet fucking hell, Christina. How did he find you?'

'Privilege and all that, Jon. You don't want me to spoil the surprise, now, do you? I work in a firm called Princeton, Braithwaite and Sotomeyer. Big firm. Big business. I'm a partner, but on my last count I think there were two hundred and seventy-seven of us.'

'Solicitors? Staff?'

'Just partners. We've hundreds of associates, assistants, paralegals. You name it. Everyone wants to be a lawyer.'

'Jesus. That's a lot.'

'It's one case or one client at a time. Our clients are all very wealthy and always in trouble. It's great for business.'

'Well, it's better than scurrying around here chasing rates dodgers. God, you have a different life, for sure.'

'Aye, well, the odd multi-millionaire pops up here now and again.'

'So, are you applying for Legal Aid for O'Driscoll, then?'

'Now, now, Jon, don't get personal. When will he be here?'

'He's on his way. I'm not interfering with security, that's a problem for someone else. I'm here for a remand. That's all, Christina, a simple remand.'

'Me, too. Let's get it over with quickly, then you can take me to Austins café. I have a real urge for apple pie and custard. The last time I was here that's where my daddy took me. And that's what I had. Can we get a table looking out over the city? I'd like that.'

169

'I think we both might need a bit of security for that.'

'Don't worry, I'm being watched over. You leave that with me, Jon, no-one will harm us.'

'Jesus, Christina, you sound like him. Very sure of yourself. What was that name of your firm again?'

'PBS – Princeton, Braithwaite and Sotomeyer.'

He glanced at his watch.

'Great name. I need to go on into court and see the prosecution.'

'I just met her. Julie Seymour. She's only young. She is just qualified and this is her first case … just a remand, sure. No problem for her. You be gentle with her now, Jon.'

'You, too, Christina. Really great to see you. I think Old Bailey will deal with it at twelve. I'll let you catch up with some of your old friends here.'

'Grand, Jon. See you in there and I'll go and see my client when he arrives.'

Valberg walked away muttering to himself. 'Julie fucking Seymour. Her first case. Jesus. Mass murder. Death and mayhem.' On his arrival in the courtroom he could see Linda talking with Julie Seymour, clearly sorting out paperwork and briefing her. Linda spotted Valberg and walked straight to him.

'Before you say anything, she's a nervous wreck. Don't annoy her. You need her as much as she needs you.'

'Her first case. Fucking joke. Who made that call? Does someone want her dead?'

'Jon, listen. You need to be civil to her. Don't undermine her. Old Bailey will love her. You do the same. She said Mr Bostridge was choking and you saved his life with the Heimlich manoeuvre. Apparently that QC guy has said the same, so you owe both of them. She's already signed her witness statement with the QC. She didn't have to. I think she's a fan of yours for some unknown reason.'

'Well, they speak the truth. I won't undermine her. I hear you. I'll have a seat here at the back of the court and do nothing but listen here for a while in peace. Just a simple remand, sure.'

CHAPTER 41

Valberg felt he didn't need to become a spectator or witness to the events outside the courthouse. If he wanted, he would watch it all on television later, plus he'd see the PSNI footage, as they would be filming it all. He noticed some journalists coming into the court already to get a seat, having surrendered the possibility of seeing O'Driscoll outside. Those who had come into the court, like Valberg, were prepared to endure the TV licensing and rates cases. Valberg occasionally came into this court for some sanctuary from contentious cases, but on a day like today it was tedious.

'Sidney Rankin. Sidney Rankin to court number ...'

Valberg looked at the court clerk calling Rankin's name through the PA system. Then he watched Bailey whispering to the court clerk and the clerk then announced: 'Summons struck out. No order as to costs. That's the rates cases concluded. We'll move now to finish the few TV licencing cases.'

'Fucking great,' muttered Valberg.

Roars and jeers could clearly be heard outside the court. The noise echoed around the building, but Bailey was unmoved. He carefully listened to each case before him, sporting an old-fashioned purple judicial robe that most resident magistrates, now called district judges, rarely wore. Valberg thought that Bailey was the sort of man his father would have liked. He was a Protestant solicitor with a long and respected history in the civil rights movement. He was only working when needed now and had been asked to do the court today, long before it was known O'Driscoll would be

171

before it. Valberg knew Bailey would relish the occasion and rise above any drama.

The intensity of the hum outside the court was getting louder. There was a lot of movement within the courtroom as well. Movement in the cells below was clearly audible, but Valberg found time to smile, witnessing Bailey ignoring it all. Like the cleaning lady outside, life would go on. Justice would be administered, and O'Driscoll and Valberg just had to wait their turn.

All the officers associated with the case started to fill the court, including Bell and Hastings. Extra civilian security staff had been brought in to deal with the situation; most of them were ex-police personnel.

Valberg sat back and waited and listened to the melee going on outside. It was obvious to him that there was a large, angry crowd there.

Then, all of a sudden, O'Driscoll was in the building. Valberg had prearranged with Linda for her to come in and give him a signal. This was it. The furnace was waiting for him.

The TV licensing representative was about to conclude her last case and Bailey was about to set the fine when a young girl, who appeared to Valberg to be wearing a red wig, rose to her feet. A local solicitor, Paddy MacDermott, drew to the court's attention that the girl wanted to speak.

Valberg recognised her at once. It was the girl he had saved from a pretend suicide at Craigavon Bridge and whom he had helped across the Rock Road with her child the day Finbar Callaghan was murdered at Magee University. His eyes fixed on her.

Bailey spoke.

'Well, madam, what have you got to say for yourself? Is there anything you would like to say to help me, madam, please?'

She cleared her throat and looked over at Valberg. He thought she was looking for his help but simultaneously was incredulous at the notion. He stared back at her and almost rose to his own feet. Believe nothing, trust no-one. Life is bleak. Darkness is always looming. Trust no-one. That is so vital. Why was she here? Why was she at Craigavon Bridge pretending to kill herself? Surely an admission to

Gransha Hospital in order to secure the lucrative Disability Living Allowance wasn't worth it? Even all the trappings that came along with the allowance weren't worth it, either. Then she was at Finbar's murder. Why? How could that be? How did O'Driscoll know today was TV licensing day at Derry Magistrates' Court? What about those light footsteps leading from Ian Haslette's house after he was shot in the head? Valberg was digging. His mind was racing. He started to grind his teeth.

The girl took her time to compose herself and looked over again at Valberg who was beginning to feel emotional as he began to have thoughts of Finbar's murder. Should she be arrested now? Could she assist police with their enquiries?

Valberg's thought processes were disturbed by the noise coming from the direction of the door to the courtroom. It was now closed and there was a clamour mounting outside. Valberg could see that Bailey was going to give this girl every opportunity to speak and everyone had to wait.

'It's okay, madam. You take your time, now. I want to hear what you have to say,' said Bailey.

'I'd just like to say. I'd just like to say, Your Honour ...'

Valberg smiled amid his confusion, as he knew Old Bailey liked being referred to as 'Your Honour'.

She continued, 'I'd just like to say ...'

Then she removed the red wig and held it in her hands. She was almost bald and looked weak and frail.

For the fourth time she said, 'I'd just like to say that on the morning the TV man came, he was very rude and aggressive. I'd just like to say that the postman, who was not so rude and aggressive, had just left me a letter. The letter confirmed my diagnosis of cancer, Your Honour. The chemotherapy hasn't worked. I'd like to say ...'

Then she began to break.

'... that I have a four-year-old son.'

She looked again over at Valberg.

'And I have two weeks to live. Thank you, Your Honour.'

She just about got that out, clearly emotional and drained.

Valberg was enraged but could do nothing. The girl who had been foul-mouthed and aggressive towards him was now polite and kindly. He shook his head in disgust. Whatever she was involved in or not involved in, Valberg detested that she was summoned to court at all.

Bailey stared over at the licensing representative.

'There is a loss of the full amount, Your Worship, for one year, and we seek an order for the full amount stated on the summons. Plus the costs of the summons as well, Your Worship.'

Bailey put his pen down, sat back in his chair and glared in front of him. This seemed to Valberg to last for an eternity and he thought the district judge had just had a stroke or a heart attack and was, in fact, dead.

The court remained silent while the commotion continued to build in the cells below and outside. Valberg thought it all felt like an unruly swelling and agitated crowd at a soccer match. Valberg imagined he was sitting on top of a volcano just about to erupt.

The silence of the courtroom was broken by the babble of an elderly woman talking to herself. Then a thud and a bump and what seemed like heavy breathing. The girl with the red wig sat down quietly now, but the noise of a thud and thump had everyone bewildered. What was it? Where was it coming from?

Valberg thought he was in a Victorian asylum. This was one of the strangest days he'd ever had in court. Bailey was still in a trance and Valberg could see that he was waiting for the noise at the back of the court to reveal itself. The security guards seemed to be making way for someone and standing back.

Valberg looked over and could see at last the top of the head of Dottie Harkin, Orla's elderly mother. She was wheeling her own oxygen bottle, refusing any help, while it banged and thumped on the courtroom stairs. She would stop every now and then to put her facemask on and breathe. The girl with the red wig got up and offered Dottie Harkin her seat and put her red wig back on. As soon as Dottie Harkin sat down, Bailey spoke.

'The application for the order is refused today. The application for costs is refused as well. Case adjourned for six weeks, for review only. I will rise now, and when ready, someone please do kindly come and get me. I need a bit of time anyway as I'm in the middle of writing a letter to my brother in Tasmania.'

The girl with the red wig was offered a seat by another court spectator and sat down, sobbing silent tears. Bailey's court clerk brought her over a jug of water from the judge's bench, poured a glass for her and left the jug. Valberg thought it was a fine act of kindness in the circumstances.

The clerk then announced that anyone who didn't have any other business before the court should leave immediately. Several people scurried out but most remained.

Valberg glared at the TV licensing representative as she left the court and he shook his head in mild despair. But as always, he was mindful that nothing about the law and the courts should ever surprise or shock anyone.

The noise outside was getting louder and louder – more intense and aggressive. Valberg was starting to wonder if the court would be stormed and O'Driscoll attacked.

As he stared over at Mrs Harkin and the girl with the red wig, now handing the jug of water back to the clerk, who put it up on Old Bailey's bench, he thought of his father. He thought of the whiteness of the snow his mother died in. He thought of Majella McLaughlin's attempts to grab her Rosary beads and of Billy Black's pleas for mercy. He looked at Mrs Harkin and tried to contemplate what her life had been like since her daughter died. He imagined Ian Haslette looking at his assassin before he got a bullet in the head. He wondered if O'Driscoll had put the girl with the red wig up to it, knowing she was dying. As all these thoughts came flooding in, he realised that these events were perhaps taking place in the wrong court from a security point of view. There was no glass partition in the Magistrates' Court to provide safety for a defendant, and O'Driscoll would need to be well protected when brought up from the cells below for his remand hearing.

CHAPTER 42

Valberg had his mobile phone on silent but just checked for any calls and to see the time. It was close to midday and there were more missed calls from a Spanish number and a text from Amanda Cleary asking for help to get into the crowded court. Valberg summoned Michael to go and help her. The atmosphere grew more intense, louder and heavy with anticipation within the courtroom. If any journalist deserved a front-row seat for the proceedings in court it was Amanda Cleary.

Amid all this, the glamorous Christina Maguire arrived to a flurry of turned heads. Valberg watched her speaking with colleagues she had not seen for some time and to the young prosecutor Julie Seymour. The press wanted to know who she was and checked her name as she handed out her glossy embossed business cards. He could see that every now and again Maguire glanced at him and touched a gold cross and chain she wore, almost pushing it into her chest.

The courtroom was swelling with people and there was just about standing room only.

Valberg could not make out what was being said between Maguire and Seymour, but the one thought he had staring at them was how much he wanted to have sex with both of them, preferably at the same time. His fantasy was disturbed by Linda Wilson arriving.

'She's consulted with O'Driscoll in the cells. They spoke in French. No-one got anything. It was very calm and there was some mild laughter. But all in French. Sorry. And a two-week remand by video-link will be agreed. Technically, she could apply for bail but she won't.'

'Anything else?'

'Just what she's wearing. Jesus – look at her. We've all been on the net on our phones checking. I thought she was dressed in Alexander McQueen or Stella McCartney from head to toe. But it's the Armani Collezioni. Look at that strong shoulder jacket. She'll need it. And that wool-crepe skirt. All in black. She's stunning. Don't say you haven't noticed. She produced a Lanvin Amalia shoulder bag from an Alexa oversized buffalo-leather satchel at the coffee counter to buy a cup of tea. And out popped an American Express Black Card. It was hilarious. Not a fake item in sight. Then there's her Christian Louboutin shoes and—'

'Linda, I'll stop you there. Your attention to detail is admirable, I must say. But to more serious matters. I've just had a thought. The magistrate, sorry, the district judge. Herbert Bailey. Perhaps something we didn't check or need to check. He's been around for years. He wouldn't, by any chance, have been the magistrate in the Derry Petty Sessions back in eighty-two? The first to remand O'Driscoll in custody? Would he? Can we check? Is this all O'Driscoll wanted?'

Wilson was about to answer, but it was too late. Old Bailey was out in the court. With a series of nods from the court clerk to the multitude of prison officers, it was clear that a direction had been given to bring O'Driscoll up from the cells. The courtroom grew silent as Constable Bell arrived with Amanda Cleary. Other family members of those killed were allowed in as well, but special provision had been made for Majella McLaughlin's family to sit at the benches where most of the solicitors would normally sit, on the prosecution side. The family were all tearful but dignified as far as Valberg could see.

Valberg noticed that mobile phones were in text overdrive. He had demanded that everyone in the court should be watched. Smartphones with access to the internet were so obviously being utilised in the courtroom, with feeds to Twitter and Facebook. It was impossible for the court staff, security and police to control this. No-one would dare to take a photograph, though. The chanting and shouting outside the court building and in the foyer were reaching fever pitch.

Bailey would not contribute to the drama and waited patiently. He sipped some water. As the noise grew even louder outside, inside the courtroom it got quieter and quieter. The guards could be heard bringing someone up the narrow stairs from the cells.

Then O'Driscoll appeared – to gasps and tears from most of those in court. He was still wearing his blood-stained forensic white suit and his face was obviously bruised. He now had a bandage over his scar as well, which looked as if it was soaking in blood. He was handcuffed to two guards and they made no attempt to release him.

Bailey took a good look at O'Driscoll and had another sip of water. 'Sit down, Mr O'Driscoll, for the moment.' He then looked at the defence table.

'Miss Maguire?'

'Yes, Your Worship.'

'Miss Maguire, you are very welcome here. In fact, very welcome *back* here is probably more fitting.'

'Thank you, Your Worship. I have been made to feel very welcome by my friends here.'

'Miss Maguire, can you tell me if there is any objection to your client remaining handcuffed?'

'He would prefer not to be, Your Worship. However, we will not object if that assists the court and makes this process easier.'

'Miss Maguire, I am not one for histrionics, but if you do not object we shall proceed as such.'

'Indeed, Your Worship.'

'Miss Maguire, sorry to keep you on your feet ...'

'Not at all, Your Worship. How can I help?'

'Well, Miss Maguire, let's deal with it, shall we?'

'Yes, Your Worship.'

Bailey stared at O'Driscoll, then sighed and shook his head mildly.

'Your client, Mr O'Driscoll, has blood on himself. I am concerned about that ...'

Valberg remembered Janice Sloan at once. She had broken down during her own attempted murder remand and the magistrate presiding then had ordered medical assistance as he had been duty bound to do. The only person who'd gone to assist her had been Maguire. Valberg could see what Old Bailey was up to. He was going to ensure O'Driscoll got a fair remand hearing. Valberg could see Janice Sloan sitting in the court smiling at him. Let justice be done, though the heavens may fall. Valberg wondered if Christina was haunted by images of Janice as well.

'I, too, have a concern about that, Your Worship. But if it pleases the court, and to allow us to proceed, I can confirm that the obvious injuries to my client were, to put it delicately, inflicted elsewhere.'

'Yes. Very delicately put, Miss Maguire. May I ask? Is your client in a position to proceed with this hearing or does he require any medical assistance? I will pass the matter and get him medical assistance at once if you request it.'

'Yes and no, Your Worship. Yes, he can proceed and no, he does not require any more medical assistance. If I may be permitted to say so, Your Worship, it was a member of the court staff who noticed the bleeding from my client's face when he arrived here from police custody.'

Maguire was experienced enough never to turn her back on the bench but she momentarily glanced back and caught Valberg's eye and continued.

'The civilian security officers then went and got a first-aid box and provided assistance. I would like to thank them for that. They helped put on the bandage that can be seen on my client's face.'

'That is very kind of you, Miss Maguire, to confirm that.'

'Mr O'Driscoll is very grateful for their kindness, Your Worship.'

'Shall we proceed, then? Miss Seymour?'

Julie Seymour nervously rose to her feet.

'Detective Chief Inspector Valberg, please, to the stand, if it pleases Your Worship.'

A bit dramatic, thought Valberg. A nod would have done. The court was silent.

Journalists had eagerly recorded the exchanges between Old Bailey and Maguire and these were already hitting the social-media feeds.

CHAPTER 43

The court clerk looked back at Old Bailey, who nodded to him to proceed.

The clerk rose to his feet. 'Mr O'Driscoll, please stand.'

O'Driscoll got to his feet with the two prison guards. Both of them were fat and nervous. One of them was wiping the sweat from his forehead with a hanky.

Maguire turned around and gave an approving nod to her client.

The clerk began. 'Are you Gerard O'Driscoll, of no fixed abode, for the purposes of these proceedings?'

'Yes.'

Then the sobbing started and got louder.

'Ah, son, how could ye do it? Blessed Mary and all the saints and angels forgive him. Who killed my Orla, son? Can anyone in here tell me?'

It was Mrs Harkin. Old Bailey let her finish.

The voice of the court clerk was shaking as he resumed.

'Gerard O'Driscoll. You are charged with one count of murder. Namely that you, on the fourteenth day of May, two thousand and eleven, in the County Court Division of Londonderry, murdered Majella Ann McLaughlin contrary to Common Law. Do you understand the charge?'

'Yes.'

'You may have a seat, with his worship's permission.'

'Yes, please do sit down, Mr O'Driscoll. Miss Seymour. Yes?'

'I see the detective is already in the witness box,' said Seymour.

180

Valberg stood up and read the oath clearly.

'And your name for the record, please?' the court clerk asked.

'Detective Chief Inspector Jon Valberg, attached to CID, Strand Road, Derry.'

'Have a seat, with his worship's permission,' the court clerk said.

Valberg was worried that Julie Seymour, who would have witnessed many remand hearings, was going to rush herself with nerves. He was hoping that she realised his evidence could be led and that it should just be a few basic questions. He was also still thinking of having sex with her.

'You are a detective at Strand Road Police Station, attached to CID?'

'Yes.'

'And you charged the accused, Gerard O'Driscoll, with the offence of murder? The murder of Majella McLaughlin?'

'Yes.'

'And you charged the accused this morning at Strand Road Station and he made no reply. Correct?'

'Yes.'

Slow down, thought Valberg.

'And, Detective, you can ...'

Seymour stuttered a little.

'I am sorry, Your Worship. And you can ... sorry, you *believe* you can ... connect the accused with the charge?'

Valberg looked around the hushed court and at O'Driscoll, then to Maguire, and answered. 'Yes, Your Worship.'

'Thank you, Detective,' said Seymour. 'The application, Your Worship—'

'Just hold on a moment, please, Miss Seymour. Miss Maguire, any questions for the detective?'

Maguire paused, too. Valberg was waiting on the question he dreaded at this stage of the criminal procedure.

She touched the cross on her chain again and rose to her feet.

'Yes, Your Worship. With your permission, may I?'

'Of course, Miss Maguire. Please do. Proceed.'

'Detective Chief Inspector Valberg. Is that right?'

'Yes.'

'Just a few matters. I won't keep you long. First of all, would you be so good as to tell the court how my client received the obvious injuries inflicted upon him? The blood on his, well, his clothing, the bruising on his face and the injury that necessitated treatment here at court, Detective. Please.'

Valberg was uncomfortable, but this was not the question he was afraid of and he was going to tell the truth.

'I am totally responsible for it all. I apologised to your client, and I apologise again, and I apologise to the court. I am sorry. It should not have happened. It was unprofessional.'

'What should not have happened, Detective? And what was unprofessional?'

'I will not beat around the bush. I should not have attacked your client.'

'So you admit you attacked and assaulted my client and left him covered in blood and bruised?'

'Yes.'

'When did this happen?'

'During the course of a number of interviews. Last evening.'

'How did it happen?'

Bailey had heard enough.

'Miss Maguire, with respect, the detective has admitted his behaviour. I now know. I even have a note and I will be reading and hearing all about it on the news after we are finished here, no doubt. So can we move on?'

Valberg spoke.

'Your Worship, if I may. I am totally responsible for this and no-one else. A number of personal comments were made and I lost my composure and behaved intolerably. I am sorry.'

'You launched yourself at my client and as a result of the severity of your attack you broke the chair my client was sitting on and—'

'Miss Maguire, I've got it. Have you anything else for the witness?'

'Detective, did my client answer all your questions?'

'In his own—'

'Detective. Sorry. I will stop you. Did my client answer all your questions?'

'Yes.'

'Thank you. And did he do this without a legal representative present?'

'Yes.'

'And did he co-operate fully with you and your colleagues at all times at the police station?'

'Yes.'

'And, Detective, did my client cause you or your colleagues any problems whatsoever at any time?'

'No.'

'And did he assist you with your enquiries, or perhaps more generally, police queries in relation to the death of a child in particular?'

'Well, he has made allegations that—'

'That will be followed up on? I am sorry to have interrupted you. I will presume the information he gave the police will be followed up on. So please tell the court how it came to be that my client was in your custody.'

'He handed himself in at Strand Road Police Station last night.'

'You mean he voluntarily attended the police station?'

'Yes.'

Valberg was calm and in control. He thought this was too good to be true. He had to admit attacking O'Driscoll. The public might love him for it. He didn't care. Valberg could nearly hear the sea at Marina-Del-Ray when Maguire said with a smile:

'Just one more thing, Detective—'

'Before you continue, Miss Maguire, may I interrupt you for a moment?' asked Bailey.

'Indeed, Your Worship.'

Bailey looked down at the McLaughlin family, sobbing and clutching together on the prosecution benches. He looked over then at Mrs Harkin sitting solemnly on her own. She took away her oxygen mask every now and then.

'Miss Maguire, are you saying that any of this is relevant to this remand hearing? I will give you some latitude, yes. But what has the death of a child a long time ago got to do with where we are at today?'

'Your Worship, if I may respectfully say, I purposely did

not ask for the information I was given. My client believes it is evidence. In any event, in view of the setting here and all those present in court, I purposely did not say the information related to the death of a child and specifically, some time ago.'

'Yes. I see, Miss Maguire. You are quite correct. Silly of me, wasn't it?'

'No, Your Worship. It was more than understandable, if I may be permitted to say so.'

'Well, you have just said it.'

'Your Worship, may I proceed?'

'Please do. I will not interrupt again.'

'Thank you, Your Worship. I am most obliged. Detective?'

Valberg was only thinking of lust and pleasure. He had to have sex with Christina soon. He wanted to maul her. He was determined to take her from behind and ensure that she remained fully clothed initially. He wanted out of the courtroom. He thought of feigning a heart attack or breaking down like his friend Francis Steen and accusing everyone in the court of being characters in a *Star Wars* movie. Anything to get out of the witness box and avoid the question coming and in order to avoid the answer he was going to have to give. But he really wanted to have sex with Christina. He felt overcome with an almost evil, lustful desire that he was going to have difficulty in controlling.

'Detective? Detective? Are you with us? Detective Valberg?'

'Yes. Sorry. What was the question?'

'I haven't asked it yet, but it is this ...'

Maguire paused only for effect. She shuffled the small amount of papers she had and put her left hand on her hip.

'Detective, how can you do it?'

'Sorry? What? Do what?'

'How can you connect my client with the charge?'

That was the question Valberg was dreading, and here it was laid before him in all its magnificent simplicity.

Valberg knew most solicitors never asked that question as they didn't want the answer they would get on the public record. Usually, all Valberg had to say was he believed he could connect the accused with the charge. That was always enough for the magistrate or district judge. Then he had to get out of the witness box and begin the evidential process of actually connecting the accused with the charge. Sometimes it didn't work out or the case would fall apart. Or, in the case of Janice Sloan, an innocent defendant would commit suicide in prison and there was no need to worry about the lie told in the witness box. But not here. Valberg needed something of evidential weight that was strong enough to protect himself. He remembered being asked the same question once before almost twenty years ago by the same solicitor standing in front of him that he wanted to undress now after his first bout of sex with her. He remembered telling the Chief Constable he could kill someone, so a bit of perjury now would be in order. The RUC lied for years in the witness box. So what was the fuss? Just do it. Blurt it out and break the hearts of his dead mother and father. This was the law. It wasn't justice. Do it.

'Salt,' said Valberg.

'What did you just say, Detective? Did you say salt? Did I hear you right?'

'Well, not just any salt. Salt very specific to your client.'

Maguire for the first time gave the appearance of being flustered and looked back at O'Driscoll.

Bailey interrupted.

'Please forgive me, Miss Maguire. Detective, I am confused. Did you just say salt? Please explain this.'

'Your Worship. During the course of discussions at the police station, and it is all a matter of record, Mr O'Driscoll spoke at length about salt. Salt from the Dead Sea. He told us how he used the salt and its purpose.'

Maguire looked at O'Driscoll, then fixed her stare on Valberg.

'Your Worship, it is no ordinary salt. From the Dead Sea, he told us. And what's more, he told us where he bought the particular salt that he uses to cleanse himself with. The market in Jordan where he regularly buys it.'

Bailey looked confused. 'Detective, I am still unclear. What is the relevance of this salt?'

'At the murder scene I found minute traces of salt. Well, I didn't know then it was salt. I thought it was crystals of

185

some sort that seemed out of place, sprinkled over the sink of the deceased's home. I collected these small traces of salt and had them analysed. I discovered that the grains of what turned out to be salt could only have come from one place in the world. The Dead Sea.'

'Detective, this is fascinating. But I am still lost,' said Bailey.

Maguire shot an indignant stare at Valberg. 'Not as much as I am, Your Worship.'

'The accused not only voluntarily surrendered himself to police, Your Worship. He voluntarily confessed to his use of this salt and provided us with samples. I would prefer not to go into all the details now, but the salt he gave us is exactly the same as the salt I personally took, bagged and recorded at the murder scene. It could only have come from one source. One market stall in Jordan. The one market stall he told us about. Taken from the Dead Sea. And we know the accused washed his hands at the sink with it. And we know now he used the salt from the Dead Sea and left minute traces behind him. That's how I can connect the accused with the charge. Salt from the Dead Sea.'

The court went into uproar for the first time and some of the journalists left. They had their first headline.

Maguire shook her head. 'This is ridiculous. Ridiculous.'

While the court clerk tried to order calm in the court, Maguire stared intently at Valberg. He looked back at her knowing full well what he had just done. He had used the old evidence bag Superintendent Kells had given him in May 2011 and deposited into it some of the salt he brushed from his clothes after he had helped clean up O'Driscoll following their skirmish in the interrogation room. He had then locked the bag, duly sealed, into his desk drawer. He would lie again to the PPS and apologise for not producing it sooner. This was all perhaps just enough to collapse the case in due course, but enough for now to get O'Driscoll into custody and let him be a problem elsewhere.

Maguire shook her head at Valberg as the court started to become quiet again.

'Right, Detective. I will sum up and tell me if anything I say is wrong,' said Maguire. The court was silent again.

Old Bailey sipped some more water. Valberg thought he was looking a bit uncomfortable.

Maguire cleared her throat. 'My client voluntarily surrendered himself to police at Strand Road, Derry, last evening. He was arrested. He assisted police with their enquiries. He also assisted police with information in relation to the death of a child many years ago. He was assaulted and attacked by you. As a result of the assault, my client was seriously injured. His injuries are axiomatic. You then charged him with murder and now you say you believe you can connect my client with the charge. The alleged murder of Majella McLaughlin, at this stage, as a result of a few grains of salt from the Dead Sea. You say that you secured this evidence at the scene of the alleged murder on the fourteenth of May, two thousand and eleven. In summary, Detective, is that your evidence under oath to this court?'

'Yes.'

Julie Seymour rose to her feet.

'The application, Your Worship, is for a two-week remand in custody to appear again by video-link.'

Maguire shook her head but bowed graciously to Old Bailey, accepting the inevitable.

'Two weeks, then. I am presuming there is no application for bail, Miss Maguire, at this time. Technically, you can, but I am sure you will have already advised your client of his right …'

Bailey started to cough and loosen his shirt collar. He took another sip of water.

Valberg needed the district judge to grant the application. He looked at O'Driscoll again. He remained unmoved by everything, as far as Valberg could see, and his stare at all times had been on Bailey.

Valberg had a notion that, in all the confusion in the court previously, the girl with the red wig had been offered some water by the court clerk and the clerk had let her pour herself some from the very jug Bailey was now drinking out of. What if she had put something in the water, unnoticed by anyone in the drama and commotion?

Maguire rose to her feet.

'Your Worship? Are you feeling okay?'

187

'I'm fine … I just need a drink of water. Sorry. Frog in my throat. There. That's it settled. Yes. Application granted. Remanded in custody. Two weeks, then, and thank you all. Detective Valberg, you are free to leave. Thank you.'

The court clerk nodded to the prison guards while the district judge tried to get to his feet. O'Driscoll stood and the crowd in the court began to shout obscenities at him while some spat in his direction. But all this was silenced by the noise and sight of Old Bailey choking loudly while standing up and putting his hand up almost as if he were indicating to the guards to stop. And they did.

Linda Wilson rushed towards Valberg as he was getting out of the witness box. 'You're right, Jon. He was the magistrate who remanded O'Driscoll in custody at the original Harkin trial. A part timer then when he was a solicitor. I couldn't approach you in the witness box. We should have checked.'

Then Bailey started roaring, trying to get his breath as he fell forwards on top of his bench with an almighty bang and scattered all the court papers everywhere, including the letter he had been writing to his brother in Tasmania. Valberg climbed up over the bench and helped Bailey onto his back. He looked for the girl with the red wig, but she was gone. Bailey was now foaming at the side of his mouth.

'Call an ambulance. Now. Fucking do it now,' Valberg shouted. 'Get everyone out of here.'

People in the court were screaming as they ran out. In the melee, Mrs Harkin got knocked over. The McLaughlin family were squealing in terror. O'Driscoll stood and watched it all for a moment before being rushed down to the cells again. The stampede from the courtroom spilled out into the foyer and onto the street outside. The news media captured the uproar and panic and broadcast it nationwide.

Valberg was attempting to get Bailey into the recovery position, but the judge retched so hard he started to throw up blood – most of it over Valberg. It was an almighty heave. Bailey then collapsed totally. He lay in his purple gown with his eyes wide open as if they were about to pop out of his head. Bailey's mouth, nose and eyes were covered in blood. What an exit, thought Valberg. Dramatic to say the least.

Valberg could see Julie Seymour, the young prosecutor who had just finished her first case, in hysterics, being comforted by Maguire. He stumbled back and wiped the blood with his hands from his face and onto his clothes.

At that moment he thought about taking out his weapon and putting a bullet in his own head. He started to grind his teeth as paramedics rushed in from a side door and urged him out of the way. He got over the court benches and made his way to the door. Linda Wilson joined him.

'You lied, Jon, didn't you? You've let us all down. You've fabricated evidence and just committed perjury. You're no better now than the likes of Dickey and Montgomery. All your smart talk and moral high ground about truth and justice.'

Valberg glared at her, unflinching. 'This is a murder scene, Linda. Get a SOCO team here and everyone out. The judge was poisoned. Rat poison or something in the water. What else could it be? Had to be. Just had to be. O'Driscoll got what he wanted. Again. I'm fucking outta here. I'm going to get the court list and the names and addresses of everyone here today. Everyone is a suspect. O'Driscoll continues to have his revenge, it seems.'

Valberg took in the chaotic scene surrounding him as he left the courtroom. He could hear what sounded like a riot taking place outside on Bishop Street. He realised that the arrangement he had with the Chief Constable's office, in relation to charging O'Driscoll and processing him, was going to be the subject of open ridicule and criticism. They had all walked into O'Driscoll's trap. Perhaps O'Driscoll had now got his final victim. He had killed the resident magistrate who was the first judicial figure to put him in custody along with Raymond the Reaper in 1982.

'*Blodigt helvete.* I need a fucking drink.'

CHAPTER 44

Valberg cleaned himself up in the court toilets and decided to walk back to Strand Road Station, despite the melee going on outside the courthouse. He refused all offers of a lift, preferring to be on his own. Valberg was worried that if he stayed any longer in court he was going to lose his temper and go down to the cells and shoot O'Driscoll. He believed that if he made a scene getting into a police car and hurrying away then this would look bad as well. So, with ambulances arriving, crowds roaring in anger and fear, and a massive police and media presence, Valberg joined the crowd and walked through the swell of people. They would all wait to get a glimpse of O'Driscoll being taken away so they could exorcise their own demons and roar abuse at him.

Valberg made immediately for Palace Street and walked down it and checked his phone again. Although still on silent, he could see that a Spanish number was calling so he answered it.

'Hello. Who is this?'

'Ah. Ah. *Habla Español*? No?'

'*Puede habla Inglés conmigo, por favor?*'

'*Si. Si.* No problem. Sure. Sure. Sure. My English is okay.'

'Yes. Well, what is it?'

'Can I ask you your name, sir?'

'Yes, you can, but who are you?'

'*Lo siento.* Oh. Sorry, sir. My name is Antonio. Not to alarm you, but I am a policeman. I am from San Pedro, just west of Marbella in Spain. You know it, sir? That is my

190

home town where my family live. I don't live there anymore, though. Do you know it?'

'Yes. What is it?'

'Well, it is a delicate matter, sir, and I would like to meet you. Is that possible?'

'Well, I am not in Spain.'

'Ah. Yes. Where are you?'

'You ask a lot of questions. It might be better if I call you back from a landline in a few moments.'

'But, sir, it is urgent. I have been calling you a lot. This is the first time that we have spoken. Can you tell me your name and where you are? Is it Val? Is Val your name, sir? My name is Antonio. Antonio Domingo.'

Valberg knew that Carolina had his mobile number stored under the name Val. He hated the nickname but only let one person use it. Carolina.

'Look, you could be anyone. I will call you back at the number you are calling from. You say that will be the police station in San Pedro in Spain?'

'Yes, sir. I am from San Pedro and visiting my father today but I work mainly from Malaga and Madrid. I am in a specialist unit but I am working with my friends here at the moment. Can I ask you one question?'

'Okay.'

'Did you have any association with a Carolina Munoz?'

Valberg knew the police language. He was talking about Carolina in the past tense and digging the way he would have done.

'Can I call you back in a few moments? What is wrong?'

'It is very sad, sir. She, ah, *muerta*. Sorry. And there is a child. She has been asking for you. Will you please call me? The child really wants to talk to you.'

Valberg hung up.

His head became flooded with a tsunami of thoughts about Carolina. What has happened to her? The Spanish police had his mobile number and were now, quite understandably, thought Valberg, doing their job. They were investigating and calling all the contact numbers she had. All her clients. And Valberg was one of her best. He could smell her. He could see her. He could hear her. Time to take that gun out again. Time for dying. Time for a bullet in the head and to fall dead on the small, narrow street. He reached for his gun but a police Land Rover came around the sharp corner the wrong way, up the one-way street with a load of other Land Rovers behind it. Valberg got up on to the small pavement and let them all pass until the whole length of the street was lined with police vehicles all the way to Bishop Street, where the multitudes had gathered.

Valberg could not help thinking that everyone connected with him was going to die. This was punishment by O'Driscoll for the sins of both their fathers. How and when could this end? Valberg thought he could only get peace if he were dead himself. He remembered the time he walked on his own from the cemetery, after Finbar's funeral, to the police station, not caring if someone shot him. Now he walked on down Palace Street, past the City Walls and the Memorial Hall and onto Waterloo Street, not caring if someone recognised him and attacked him. Even killed him. By the time he got to the Strand Road, still no-one approached him. It seemed as if the whole of the population of Derry was up at the courthouse in Bishop Street.

He made it to the Strand Road Station in the company of Cameron De La Isla in his head, singing and clapping and playing guitar with Paco de Lucia. He remembered Carolina always played that music in her apartment. The image kept him focused. Valberg thought of the many nights and into the mornings he'd made love to Carolina with Cameron's haunting voice in the background.

Immediately upon his entry, a civilian security lady advised him that a young girl with a red wig was at reception and that she would not speak to anyone but him. Valberg went to her immediately and took her into a private room on her own.

CHAPTER 45

'He's got my son. You have to help me. He said he'd kill him if I didn't do what he said.'

'Who? What? Who?'

'You have to help me. You have to help me. I can't even cry anymore. It's the medication. It's a side effect. Crying with nothing coming out of your tear ducts is painful. I'm dying. He's got my son. He's only four. I had no choice. He said if he saw me talking to you, Pearse would die. I had to do exactly what he said. I killed the solicitor Haslette, and the judge. It was me. I had to do what he said. Just point the gun at the lawyer and shoot. And so I did. I pretended I was leaving down my TV summons. On fucking Christmas Eve night. The solicitor knew I was upset and he told me to come on in. O'Driscoll told me exactly where to go. And I did. Because of Pearse. He had him. He said I could only confess after the court hearing. Everything. He stole your gun, and I put it back when you were out. He said he'd kill Pearse if I told the police anything before my court case.'

'What's your name?' asked Valberg.

'I'm Debbie Sloan. Janice's younger sister. We were fostered out. Split up. You don't know me, but I got to know about you. You tried to help my sister. So help me now. I'm begging. My son. My wee boy. He's only a wee boy. He told me what he would do to him if I didn't do what he said. There's the packet with the stuff he gave me to get into the judge's water. If that didn't work I had a knife. I would have got him. For Pearse. As long as Pearse would live, I didn't care.'

'I didn't know Janice had a sister.'

'We were fostered out, then adopted. An easy way to wipe the memory. What am I to do?'

'Have you told anyone any of this?'

'No.'

'Then don't.'

Valberg lifted the material Debbie put on the table. It was clear liquid rat poison called Coumatetralyl.

As he read it, Debbie said: 'He told me to tell you that the use of liquid poison is a highly successful way of controlling rats. And I killed that nice man who was so nice to me. Just like you have been. I killed him. I thought he might just collapse later. But it was for Pearse.'

Valberg looked at some of the symptoms of involuntary ingestion of the poison which included bleeding of the gums and nose. That explained why he was covered in so much of Bailey's blood. He could see Bailey in front of him, lying dead on the bench of the court.

'Listen to me very carefully. I'm taking all this stuff from you and I'll get a bag and seal it. Listen to me. You have come here to make an allegation that your son has been kidnapped. Forget everything else for the moment.'

Debbie sat down and her wig fell to the floor as she lowered her head. She sobbed inconsolably.

There was a knock on the door.

'Inspector Valberg. Are you in there, Inspector? Is everything okay? Can I help?'

It was the civilian security lady whom Valberg did not know. He called back that everything was fine.

'Listen, Debbie. Look at me.'

Debbie was shaking now.

'I need my stuff. My meds. I'm going to throw up.'

With that, she vomited profusely, but Valberg managed to get the rubbish bucket at the corner of the room to catch most of it. He got out his mobile phone after he tried to clean the vomit from the floor and checked the time. He could see that the policeman from San Pedro had been calling him constantly since he hung up. He switched the phone off.

Time to think. Time to be calm. Time to rationalise. Don't overreact. Believe no-one. Trust no-one. Don't even think for a second of detaining this girl under the Mental Health Act.

Debbie was getting out a bottle of water and taking her medication.

'Right. When did he take him?'

'The minute I realised he was gone my mobile phone rang and I knew it was him. I was in Foyleside. He said it will all be on the CCTV footage.'

'It might just be a threat, Debbie.'

'Mr Valberg, you have to help me. I can't die knowing that my son is dead. This is all fucked up. He's going to heaven and I'm going to hell. I won't even see Janice. Nothing. The devil is going to get me.'

'We need to move fast. Did he say anything else?'

'He said I could only talk to you after the court and only here, so I came straight down. He said he would tell you the address when he was in the police station, and only you. It was last night. He said he would make Pearse safe for the night, but that if anything went wrong, or if I didn't do as he said, Pearse would die. He said he would sedate him but that he would be okay.'

'What's the address? Did he tell you? Do you know?'

Debbie shook her head.

'Sorry, Debbie. I've a load of questions. But where on earth did you meet him?'

'He was at the clinic I went to when my results came back a while ago. He told me he was there privately and he chatted to Pearse. I just assumed he had cancer, too. Or some other fucking horrible disease. Perhaps dying as well. Then his name was all over the place and all that stuff last May. I couldn't believe it. Who killed that wee girl anyway, Mr Valberg? Tell me it wasn't him. Please. Can you tell me he wouldn't harm a child? Am I going to jail?'

Debbie broke down again and fell into Valberg's arms and he held her tightly.

Valberg remembered debating with his father whether or not Columbo was right to let Janet Leigh go in *Forgotten Lady*. She had killed her husband and was dying herself. What would a prosecution have achieved? It was a real legal and moral dilemma. Valberg thought she should have been prosecuted when he first watched that episode with his parents. However, as he got older he came firmly around to the view of his father and his favourite policeman.

He finally let the female civilian security woman help him and asked her to look after Debbie until he came back to collect her.

Within a few minutes, Valberg found himself standing in the office of his Chief Superintendent as sirens blazed around Derry.

'Jesus, Jon, what is going on? What's the sense of it all? I'm ready for Gransha.'

Valberg sniffed at his shirt knowing that he looked awful.

'Don't go just yet, sir. Do you trust me?'

CHAPTER 46

The focus moved away from the Derry courthouse once O'Driscoll was driven off in a secure prison van and the mob had vented their emotions. The media got their story and photographers got their pictures. All predictable and all inevitable, thought Valberg. He watched the gathering crowds at the bottom of Clarendon Street and at its junction with Queen Street who had made their way down town to the new drama. The public knew something big was happening once the police started to clear the area and a British Army bomb-disposal squad arrived.

Valberg wore, for the first time in years, a black bullet-proof vest with the word 'POLICE' emblazoned across it. He had got showered and cleaned at the station. Chief Superintendent Kells gave him the full official PSNI uniform: white shirt, dark trousers, boots, jacket and baseball cap. Everything fitted perfectly. The finishing touch was the thin police-issue tie that his superintendent gave him as well. Valberg felt like he was dressed as a real policeman. He liked it.

Number 107 Clarendon Street was about to be stormed, so the area was cleared. Valberg was convinced Pearse was in there, but care had to be taken. It could be another O'Driscoll trap. Valberg had checked with the custody sergeant in the presence of the Chief Superintendent as to whether anyone else had been in to see O'Driscoll on the night he was in captivity, but he confirmed there most definitely had not. So O'Driscoll's reference to 107 Clarendon Street had to be the location of Debbie's son. It had been a reference Valberg

197

had chosen deliberately to ignore at the time, thinking it was just a wind-up.

By now, Wilson, Bell and Hastings were all down from the court and wanted to help. The building was just around the corner from the Strand Road Station and in hindsight, thought Valberg, an obvious location for O'Driscoll all this time. It was boarded up and on the market for sale.

Valberg watched the bomb squad from the British Army get ready. O'Driscoll had indeed managed to get the army in the sky and back on foot on the streets of Derry.

Valberg stared at the huge black door of the graceful Georgian building that was to be assaulted. He watched the Tactical Support Unit getting ready to move forward, waiting on the order from him to bust the door open. Time was of the essence. The life of a young child was at stake. The officers had to move.

'Go! Go! Go!' Valberg shouted the order.

Debbie Sloan looked on, protected by other PSNI officers from a safe distance. Ambulances with full medical crews were also on standby.

Valberg and his three fellow officers got behind the first unit in. There was an almighty bang as the heavy black front door was burst open. Valberg had his gun out as the masked officers in front of him cleared every room on the ground floor. It had previously been a dental lab and lay disused but not damp. The heating had been on. Hundreds of sets of white moulded teeth sets greeted everyone. They were laid out in different shapes and sizes in different locations all over the ground floor, but especially in the back room. Skeletal in appearance, they represented the shape of the mouths of many dental patients. The tools of the trade of the dental lab technician lay everywhere, too. It looked as though someone had just abandoned the place and time had stood still. The police officers' boots crunched on the bone-dry materials strewn on the floor.

'Wait. Listen.'

Valberg signalled to everyone to stop moving. He pointed upwards. A floorboard gently creaked above him. Valberg rushed up the stairs, barely allowing the Support Unit to clear the way. They stood motionless on the landing of the first floor. There was a key in one of the doors and Valberg was about to touch it when he heard a cry.

'Mammy, Mammy, Mammy. Is that you, Mammy? Mammy. I want out, Mammy.'

Valberg signalled to everyone to lower their weapons and he opened the door.

Pearse Sloan saw him and backed away.

'Mammy. Mammy. I want my mammy.'

Valberg swept him off his feet and rushed the child down the stairs and out, much to the relief of all the police officers there. He came out of the building with Pearse in his arms and safely placed him into the weakened arms of his dying mother. The massive crowd that gathered clapped and cheered. A lone male voice from the crowd shouted, 'Valberg for mayor!'

Valberg looked over at his Chief Superintendent who just nodded.

Valberg looked back at the building, realising the number of officers inside it and wondered what they were doing. Why were they still there? Then he thought it really was a trap, and incendiary devices – which O'Driscoll had used frequently before – were about to be set off. He rushed inside and up the stairs with the intention of shouting at everyone to get out but was met with their faces staring at a computer.

A large screen was flashing up the words: 'I killed Orla.'

The room they were standing in was covered in pictures, diagrams, photographs, maps, newspaper articles and information, all about the case of Orla Harkin. Everyone O'Driscoll had killed since May 2011 had a section of their own. Their lives were all mapped out and displayed in legal wallet folders. The other rooms upstairs were similarly bedecked. Valberg and his team went through them in a daze. Even the loft rooms were covered with information. The ceilings were covered, too, in police documents and folders and barely a piece of wallpaper or plaster could be seen anywhere. Everyone there was amazed and stunned into silence.

One of the rooms had a placard outside it reading 'The Room of the Forgotten'.

Michael recognised some of the names and folders from

his own local knowledge of Derry. They contained the names, with folders in pristine condition, of unsolved murders and deaths at the hands of the paramilitaries, the British Army and the RUC. The files contained information for family members especially.

'Jesus. He's spent all his time on all these cases. So close to us. So close to us he could touch us. So close.'

'Putting right the wrong, sir?' Michael asked.

'Get this all sealed. Get everything filmed and photographed. I almost don't want to touch anything, it's all in such good shape. Everyone get gloves on.'

'Well, did he kill Orla Harkin, sir? Is that a confession on the computer screen?'

'No, Michael, he did not. Let's read on and you can see who did.'

Michael, with a pair of blue forensic gloves on, clicked the mouse to begin playing the computer. It was ready to activate. It immediately showed a video of Ian Haslette confessing to the killing of Orla, but not murdering her. The confession didn't reveal the involvement of Valberg's father. Valberg believed this was an act of kindness on O'Driscoll's part. Another secret to the grave for the moment.

'Sir, if you don't mind me saying. It's not my place. And in this moment. But you really look like a policeman. I can't believe it,' said Michael.

'Well, Michael, what do you make of all this? Fuck me, look at it. Everything. He was under our noses all this time. Sealed up behind a building for sale.'

'Incredible, sir, just incredible. Never thought I'd be in a case like this in all my life. I just can't believe it.'

Valberg looked for Linda. He found her in a state of wonder as well, looking at the detail of the work that covered the rooms.

'Jon, I never thought this would happen. Sometimes the simple things are just too obvious. I checked the child's room. He left him enough water and food and a bed. It was en suite. But what if we hadn't got here?'

'But we did, Linda. So forget it. Do you have Christina Maguire's number, and can I use your phone? I didn't get one of her cards.'

200

'Aye. I've got it here. I'll call it for you. Here. Let me look at all this, it's unbelievable.'

Valberg took the phone from Linda and it was ringing. Christina answered.

'It's Jon, Christina—'

'I'd like to report a crime ...'

'What? A crime? What a day. What crime do you want to report?'

'My bloody overcoat. Someone stole my coat in that court nightmare. My Louis Vuitton, full-length cashmere over-coat. Got it in Barcelona. A simple remand, you said. Then there's that apple pie and custard. When?'

'Where are you?'

'City Hotel. I'll text you the room in a moment, I'm just checking in.'

'Well, I'll be a while. Relax there, it's crazy here. We've a lot to talk about.'

'That grain of salt?'

Valberg remained silent. He looked at the others, still fix-ated with everything in the rooms. The Chief Superinten-dent was present now and he had the same stunned look, Valberg thought, about the scene confronting him as he'd had at the bloodbath at Long Tower Church on Christmas morning.

'Jon, Jon, are you there?' Christina asked.

'Yeah. Yeah.'

'A grain of salt? My client was very disappointed. He men-tioned something about Richard Rich, was it? A Man for All Seasons who sold Sir Thomas More out for Wales? Anyway, I'll text you the room. I have a proposal for you. An invita-tion to treat, if you will. An offer you might not be able to refuse.'

'Okay. Text the number to my own phone. Not this one.'

'Don't worry. I know it. Checking in here now. See you later.'

Christina hung up.

Superintendent Kells approached Valberg.

'A full confession, then?'

'Seems that way.'

'The Orla Harkin case solved at last?'

201

'Yip.'

'A saved child?'

'He seemed fine to me. The best place for him is with his mother.'

'O'Driscoll in custody?'

'Yes.'

'A grain of salt?'

'More than just one grain, sir.'

'Salt, you say? From the Dead Sea?'

'Yes. The Dead Sea.'

'A complete case analysis of Orla Harkin's botched investigation and the framing of an innocent man? All contained, no doubt, in the plethora of paperwork that plasters the walls of this building?'

'I think so.'

'A dead solicitor and a dead judge?'

'That's unfortunate. But, yes.'

'The RM. It was the same man who put O'Driscoll in custody? Old Bailey? Dead?'

'Yes. Most definitely dead.'

'No clues, suspects or leads on those two murders?'

'No. Nothing at this stage. But I have a couple of lines of enquiry.'

'The finding of the boy will save our bacon. You know that? *He* knew that. A PR triumph in the fog of war.'

'A matter of comment, sir. I couldn't possibly say. But the boy is safe.'

'Now I, the arsehole with the poker up my backside, must do a press conference and explain all this?'

'Part of the job, sir. Professional when you least want to be.'

The Chief Superintendent pulled Valberg to one side to talk more quietly.

'Jon, Anna has had a call. She's been trying to get you.'

Valberg's heart sank. He thought it was the Spanish policeman.

'Who was it? Is it important? I'm sure she gets a lot of calls.'

'Listen to this. Langley, Virginia. Ringing bells?'

Valberg sighed.

'Some guy called Samuel Leadbetter.'

'Not a name you are likely to forget, sir.'

'He has an interest in O'Driscoll or "The Necromancer" as he referred to him. Does this mean anything to you?'

'Nothing. Nada. Zero. Not a thing.'

'Right, Jon, let's leave it for the moment. The CIA. That's all we need. Anyway, I'm looking forward to seeing all this written up. Anything else?'

'Let Amanda Cleary from the *Derry Journal* in with a photographer to see all this. Give her a statement, but only let them photograph enough from a distance.'

'Can't do it. Not fair. What about the rest of the media?'

'Let them all in, then. But Amanda first. Do you trust me?'

'Has anyone told you you look like a real policeman for once in your career, Jon? Trust *you?*'

CHAPTER 47

Valberg could hear *European Super State* by Killing Joke being played loudly in the Amelia Earhart suite of the City Hotel as he knocked on the door. When Christina opened it she was singing.

'*From the Baltic to the Straits of Gibraltar ...*'

'Hello, Christina.'

'Great song.'

Christina was still in the same clothes she had worn in court. The brands and labels of which Valberg knew now, thanks to Linda.

'Oh, fuck, I love it. Come on in. I just got it on the radio there. Couldn't believe it. Searching for something different to get away from the news. Fuck the news. Come on, Jon, let's get wasted. Where's your uniform? Seen ya on the telly. You looked good in that PSNI garb.'

'You look a lot better. Can we eat here? I don't want to go downstairs. Too awkward for me.'

'You're the king, Jon. The punters think you're the next Chief Con. Even though you are perjurious.'

'Are you safe, Christina?'

'Stop being a cop, Jon. Live a bit.'

'I need help. I need a lawyer.'

Christina turned the music down. 'Before you say anything. Before we do anything ...'

Valberg looked at the bed. She smiled at him.

'Let me make you an offer.'

'An offer? What do you mean?'

'A job offer. Here's the way I see it. I hear Linda is off to

204

the HET. You are out of the O'Driscoll case. Maybe a witness. I dunno. He's off to God knows where. He'll be out of that prison – if he even gets there – in no time. A matter of national security. Public interest. Blah, blah. Health, even? Whatever. Right? So what have you got? Move to the HET yourself? Get all moral and dig up the past? You're too tenacious. You don't really want to head off to Iraq or Afghanistan on security detail for some company, do you? Do you? You'd get a few grand a week and come home, or part of you would come home, in a box. So why not work for us instead?'

'What? I'd never be any good as a lawyer. Fuck. Having to go back and do all those professional exams? Law Society would never let me in. I've assaulted and threatened so many of their members.'

'No, no, no. As an investigator for me. You'd be as good as self-employed. Name your price. We have clients with so much money they could buy all the freeholds in England. Multiple nationalities with vast sums of money. People vanish. People steal money. People spread gossip. People die. Children die. Children vanish. We need investigators. Freelancers to get us results. Information. Intelligence. Evidence. The clients we have will pay anything. Fucking anything for someone like you. You pick where you want to be based. Anywhere in the world. We have offices everywhere.'

'Oh, I get it. You get me out of the way then?'

'Think, Jon. Life is so short. Princeton, Braithwaite and Sotomeyer will still be around long after we shake off this mortal flesh. Law firms will never die. But we will. Do it. Resign. They'll send a private jet for you to Eglinton.'

'Are there any illegal substances in your body, Christina?'

'Not yet. But I'm game if you are.'

Valberg shook his head uncertainly – but not ruling anything out.

'I need a few weeks. And I have one request or call for assistance. Can you help me?'

'Sure. If I can. What is it?'

'Can you have your people find out what happened to a Carolina Munoz in Spain? Marbella, Malaga region. I've been told she's dead.'

'Okay. I only need the name for now. That's enough, leave it with me.'

'Thanks. I'll give your offer some serious thought.'

'Sure. Up to you. Don't hope too much on this side of the grave. You know that well. We've watched you from afar. Good on your own, Jon. Good at keeping your mouth shut. Very important.'

'Yeah, but all this O'Driscoll stuff. The public inquiry. Perhaps next year?'

'Are you joking? It's goodbye to Gerard for a while. Just one rule, though.'

'What's that?'

'We never talk about him again. No questions. Nothing. You'll be working on other stuff. We'll double, triple, quadruple your salary, buy you anything you want and—'

'You've travelled far, Christina. You're not that young solicitor, modestly-dressed, defending Janice and chasing trippers and whiplashers anymore. Or chasing the DOE all the way up to the dizzy heights of the County Court in Derry.'

'Do you want a drink, Jon? Brunello? You know where I got this? Tesco. Gerard did say that there will be no Puro Caviar Black where he's going for a while. But that shouldn't stop us. So let's have a drink. Shall we?'

'Of course. Go for it.'

'I've just one other personal matter to mention, Jon.'

'Go on.'

'I've only got a change of clothes for one night. I'm leaving in the morning. Plane to catch. People to see. So call me when you're ready. This may be the last sensible conversation we have for now.'

'Okay, let's drink. Do you have offices in Madrid or Malaga?'

'Both.'

'Do you know anything about Spanish adoption law?'

'Absolutely nothing. But I know a beautiful woman who does.'

'Then let's drink to that.'

Valberg remembered starting to drink with Christina but not much else. He wanted to have sex with her, and he wanted Christina to keep her clothes on when they were having sex. Something about the labels. It was a notion he took. She obliged then went for a bath. Valberg remembered her taking her iPad and mobile phone with her to the bathroom and her talking. But he had no interest in whom she was talking to or what about. He switched off his own mobile phone.

The next thing he was doing was staring at Christina with her eyes wide open, motionless beside him, with nothing on but her bathrobe. He started to panic. She wasn't breathing.

'Sweet mother of fucking Jesus Christ,' Valberg said. He wanted to jump out the window. What a mess. She had coked up and overdosed, he thought. He was in serious bother. He grabbed her and started shaking and roaring her name, then Christina squealed out of her after a huge gasp.

'Stop, Jon, stop. Jesus. Fucking stop.'

Valberg fell off the bed and got up.

'I thought you were dead.'

'Sorry, sorry. My fault. Happens now and again when flying. My blinkers. I forgot to say and forgot to put them on. Nocturnal lagophthalmos. I sleep with my eyes open. Whoops.'

Valberg sat on the side of the bed with his hands on his head.

'Fuck me. What a shock. That's a new one on me.'

'Sorry. I should have said. I come with a health warning.'

They both laughed and got back into bed and fell asleep, both completely exhausted.

Christina was picked up early the next morning and taken straight to the airport and Valberg cleaned up and headed for Strand Road Station. He said he would call Christina soon. He needed to mull over her proposition and sort things out.

CHAPTER 48

The afternoon after the rescue, Valberg headed for the City Cemetery.

It wasn't long before he was standing at the grave of his parents and brother. He had previously found it hard to let his emotions out – he was too angry. He stared at his mother's gravestone and the words 'Died On Her Birthday'. It made no sense now. Nothing seemed to. O'Driscoll had got to him. He could hear Rush playing *Hemispheres* interrupted by Ian Haslette's Jag, crunching to a stop on his parents' driveway. The whole spectacle angered him. Now he knew there had been a dead body in the boot. The body of Orla Harkin. He shook his head.

'How could you, Dad? How could you do that?'

Still angered, he walked away and caught sight of Janice Sloan's grave. It was, like all the graves, battered by the rain, where now just one large bouquet of new flowers lay carelessly.

Valberg fixed them.

'Who has sent you flowers, Janice?'

Valberg got down to look; the flowers were from Christina. Valberg wondered again if Christina felt Janice's presence in her life. She had deeply affected both of them. But where could Janice be now? Barely a woman before she was taken, and the same story for her sister. Derry wasn't the worst place in the world. Evil was everywhere, but was Derry cursed with tragedy? The only way out of this thought process for Valberg was alcohol. But not today. He wished he could come to the cemetery and leave without being angry.

Perhaps one day. But not today.

As Valberg was leaving the cemetery he called Christina.

'Christina, it's Jon. I'm up for it. Where are you?'

'Rio. Rio de Janeiro. God, it's great to hear from you. I knew you'd call me.'

'My God. From Derry to Rio in a day. No bother to you.'

'Well, to London first, then a private jet.'

'Okay, what do I do?'

'I'll meet you in London – in the Savoy on the Strand – in a few weeks' time. My PA will book a room in my name and will contact you with the date and details. See you there. We'll be having an office party thing soon so the timing is perfect. Oh, must go. I'm being called. I'm on the red-eye later this evening.'

'No problem.'

'Jon, just before you go. Quickly. Carolina Munoz.'

Valberg felt an invisible bullet pass through his body, left to right. He had a sense of doom.

'What is it?'

'Just briefly. I made a call before I got on my flight to Rio yesterday, and when we landed I had all I needed. I assume you knew every part of her body? Did you know about the bar code?'

'Bar code?'

'Tattooed. She had a bar code tattooed on the upper inside of her right thigh.'

'Jesus. I never saw one when I was with her.'

'For identity purposes, it seems – for ownership. She got mixed up with some Russian or Romanian gangs. Perhaps even Serbian. Dangerous crews. Very dangerous. Murder. Violence. Drug trafficking. And prostitution. We know one of the cops heading the investigation. They starved her to death. Chained her to a radiator. Her daughter is in an in-stitution. No family. But I'll tell you everything when I see you. I really have to go. Bye.'

Christina hung up. She sat naked on the edge of the bed, only a gold cross and chain touched her skin. She yawned and stretched out. She put her head back and let her long blonde hair fall into the hands of Seán Carlin.

'Well, Pontiff, he's in. Gave him enough to keep him keen.'

'Do you sleep with all your clients or just me, Christina?'

Christina turned around, got up and straddled the Pope, then let him ease into her.

'That is so good, Seán.' She smiled down at him. 'And, no – only the ones I like.'

CHAPTER 49

Standing in the cemetery among the dynasties of the dead was not a good place for positive thinking. But it had always been a good place for reflection for Valberg.

Now there was something else he was responsible for. Carolina's death was probably his fault, too. Could he have saved her? Should he have done more? *Could* he have done more? Pearse was soon to be without his mother, and Maria's mother was dead. She died slowly and painfully and unnecessarily. Why? Why did he always feel such a burden of responsibility? For what? Time to be selfish and think for himself. He had to do something to avoid bipolar land.

He called Chief Superintendent Kells.

'I've made the contact. That's it, I'm in. As soon as I can get organised you'll hear from me. And, David – thanks for your support. Thank Anna, too.'

'Do you really know what you're doing, Jon?'

'You do trust me, don't you?'

'I do, Jon, but we need to meet first. We have a lot to talk about.'

'I'm not meeting you at Strand Road.'

'Where, then?'

'Number one hundred and seven. One hundred and seven Clarendon Street. The forensic guys must have all they need now for the Serious Crime Unit.'

'They shelled the place and sealed it. You know that. Every scrap of evidence had to be gathered. They took skip loads away. And all the material on the walls and computers and files left by O'Driscoll for us, that's all forensically sealed and safe.'

'Six tomorrow morning, David. See you there.'

'Okay, Jon, six in the morning it is. I'll arrange entry.'

***

Valberg rang Kells at six the next morning.

'Change of plan, David. I'll pick you up outside number one-o-seven now and you come with me. The Provos and the Brits used to do this all the time. Change the location for security reasons at the last minute.'

'We'll be followed, Jon. You know that. For security.'

Just then, Valberg pulled into Clarendon Street and Kells got into Valberg's car.

'Good morning, Jon. And where are we off to?'

'It's dark at the moment but the light is coming soon. I thought out the old railway line. Out where Orla Harkin lay dead and I used to fish with my father. We'll go on a bit down from Milltown House. No-one will suspect us there. I just thought a drive and a little walk would do us good.'

'Okay, Jon, whatever you want.'

Valberg drove out the Foyle Road; the lights were red just as they came to the lower deck of Craigavon Bridge. Both men looked in the direction of where Billy Black had been left hanging but all Valberg could think about, as he always did in that area, was Janice Sloan, dazed and confused, after being arrested on the far bank of the river. Valberg pretended not to notice the two white PSNI Land Rovers following them.

The roads were quiet apart from the police presence.

After driving a bit out the Letterkenny Road, Chief Superintendent Kells asked, 'Are you turning down at Balloughry? There's a gun club out here. I know some of the members.'

Valberg didn't respond but did turn down left onto Balloughry Road.

'It's beautiful out here. And so close to Derry,' said the Chief Superintendent. 'Am I getting the silent treatment, Jon? We need to talk.'

'Sure we do. Let's pull in at the layby out here. Not too far out this lovely road.'

Valberg pulled in at a layby leading to a walkway and cycle track that turned back in towards Derry on the left hand side of the Ballougry Road. He was able to park his car there.

'Let's walk from here, David. The guys coming behind us will watch my car. I'll not make that mistake again. Down the track and towards Derry.'

'Sure, Jon. That's the gun club just down there to our right, just before the border.'

As both men walked towards the River Foyle, the sun was attempting to rise.

'I've listened to the tapes, Jon. The O'Driscoll tapes. They make uncomfortable listening. That along with the stuff on the memory pen. He set us up, didn't he? And we helped, in effect, murder the judge, didn't we? By charging O'Driscoll and delivering him to court?'

'As dear old Seán Ignatius Carlin once said to me, don't be so hard on yourself. It's all my fault really – or more accurately, my father's.'

'Jon, we're in the mire here. But you must find a way to forgive your father. You have to because there is no resolution for you otherwise.'

'O'Driscoll got to me, David. I trust you completely, but not Strand Road, and that's why I came here. Paranoia. That's cool with me but I haven't gone into an alcoholic downward spiral in a while. I'm getting better. And I know you will find this hard to believe, but for the first time in years I actually felt like a policeman when I had ... well, your uniform on. Why can't it be simple? Someone dies and we just investigate. Solve and provide closure. Move on.'

'It doesn't work that way, Jon. It never does. Never.'

Valberg shook his head as they walked along the tree-lined pathway towards Derry and the rising sun.

'There's a number of breaks along here, David. I know most of them. They take you right down to the river. So let's walk in to where this all started and we can get a lift back. I noticed the uniforms following us and I know my car is safe this time.'

After a moment's silence, Chief Superintendent Kells replied, 'This time? That's another delicate matter, but Mr Haslette first. The solicitor. We think we know what was missing from his office. We bagged all that could be bagged and tagged. But we found a cabinet with a set of title deeds missing. For a plot of land in County Derry that it appears he planted a little forest in.'

'The trees. They'd be difficult to cut down, David.'

'Look, I don't know where it's all going, but whoever murdered Haslette took nothing from his office that we know of but those deeds. Perhaps the only thing that was on his desk that night. It was just luck that lying in one of his cabinets we found a list for the deeds. Young Constable Bell had the idea to do a search in the local registries. The address corresponded exactly with the tab on the deeds cabinet in his office. Up near Downhill. Beautiful area, too.'

'Let's go in here, David.'

Valberg found an opening in the trees lining the riverbank and both men made their way as close to the river as they could.

'What lies beneath, David?'

'The river, Jon?'

'No, the trees. That's what you mean, isn't it? And what more did my father know about Mr Wonderful, as O'Driscoll called him? The prospect is frightening.'

'Here, Jon. Take this.'

Valberg opened up a copied Department of Agriculture map outlined in sections with the names of various tree species that had just been handed to him.

'Ash, Oak, Beech, Sitka Spruce, Larch, Mixed Broadleaves, Scots Pine, and Michaela. A lot of Ash and Michaela in one particular area. Looks beautiful, David.'

'Stick it in your pocket. There are some other matters you will not be happy with ...'

'I hate that word. Happy. I hate happy people, too. I once met a girl who was so fucking happy I thought about cutting her into little pieces and—'

'I'll stop you there, Jon. I'm not in the mood. Constable Hastings ...'

'What about her?'

'I read all the reports. When you arrived at the reception area when O'Driscoll presented himself, what is the first thing you did?'

'I took out my weapon and thanked Jenny.'

'She didn't.'

'Didn't what?'

'Produce her weapon.'

'Oh, come on, David.'

'She can't tell me why not.'

'That Nesbitt guy pissed himself. She protected his dignity and raised the alarm. She should be commended, not criticised.'

'I agree, Jon, but procedurally—'

'Fuck off, David. Don't procedure me when she calmly and professionally dealt with a mass murderer.'

'She also said the only thing that stopped her producing her weapon was you and the others arriving. She said she was about to.'

'Fair play to her.'

'You need to know that the whole thing, because of the PACE mess, is under some scrutiny by O'Driscoll's lawyers.'

'She acted nobly and with great fearlessness. I will defend her to the hilt.'

'As I will. And who will defend you, Jon?'

'From myself?'

The Chief Superintendent didn't answer and stood for a while looking at the river.

'The sun is well up now even though it's still early. I can see the attraction of this place.'

'It's very peaceful. Beautiful. There's so much of nature to see here. Especially on the eve of spring. So much that is pure. David, let's walk back to the path and on down a bit. Just past Milltown House we'll come to Orla's last resting place. Come on.'

Once back out on the path the men began talking again. Armed officers were now in clear view, but a distance back.

'Jon, you'll hate this, but O'Driscoll's lawyers and some of our colleagues want to know why you let O'Driscoll leave the City Hotel when you spotted him during last year's debacle. The lawyers, somehow, got access to your statement.'

'Do I have to dignify that with a response?'

'To me? Aye.'

'You know the answer, and I have given my statement. It was to protect everyone. I mean everyone. The thousands there that day including women and children.'

'And you directed every available armed officer to the Memorial Hall. Do you know what I had to put up from Mr Fluckman because of that?'

'Is that his real name? Richard Fluckman. Dick Fluckman? Seriously? Grand Master Fluckman?'

'Jon, the police arrived in multitudes and stormed the building and the tower on your tip-off.'

'It was the right thing to do. And you know it.'

'Yeah, but the complaint to the Police Ombudsman's office is awkward.'

'Claim the golden oldie – as will happen at any public inquiry – National Security. Refuse to answer.'

'And we also have the Bostridge strangling episode to contend with. You have that QC Charlie Creswell to thank for saving your bacon there. Thank him.'

'I will.'

'His evidence and that of the young female barrister will scupper any criminal action, too. So thank her as well.'

'I will, I will.'

'There's just a couple of other things.'

Valberg stopped. He looked around him. 'Look. We're here. It's changed a bit. But not much really. I caught a lovely trout here once. We can walk up the little path and uniform will take you to the station and me to my car.'

'You can see Craigavon Bridge from here, too. God, it really is lovely here.'

'This river will keep flowing and the pain still hurting unless we do the right thing, David. And before you tell me, don't worry.'

'Tell you what, Jon?'

'That you have no choice but to suspend me. I'm not going off on the sick.'

'On full pay, of course.'

'Of course. Or perhaps not. I don't care. We have an understanding, then?'

'We do, Jon. So, to move on. Two women – Linda and Anna. Let's start with Linda. We listened to the calls. Your calls with O'Driscoll the day the Peace Bridge opened. His allegations about Linda.'

'We?'

'Jon, don't do this unless you want a procedure lecture.'

Valberg shook his head.

'Okay.'

'She's looking for a move and I'll tell you what I think.'

'Go on, David.'

'I think you've been playing her along recently. Humouring her and so forth. I thought nothing of O'Driscoll's accusations until I listened to the PACE tapes afterwards. The tea – for O'Driscoll.'

'No sugar and a little milk.'

'That's it. How the fuck did she know that? An obvious blunder. She knew him from before – or something about him.'

'She didn't want him charged, either.'

'Who can you trust, Jon?'

'Anna, of course. And Linda. Well, I want to trust her. But now I'm filled with doubt. I keep telling myself to trust no-one. But that's not realistic, is it?'

'Then can you leave Linda to me?'

'I will.'

'Can I leave Anna to you?'

'You can.'

'This is done now. You're suspended. So you can go your own way while I clean the stains.'

'Okay. We sound like two old RUC Special Branch men. I already had my gun taken from me for forensic tests.'

'Young Michael said you didn't touch it the day he called. Just stared at it. And the forensic report says yes, it was your gun that was used to kill Haslette but that the fingerprints on the weapon – well, the clearest last ones – seem to be those of someone with a small hand. Or a woman. And you are, thankfully, timed as present at Long Tower, tied up on that hellish night.'

'Right. Is that so?'

There was another pause between the men.

The Chief Superintendent looked away from Valberg again as if admiring the river view and examining Orla Harkin's last resting place. He looked a little embarrassed, then drew a deep breath.

'Did you hear about the electrical fault that caused the fire in the custody suite at Strand Road?'

Valberg stared at where O'Driscoll must have sat all those years ago, just yards from the body of Orla Harkin. He didn't answer the Chief Superintendent.

'It happened inside the store where all the PACE tapes are kept. Just last night. So you wouldn't know. Everything melted. Everything. Every tape in there from the last couple of months has been obliterated. I was called down to see it. What a mess. Just that tape store. It got the brunt of the fire and they managed to contain it within the store. It was just an electrical malfunction.'

'I didn't hear about it, David, no.'

'Go to Anna, Jon. Stop being a policeman for a while. She wants you and you need her. Would you do that for me?'

'Okay, David.'

'And not a rat in sight.'

'Not one, David. Not here anyway. We better go our separate ways. I dream about something else now. Not rats anymore.'

'What is it?'

'A red gurnard.'

'A fish?'

'A tough one. Very tough. Swims mainly in the darkest depths. A bottom feeder. It just stares at me with its tentacles up and fins expanded. I can't get past it. We don't talk. We just stare at each other. One of us is waiting to make a move. Its eyes are big and black. Not a popular fish, but I remember my father saying it was the chicken of the sea. It has a tough exterior. Very tough.'

The Chief Superintendent continued to examine the area and shook his head.

'Leave the mire with me. Safe journey, Jon.'

Both men turned to walk away, but Valberg stopped.

'David. My father always said that. Safe journey. I want to go and see Mrs Rankin, Sidney's widow, before I leave.

She's been calling the station a lot. Michael and Jenny already visited her. Is that okay? And I need to make a few trips to Strand Road to get a few things.'

'That's fine, Jon, do that.'

Now, with the armed officers gathering, it was time to walk up the embankment to the Letterkenny Road away from the river and go their separate ways.

Valberg began to think of Anna now and how much his father had liked her.

But in his confusion his thoughts also drifted towards Linda. Could O'Driscoll be telling any truth about her? Valberg was reinterpreting events in his head, on purpose, to suit O'Driscoll's line to see if he could fight a way back from it. He remembered Linda saying O'Driscoll needed to hand himself in, her demonisation of Father Doherty, O'Driscoll confirming that Linda was very fond of Coco Chanel perfume, and the no sugar and little milk provision for O'Driscoll's tea. How could she have known? Above all else, there was the horrific possibility that she knew Finbar was going to kill himself when he turned the ignition on in Valberg's car. All significant points, Valberg mused. She was also sharp with Finbar on the Derry Walls, saying some bomb family victims had a lot less to bury than a piece of flesh on a ribcage over the years. That had to be a reference to her father.

Valberg let all that rest with him for the moment. Only time would work it all out for him.

CHAPTER 50

Mrs Rankin recognised Valberg at once. She smiled thinly as she welcomed him.

'Come on in, Mr Valberg. They're letting me stay another while before I'm evicted to the cemetery. Mind all the boxes. Mainly rubbish. I'll make you a cup of tea.'

'That would be great, Mrs Rankin.'

Valberg was invited to sit in a living room which was in a chaotic state. He knew Mrs Rankin wanted to talk to him. He felt morally and duty bound to let her.

'When you held him, Mr Valberg, what did he say?'

'Not much, Mrs Rankin. He was tired and in pain. Well, perhaps not pain, some discomfort. But he was peaceful and relaxed.'

'We never got to bury anything. He threw his grandfather's War of Independence medal to one side. That's all that survived. A lovely young policeman and woman, Michael and Jennifer was it? They called to see me.'

'That's right. Two great young officers, Mrs Rankin.'

'Well, they brought it home to me. Sidney's last act of defiance. Throwing the medal away so it would survive. We put a wooden box in the ground and I filled it with all his clothes and some personal things to give it weight. It was a closed coffin. Obviously. But only the policemen and women on the scene knew that there was nothing left of Sidney. You were all very good. Thank you.'

'What was his name? His grandfather's?' Valberg asked, sipping the nicest cup of tea he'd had in ages.

'Michael Davitt Rankin. Son of James Peter Rankin.

220

Michael's brother, Sid's great-uncle, died at Loos. This brother thing.'

'The Battle of Loos? I know that. But in the British Army?' queried Valberg.

'Oh, aye. An outcast. The family disowned him. I can't imagine the desolation. A young boy sent to fight. For what? For the world? For Ireland? What? Sid always admired him. Admired his obvious bravery. You see, Sidney was angry, too, at times. Couldn't understand why there was so much hatred for his great-uncle. His grandfather got the medal. Aye, he admired him, yes. For Ireland or for what? But he worshipped his great-uncle. For the world I suppose. Sidney found out everything he could about him. But that's all buried with him now. Or in that coffin. In the damp graveyard earth. I buried the past. Not a body. Not a person. Just the past. And if we don't respect the past or treat it with dignity, it comes back to haunt us – always.'

'What was his name? Your husband's great-uncle.'

'Matthew. James Peter Rankin had two sons. Matthew and Michael. One joined the British Army and the other the Irish Army. Or the Free State Army. The Collins crew. Sid always talked about Matthew, dreamt about him and wished he could meet him. It was a bravery thing. I just wondered; did he mention him? Or me? Or anyone else?'

Valberg thought he should have lied – again. He should just have said something to ease the blow. He remained quiet.

Mrs Rankin asked, 'Do you think he is with his great-uncle Matthew now, Mr Valberg? After all this time? Perhaps he has finally got to meet his hero. I can see them embracing each other. The two of them smiling and hugging one another. The generations meet. No shame anymore. Forgiveness at last. They shall overcome. Someday.'

Mrs Rankin tried to smile. But she couldn't.

'I'm sure they are together, Mrs Rankin.'

Valberg had just lied and he knew it. He was not sure at all. He wanted to have faith, but the last couple of years had been punishing, personally and professionally. He found it difficult to have faith in anything. Or anyone. He was searching for his own faith. He had fallen into the habit recently

221

of visiting some of the city's finest religious buildings: Saint Eugene's Cathedral, Long Tower Church, Saint Augustine's Church and Saint Columb's Cathedral. He spent ages sitting and reflecting and trying to find what his mother had found and, in a strange way, his father. He was trying to find solace and peace. But nothing came to him. He wondered why the people around him in every church, chapel or cathedral appeared to him at least to have so much faith. Was there something he didn't know? Was there some big secret that made it easier to have faith in any God? The harder he tried to believe in what he was brought up to believe in, he felt he was drifting away from it.

'Perhaps,' continued Valberg, 'it was, or is, his great-uncle Matthew who is providing the forgiveness. Not asking for it. He doesn't need to. One by one, he has forgiven them.'

'I hope so, Inspector. I hope so. Desolation. It's all desolation. What will become of that boy? Gerard O'Driscoll. I say boy, but he is a man, like you.'

'As far as I know, he is unwell and in a secure location getting medical assistance. I'm merely a witness in the whole debacle. The Serious Crime Unit have taken over everything. Then the FBI, CIA and Interpol. You name it and they are looking for him. I have no real direct involvement as an investigator anymore. The whole thing became very personal. I finally fell foul of every PSNI rule, protocol and procedure. It all caught up with me eventually, Mrs Rankin. And I don't feel ashamed to say that to you or admit it.'

'Has he had some sort of breakdown? Is he mad?'

'It's not for me to say. I have my doubts.'

Mrs Rankin paused and sighed.

'You know the bank and the Inland Revenue took everything. They moved fast and had already been moving even before Sid died. And he died horribly. I've nothing. No pension. Nothing. Penniless. Surviving on hand-outs. The Solicitors Benevolent Fund didn't exactly help much. So many lawyers are killing themselves these days, there's not much to go around. Sid worked up so many debts. He never told me a thing. Too proud. Too terrified. Awful. Why are men like that, Inspector? Mr Valberg, why?'

'I dunno, Mrs Rankin. We suppress everything to protect others.'

'And you went to try and help him and your mother had just died. I've heard all about it. I'm so sorry. Your own mother wasn't even resting in her own home and you went to help my husband.'

'No. Don't worry. I was doing my job. That's what I do. It wasn't just me. All the police officers there went to help.'

Mrs Rankin looked away from Valberg and he could see she was lost in thought. Staring at nothing. She kept looking away and then said, 'He spoke about you once. I didn't understand. Remember when he went missing that June time?'

Valberg's attention increased.

'Yes, I remember.'

'Well, he arrived home the evening that the Peace Bridge opened. When he came back he was a different man. He was always in that police station. He overheard someone talk about you. It was a woman, if I recall. He always wrote everything down, but I buried a lot of his notebooks with him – most of them had research on his great-uncle. Then there was his will. That was made with Mr Haslette, the other dead solicitor. They never got on, you know. Mr Haslette arrived in Sid's office one day. He was very upset, but Sid wouldn't see him. Then Sid picks him to do his will. Of all the solicitors in Derry he chose Mr Haslette.'

'Sorry to drag you back, Mrs Rankin. What did he say? What did your husband say about me? We had him in the station at the time, but he did not give us much to go on.'

Mrs Rankin turned and looked at Valberg.

'Oh, I can't remember it all now. Somebody in the police was worried about you. He never really talked about his work. That was the first time. Something moved him. Disturbed him. Then he got more withdrawn as the months went by and lost it at that bloody bank. Then the bank and the Revenue took our home, his office and everything else he had. But that's why I really wanted you to come.'

Mrs Rankin got slowly to her feet and took from the back of an old mahogany china cabinet a rusted and dated tin box.

'What is it, Mrs Rankin?' asked Valberg.

'His grandfather's medal. I've not long to go. I hope you don't think I'm a confused old woman but I am a dying one. And I want you to have it. You tried to help him, you were kind to him. You held him in your arms when he was dying. You held his hand and didn't let it go. You were the last person with him. I insist, go on. Take it. Please.'

She just about had the strength to open the tin box and show Valberg what was inside. Valberg didn't want to have to help her and he was glad when it popped open.

'Mrs Rankin, you could auction that and get something for it. Please don't.'

'I insist, Inspector. I'm begging you. I've hidden it from the bank and the Inland Revenue for long enough. How ironic that the proceeds from an auction of an Irish War of Independence medal could end up with Her Majesty's Customs and Revenue or even that bloody Emerald Bank. Only a policeman like you could put a stop to that.'

Valberg wanted to smile. He took Mrs Rankin's comment as a compliment even though he realised full well that a degree of illegality was involved in what she proposed. Valberg was now a willing and eager accomplice in preventing any bank, or the Inland Revenue and Customs and Excise, from torturing Mrs Rankin further.

'What about your children or your grandchildren? Is that some of them in the photograph?'

Mrs Rankin turned around and lifted a photograph of two young girls arm-in-arm. She looked at the photograph and kissed it. She went silent again and looked away from Valberg. He could see that her eyes were full of tears. She held them open for as long as possible and the moment she blinked her tears fell, but she made no sound.

'These were our girls, Inspector. Not our grandchildren. That's how we always remembered them. Arm-in-arm together. And the way we wanted to remember them.'

'Were?'

'You don't know, do you?'

'No. Sorry.'

'The death of Orla Harkin overshadowed everything in Derry back then. Just as her death has done recently. Before she died, the girls drowned. From all Sidney could find out from the police – and it wasn't much – we think Ashley fell in first, then her younger sister Michaela went in after her. To the day he died, Sidney was certain someone was chasing them. That theory became fact in our home and that is how I believe they died. Both drowned. Someone chasing them. That's all I see and imagine. It is horrible. Their bodies never found. We never had a funeral for them.'

'My God, I am so sorry. I didn't know that.'

'There were more over a long time. And, of course, that poor policeman – or should I say policemen and women. That bomb in Coleraine that day. But I always remembered Mr Wilson and his daughter because she cried so much at his funeral. Really cried. Really hard. It was horrifying. You know I lost two girls, but the uncontrollable crying of that wee girl at her daddy's funeral really upset me. I still hear her sweet little heartbroken voice.'

Valberg took a deep breath and shook his head. He realised Mrs Rankin was referring to his colleague Linda.

Mrs Rankin wiped the tears from her face and composed herself and continued.

'Sidney said the police wouldn't listen to him, and all their resources the day the girls vanished were directed at the bomb. They were forgotten. Nothing. The police promised to help him if he helped them. They fed him scraps of information over the years if he ... well ... did not cause them too much fuss at the police station. Or court.'

'I'm sorry to hear that. That's awful.'

'Sidney never recovered. He wasn't the most popular solicitor in Derry, I know, but when he closed his eyes he wasn't sleeping. I know everyone accused him of sleeping in court and at the police stations. You see he was dreaming about Ashley and Michaela. That's all he was doing. Dreaming. Wishing. Fantasising. The thing we all do in our own secret worlds. He was praying they would walk through the door and rescue him from whatever he was doing. He never wanted to be a solicitor. He found himself in an awful compromised position. And for me. He'd spend all his time chasing false leads that some policemen gave him – not policemen like you, but officers like Dickey and Montgomery.

225

There were others. But those two especially.'

'My God, Mrs Rankin, I am very sorry to hear this.'

'That's okay. He hated being a solicitor and what the profession had become. It seems to be very common now, lawyers who hate being lawyers. He never stopped thinking about his daughters. His two pieces of gold. His angels from heaven sent by his great-uncle Matthew. He never stopped thinking about them. Never. And we have a son, Dominic. And grandchildren. But Dominic won't mind. He's a beautiful boy but not well, either, I'm afraid. Sadly. Especially recently since all that trouble and the way his father died. His shooting licence was revoked by the gun club. He's not too healthy but is being well looked after. So I'm begging you. Begging you. I'm just waiting to meet my daughters. I'm begging you.'

'Please don't beg. I'll take it. But in trust. I'm holding it for you and your son Dominic. It will always belong to you and your son. I am a trustee. Nothing else.'

'Well, you are taking it. That's all that matters to me. And here. As you can see, it's an old tin box with old pennies in it. That's where Sidney kept it safe. It's safe from the bank and the Inland Revenue now with you, Inspector. My God, some younger people with children have to decide between feeding their family or paying their mortgage. The bank and the tax people have eaten enough of me and my dead husband. Anyway, this tin box has been rattling around Sid's family for years. It was thought to belong to Matthew first then his brother Michael, Sid's grandfather. Look at the state of it. Sidney's grandfather kept his War of Independence medal in it as Matthew was dead by then. Blown to bits. All this time. Take it and the tin box.'

'Thank you. I'm very touched. Thank you.'

'Find out about Matthew Rankin, Inspector. Battle of Loos. The little brother of the Somme. Matthew's father, James, apparently burnt the telegram bringing the news of his son's death. James died then within three months of a broken heart. That really upset me hearing that. His own son. Blown to bits as I say. Nothing to bury. At least they had that in common. So many dead brothers. And dead sisters. Dead children.'

'It is a very sad story, Mrs Rankin, but a respectful one.'

'But you know what, Inspector?'

'Yes, Mrs Rankin?'

Mrs Rankin turned away and paused again. Valberg allowed her to gather her thoughts then she faced him again.

'There's something truly horrifying about a dead child. Dead children. The sight of a dead child is the most terrifying thing imaginable. A dead child. Absolutely horrifying and unnatural. Inspector, will you look at their files for me? Ashley and Michaela Rankin. They were both like the tree of life for us. Would you do that? There were others. All below the radar for some reason. Other forgotten families who lost children. A child or children vanish on the European continent. In America or Africa. Not from the north coast of Ireland. The police then, I think, even doubted that my daughters existed. But they had their hands full that day with that bomb attack. Talk about trying to convince them Ashley and Michaela vanished.'

'I will see what I can find out, Mrs Rankin. It's all terribly sad. Can I ask you a question?'

Mrs Rankin was still clutching the photograph of her daughters.

'Aye, Inspector, go ahead.'

'Is that Mussenden Temple in the background?'

'Aye. We took them there that terrible day. This is the last photo we have of them. Not long after, they vanished into the sea, we were told. It was an awful day going to the chemist to leave off the film from the camera and a worse day going to collect the prints. Collecting the prints was really sad. There was almost an element of going and collecting the girls. The last image of them. I wanted them to come back to life from the photos.'

For Valberg, this was what listening was all about. His father taught him well. Always listen and don't interrupt. Let people talk, the way lawyers do, until they can talk no more. Be a good and respectful listener, especially to someone heartbroken and sad. Be patient and listen. Always listen.

Valberg then felt a cold shudder pass through him. He remembered his father taking him to Mussenden Temple during one of their fishing trips up to the lake at the top of

Benevenagh Mountain. Now Valberg realised that yet another pleasant memory was destroyed, as all he would think of now was the two dead children.

'I hope I'm helping you in some way, Mrs Rankin.'

'Thank you so much. Well, anyway. That's Ashley and Michaela. Now they celebrate Matthew as an outcast a hundred years after he died. An outcast. I wonder, Inspector?'

'Yes, Mrs Rankin.'

'Are we all outcasts?'

Valberg dropped his head. He had no answer.

'Thanks for coming, son. I wanted to see you and meet you. I'll let you go now.'

Valberg was on the verge of making something up that would settle Mrs Rankin, now that he had heard more about Sidney, but he thought the better of it. Valberg had already physically been involved in too much noble-cause corruption lately; behaving that way now with Mrs Rankin on a mental level would be unforgivable.

Valberg noticed Mrs Rankin still holding on to the photograph of her dead daughters as he said goodbye to her. Once he was in his car, he rang Anna on her personal mobile and got her straight away.

'Oh, I was expecting to leave a message. How are you?'

'On my way to Derry. I'm meeting David and some others. You and I have no more secure quiet locations to meet anymore, Jon.'

'What do we do? I need to speak with you.'

'Need to, Jon?'

'Yeah. Need to.'

'There's no point talking to you at Strand Road. You'll be agitated and cross. I'll just see you at my sister's again for the moment. The place is still vacant and you still have a key. But my entourage will be waiting on me outside. We'll have about an hour.'

'What time?'

'About eight tonight. See you there.'

'Okay.'

CHAPTER 51

Valberg arrived early at the apartment in Eglinton which was now up for sale. He noticed a security man covering the block that he was entering. The other apartments on that block remained unsold by the developer. They were now in the hands of the Bank of Emerald and marketed by them. Valberg paid no attention to the guard and assumed the bank had to have him in place for insurance purposes.

Valberg surveyed the apartment thinking of all the time he had spent with Anna there.

The Chief Constable arrived not long after Valberg amid tight security, but it seemed to Valberg that residents in nearby properties were none the wiser.

Valberg watched Anna in full uniform leave the car and he held the ground-floor front door of the apartment open, just like he had always done before when waiting for her.

Valberg's greeting to Anna was: 'Is this what it boils down to? We have an hour?'

'Jon, you are suspended and you've had a punishing time recently. Again.'

'All in the line of duty, sir.'

'Jon, you will take care of yourself? My ignorance is my protection. I need to be able to swear truthfully on oath. You do understand that?'

'I do. I miss you, Anna, I miss you.'

They moved quickly towards each other, clasping the other tightly.

'Time is so punishing, Anna. We dive here, there and everywhere then we die. It is precious. This is what we are

229

reduced to. Like two teenage criminals sneaking away. Could we even take a holiday together? Fuck, I sound so stupid. So pathetically melodramatic.'

'What is it, Jon? Something is eating you.'

Valberg broke from their embrace and turned to look at the security presence outside.

'What if O'Driscoll speaks the truth? The truth about my father. Where does that leave me? Personally and professionally? I'd be finished. Dead. The allegation alone would destroy me. It doesn't matter about the truth.'

'Jon, I haven't heard the tapes but I hear they're bad.'

'Bad? They're horrific, and I lost it with him.'

'You? Well, no-one can believe a word he says, Jon. Not a word.'

'Oh, there were things he couldn't have made up. He had to have been told. Haslette had to have told him before he had a bullet put in his head. With my gun, it seems. I'm in serious bother enough over all that. Leaving my weapon lying around. Fuck me. How could I have been so fucking stupid?'

Anna didn't answer.

'I haven't been drinking as much lately. All the same, I'm slowing down and stiffening up, though. I felt fitter when I was drunk most of the time. And I was. Drunk that is. More like rubber. Technically. I don't have those cravings anymore. My libido has left me as well. I'm not living, just existing. Moving and walking about.'

'Join the club. Join the human race. Look, Jon, I want you to be safe, and safe in what you are doing. You'll be back in no time, you'll see.'

Valberg continued to observe the security presence outside the window.

'Anna, who knows we're alone here?'

'No-one at Strand Road or anything. Just my security ...'

'My gut is telling me something is not right. Are you armed?'

'No, I'm not armed.'

All Valberg could think about was a vantage point for a sniper. He couldn't see one.

'And you didn't tell anyone?'

'Only those outside. This place is up for sale now as you can see. Our lust den. Our private palace. My sister got no use out of it. We got more.'

Valberg was ignoring Anna.

'When I called you, who was with you?'

'No-one. Just the driver and—'

'Where were you?'

'In the back of my car. I was being driven.'

'Just you and, I presume, at least two other officers.'

'Yes.'

'So you weren't alone.'

'But they couldn't have been listening in.'

'Fuck, that's it. It's my fucking phone. Listening in. From months ago. From May. It's been tracked since then – with my fucking consent.'

Anna didn't answer.

'What arrangement do you have for leaving here?'

'I'm just to phone or radio that I am on my way out. I'm in full uniform here, Jon. Haven't you noticed?'

'Don't do either. Don't phone or radio. We must get you out unexpectedly. We've arrived early and you're leaving early.'

Valberg could hear O'Driscoll's voice in his head from the previous June on the Peace Bridge. *The old RUC doesn't want the new PSNI. They don't want Anna, that's for sure. Or you. Or perhaps there's another force within a force again? A new one?*'

'Anna, if I were to attack you now here, who would know? The guys outside are too far away from the building.'

'Jon, it is a matter of reality that the road is where it is and your car is in the driveway.'

'They should be closer. As a Personal Protection Unit, they should definitely be closer.'

'What is it, Jon? What's wrong?'

Valberg closed the blinds in the front living room where they had been standing. 'This is the first time we have been alone together in months. On our own. Just the two of us.'

'Why does that not surprise me?'

'We should leave now. Walk behind me on the way out. I want you to almost touch me. Keep tight.'

Valberg did not want to unsettle Anna any further. He

gingerly walked to Anna's car and got her safely into the back of it. He nodded to the other police officers there with a sense of relief and was just ready to close the heavy car door.

'Back to Belfast, Anna. Call me when you are—'

Then there was a massive explosion from the apartment. Valberg slammed the car door shut and ducked. The building collapsed into itself. Valberg was protected from the blast by the car. He shouted to get Anna away, and the Chief Constable's entourage left at great speed, sirens blazing, as other members of the security team arrived.

Valberg's first thought as he gathered himself and examined the scene was that if they could keep it quiet that the Chief Constable had been here at all, that would be a success. His second thought was that it had been a familiar bang. That sickening noise of a paramilitary explosion. Not O'Driscoll's white phosphorous hissing through the cold thin air. It reminded him of Finbar's explosion. Then the next realisation was that his own car was destroyed. Another one. But the blast came from the apartment. He was sure.

One of the security team for the Chief Constable ran to Valberg. He had an English accent. Valberg recognised him from other duties before.

'Fucking lucky you got her out of there. That place should have been checked before she went in. Thanks. You saved my bacon, mate, but I'll still be in the frying pan, I expect.'

'Okay. As long as she is safe.'

Valberg knew the bomb was meant for both him and Anna. He watched a familiar scene developing as multitudes of police and ambulance crews began to arrive, then the media, amid the thick cloud of dust covering the area. That was his cue to vanish, if he could.

There could still be fatalities yet, however. Valberg stared at the collapsed building and instead of leaving, he ventured into the rubble. He started to clear bricks and debris with his own hands, frantically, not really knowing what he was looking for. Then a call went up to evacuate the area, as there was the acrid and pungent aroma of gas in the air and another explosion was feared.

Valberg heard Linda, now on the scene, calling him. He stood up with a large brick in his hands, looked at Linda and paused. Everyone was screaming at him to get to safety. He dropped the brick and made a hasty exit from the area.

'Get me out of here, Linda. I don't want to talk. Just get me fucking out of here.'

Then he remembered the guard. He quickly rushed back to the collapsed building amid the sounds of sirens and mobile phones ringing.

'There was a man at the back of the building. The caretaker guy. Where is he?' Valberg was shouting.

Valberg got to the middle of the rubble with others not concerned for their own safety, either, and helped them search through the wreckage. Valberg saw some movement underneath the remains of the thick back door of the apartment block and heard groaning.

'My leg is trapped. Can't fuckin' move it. Can't move my legs.'

Valberg got the door clear.

'My legs are trapped underneath me. Just roll me over so I can get free.'

Valberg attempted to help the man but as soon as he did he noticed the injured man's legs were not underneath him. They had been blown off from the waist down. Valberg ran his hands underneath the man as best he could, but all that came out was warm lumpy flesh and blood.

The injured man then reached for his mobile phone, which had been ringing in his top jacket pocket, and took the call. He seemed to calm himself and steady his breathing.

'Oh, is that you? I left the spuds. They're all peeled and the washing is out love. The weans will be over with—'

Then he died. He was staring at Valberg who was staring at him. He still had the phone up to his ear and his mouth and eyes were wide open.

The two firemen who were helping Valberg looked at him and he looked back.

The fire officers who were helping him listened to the caller who was shouting, 'Mickey, Mickey. What's going on there? Mickey for God's sake. Did you drop the phone? You better not be talking to me from sitting on the toilet again. You didn't drop the bloody thing down it, did you? Call me later and I'll get the spuds.'

Valberg was relieved that the caller hung up. The paramedics arrived to do their job. But there was no hope for Mickey. At least the spuds were peeled and the washing was out, thought Valberg, covered again in blood, sweat, dirt and the smell of death.

Valberg noticed other Fire Service personnel secure and remove propane-gas appliances from the area, then he had another thought. Anna's sister would get the money now for the apartment through a criminal damage claim or insurance. So would the Bank of Emerald.

By now the media were everywhere and politicians started arriving, getting ready for interview. Then the English member of Anna's security team came to him with his Black-Berry saying, 'Jon, the Chief Constable wants to talk to you.'

Valberg nodded, looking at the chaos around him and took the phone.

'You are okay? I'm told you're okay. Is that right?'

'That's right, Anna, just great. But I need a drink, I think.'

'Do you need to go to the hospital or anything?'

'Fuck, no. But we've one for the morgue. I couldn't save him. Mickey someone ...'

'Mickey Clarke. The watchman. Oh, that's terrible. Poor Mickey.'

'Aye. Poor Mickey.'

Valberg hung up and tried to wipe the blood from the phone onto his clothes but only made it worse.

'Sorry about your phone there. What's your name?'

'Charles ... Charlie,' he said as he removed a handkerchief from his pocket and cleaned his phone.

'Charlie, can you get me to DS Wilson? She's here somewhere – I want to get out of here.'

'The Chief told me to make sure of that. Here, follow me and we'll get you away from this mess.'

Within an hour, a claim of responsibility by a dissident splinter group of the Real IRA known as the Permanent IRA was telephoned to Amanda Cleary of the *Derry Journal* with a recognised code word: 'Rosebud'. Amanda rang the PSNI straight away and then Valberg personally, but he didn't answer his mobile phone.

CHAPTER 52

The day after the Eglinton bomb, Valberg texted Amanda Cleary a new mobile number to contact him on. She rang straight away.

'Can we meet, Jon? Please. We need to meet. I can't stop what is breaking.'

'My mind is broke. Can you fix that?'

'Two things. Don't answer if you don't want to. Are you suspended, and was the Chief Constable at the Eglinton bomb? I mean, before the bomb exploded? I hear the caretaker guy set the thing off. It was a booby trap and he got sucked into the building with the implosion. That's what I hear.'

Valberg stayed silent for a while and so did Amanda.

'I like the way you kept it to two questions with no rejoinders or additions,' Valberg said.

'That depends on your answer.'

'Yeah, but most journalists and lawyers say two questions then ask twenty-two questions.'

'Well?'

'Have you given your statement about the call? The call of responsibility for the bombing.'

'Yes. Just the facts. As you taught me. The facts and no comment.'

'Was it genuine?'

'The call was certain.'

'Was it genuine, Amanda? Did you believe it?'

There was another pause and Valberg waited. He could hear Amanda sighing.

'I'm not sure. Was that a test, Jon?'

'No. I respect your opinion. I treat it with honour.'

'Well, you are – surprise, surprise – the only one to ask me that. I'm full of doubt. And fear.'

'That's healthy.'

'I wonder, Jon.'

'We don't need to meet, Amanda. No offence – we can talk here as long as you want. And as regards your questions, you may interpret my silence as consent.'

'Consent? You mean affirmation?'

Valberg went quiet again.

Amanda continued.

'That crazy anti-PSNI blogger guy, I hear, is about to run with something or suggest something. Then the Sundays will pick it up and embellish it more. I have no interest in it but I have been contacted and asked if it's true? What's his name?'

'He's an idiot. I'd like to say a harmless idiot, but an idiot who couldn't get into the police. I forget his name, too. It'll come to me at about twenty past three in the morning.'

'Okay.'

'What did you say?'

'Nothing. But I'm calling you. What happened to your old number?'

'Can we get back to the bombing, Amanda?'

'Sure.'

'Do you think those new guys have the capability? I mean, hypothetically, if me and the Chief Constable were alone in a building, very few people would know the location, right? In advance, to have a bomb in place set to go off at a specific time. Right? Common sense, surely? And then when there is this admission to you, they don't mention anything about me or the Chief Constable. Seems odd. They didn't even say they only had to be lucky once.'

Amanda sighed again and didn't answer.

'Would someone from the Permanent IRA meet with me? Do they exist at all?'

'Jon, the first day we met – well, not the first day, the day Mr Black was found on Craigavon Bridge – you said something that stuck with me.'

'What was that?'

'When I suggested that things were different now ... well, you didn't agree. You said you weren't sure. Do you remember? Are you sure? Do we have a new police force or just the old one with a new name?'

'Let the bloggers blog what they want. Let the papers write what they want. Something is rotten, Amanda. Perhaps at the core. But that's all I can say.'

'Jon, you don't accept your talent as a police officer. You fight it to reject it. You can see round corners. You can solve things instantly most of us would take ages doing. You have that reputation. That is the perception of you. And I know you fight it, reject it. It's almost as if you are ashamed of it. I'll leave it at that. Sorry. I'll let you go. I shouldn't have said those things. Sorry. But I'm just thinking if anyone can see through all the bullshit that is going on ... well, it's you.'

'Amanda, we have a lot to talk about. Anyway, your sources within the police and beyond are better than mine. We both know that. We need to talk.'

'I know. Everyone says that. But not now, you will say. Anyway, it's the Year of the Dragon, by the way. My daughter came home and told me they celebrated it at school. Two thousand and twelve. Hard to believe. City of Culture next year. We won't be allowed to report, let alone publish, bad news soon.'

'The wooden dragon, by the way, for me. I was born in the Year of the Dragon.'

'So maybe this is your year.'

'Maybe. We'll see.'

'News soon becomes history, unless you can prove the Bank of Emerald blew the apartments up and poor Mickey Clarke.'

'Poor Mickey ... Amanda, I'll be away for a while.'

'The suspension? Is this confirmation?'

'Not too long, but a while. Leaving in a while. We need to find a way so that I can record things with you.'

'That's easy. No problem.'

'On my terms. In the strictest confidence.'

'You have my word.'

'I didn't need it, but thanks anyway. Bye.'

'Bye, Jon. Take care.'

'Woo. Stop. Barry "the Bastard" Brannigan. The blogger.'

'Right. How did we forget?'

'How could we forget? He's resurfaced under many guises as the High Court keep shutting him down. I fucking hate the internet.'

'Bye, Jon. See you soon.'

'Cheerio.'

CHAPTER 53

Valberg didn't know anything about Irish adoption law but wished that he did as he watched Debbie Sloan being lowered into the ground, for the worms and maggots, at her small rain-swept funeral. It was just six weeks and three days after his nocturnal lagophthalmos episode with Christina, Debbie Sloan's court appearance and the dramatic rescue of her son. Valberg was cutting up at the sight of young Pearse crying 'Mammy'.

If he couldn't help Debbie or her sister when they were alive, Valberg had at least to be respectful in their deaths. He had visions of being interviewed by a twenty-three-year-old social worker with a third-class degree in geography about the adoption process and being told why he was, sadly, not suitably qualified to adopt a child.

Debbie had exactly six weeks with Pearse. She died the day scheduled for her review hearing for her TV licence summons. Valberg asked Michael to attend the court and, sure enough, her name was still on the list and read out.

Michael let Valberg know later at Strand Road Station that the licence prosecutor had tried to apply for a fine to be imposed and an order for costs made. Michael told Valberg he had informed the court clerk that Debbie had died that morning. The court clerk passed this on to the district judge who then informed the prosecutor in open court.

'Did she still apply for the fine and the costs, Michael?'

'Believe it or not, sir, she did. Against the estate of the deceased. The judge said the summons would be dismissed. Justice, sir? Anyway. She died without a criminal record.

Not a blemish on her character. Straight to heaven, I'm sure, the poor girl.'

'Indeed. God be good to her,' said Valberg. 'Though no-one gets to their heaven without a fight.'

Derry had been calm since the Eglinton bombing and Valberg was being pursued relentlessly by the Spanish policeman Antonio Domingo. Valberg didn't go to Carolina's funeral but did intend to go to Spain and face the music over his involvement with her eventually. But only when he could find out as much as possible about what happened to Carolina via Christina's law firm.

O'Driscoll was excused from his remand hearing on health grounds, which was to be by video-link to the court. Valberg didn't believe the excuse at all. He didn't care where O'Driscoll was now. It was farcical to Valberg that O'Driscoll's case was adjourned 'generally' until a date was agreed with the 'defence' and their client's health improved.

'What fucking bollocks. History repeats. It's gonna happen. I'm in "I-don't-give-a-rat's-arse" mode, Michael. I tend to fuck things up when that happens to me. So stay clear. For your own protection.'

'You got the boy six weeks with his mother. If it hadn't been for you, sir ... well, I was talking to Jenny about it. These last few weeks have changed her life forever.'

'Michael, you and Jenny are two great officers. I would trust my life to you.'

Michael steadied himself.

'Nobody ever said that to me before, sir.'

'You saved my life. Don't you remember? It wasn't that long ago, for fuck's sake.'

Valberg rolled his eyes and turned his back on Michael.

Michael nervously paused again, building up the courage to speak honestly.

'I miss Finbar, sir, I really do. He was so good to me. Really patient.'

Valberg could sense Michael beginning to cut up but ignored it.

'Do you know the scene in *Enter the Dragon* where Bruce Lee visits the graves of his parents, Michael?'

'No, sir. Sorry.'

'He says they won't agree with what he is about to do. He asks them to find a way to forgive him. It's moving in its own way. How many times must we all think that? I dunno. But, Michael, take care of yourself. And look out for Jenny.'

'I will, sir. You did all you could for Debbie and her son. And, sir, it may not be my place, for her sister as well. I've heard all about you and that solicitor, Miss Maguire. I'm taking a bit of time off. Heading away for a while.'

'Do that, Michael. Safe journey.'

Valberg had fallen into a degree of recklessness and carelessness but not as serious as before. He had so many things to sort out, including his mother's estate, but was ignoring it all for now. He needed to tidy up his desk in preparation for what might be a lengthy suspension and remove anything he might need.

The fresh spring air suddenly turned sour for Valberg at the sight of the unfashionable brown crocodile-leather shoes of Detective Sergeant Walter McMurray.

'What the fuck do you want, Wally?'

'A word with you, Detective, about Ian Haslette. Sir. The dead solicitor. It's a delicate matter, but I've been tasked with my team to look at it. We'll leave the Bostridge Strangler episode for now. You fucking that little cutie for the PPS now? Seymour?'

'Your team?'

'Aye. Do you have a problem with that? Sir.'

'No. But a big problem with you, you fuckwit. You really are a twat.'

'Well, glad to see you survived the bomb attack by those terrorists.'

'Wally, fuck off.'

'I can have you arrested now. In front of everyone. Or you can come quietly with me so we can have a chat. Up to you. Sir.'

'I'm going fucking nowhere with you. I'm back in here sorting stuff out with permission and you know that. What is it? Say it. *Digami.*'

'Just as well you are on that Long Tower Church footage with your mucker O'Driscoll. We checked all the timings. Worked all that out. He gave you an alibi. Well, for yourself.

241

All timed. Then Father Doherty. Out of his coma now. Looking for you but not at all well. Very unwell. Nasty mental stuff. Fuck, who's going to hear his confession?'

'Very technical, Wally. What the fuck do you want?'

'Your gun. The bullet. It's traced back to your gun. You couldn't have fired it, but—'

'But what, arse-wipe? Is there a sale on in Dunnes, Wally? You're eating your way into a forty-inch waistline there. Or do you think you're in Miami Vice with those shoes?'

'You could have put someone up to it. Gave them your gun, maybe? Then there's the small matter of you leaving your gun lying around and that. That's not in the procedure.'

'You toe-rag idiot. Fuck off. Arrest me when you're ready, Crockett.'

'Okay. Just doing my job in the new PSNI. Don't take it personally.'

'Piss off. The new PSNI. Don't make me vomit.'

'You'll be hearing from me again. Just touching base.'

'I'm clearing out my stuff, you moron. I'm going to tell you one more time to piss off. It's a phrase I am sure you are well used to hearing since you were born.'

'Any more unused evidence bags in there?'

'Fuck off.'

CHAPTER 54

Valberg could see a young girl doing something very unusual. He was sitting in a first-class carriage on the Heathrow Express. He always enjoyed the quiet journey on the way into Paddington Station in London. The young girl wasn't talking for everyone to hear on her mobile phone. She wasn't listening to music, either. She was reading a poetry book, and Valberg could see the names of Samuel Taylor Coleridge and Rudyard Kipling. *Kubla Khan* flashed before Valberg.

But then his emotional angst hit him. His eyes felt heavy. What a waste. What a death. What a life. What a contrast. He started to think about Matthew Rankin. The young man from the Bogside in Derry who died at the Battle of Loos in Belgium in the First World War. That made him think of Rudyard Kipling's son, who at least died a hero and with dignity, to a degree. He had a supportive and loving family. They cared about him when they should have cared about him. Not one hundred years later when it was too fucking late.

Poor Matthew Rankin. Death and dishonour. No poems for him. No posthumous glorification. From the Bogside in Derry to the bog at Loos. He fought for the British Army. Or was he fighting only for himself? Just to live? To survive? Buried forever in pieces in the dirt. A life and soul scattered in the mess. It took nearly a hundred years for a family and a community to understand him, let alone forgive him.

Sidney Rankin, the dead solicitor, loved the great-uncle he never knew, the one who was never spoken about. That was obvious to Valberg now. If only his father were alive, Valberg thought, they would both together research and find out everything they could about the Battle of Loos and in particular Private Matthew Rankin.

More generational family secrets from Derry. There was no escape from the past, even in the clean, quiet and peaceful journey in first class on the Paddington Express into central London.

***

Comfortable now in the back of a black cab on his way to the Savoy Hotel on the Strand, Valberg remembered he had a copy of Judge Bailey's last letter to his brother Wilbert in Tasmania in his inside jacket. The original was evidence from Judge Bailey's murder scene. It had been scattered into the air by the judge just as he fell dead over the bench. Valberg read it, hearing Old Bailey's voice in his head.

My Dear Wilbert,

I hope you are recovering from the operation and that your prostate has settled. I love writing letters. You know that. I love the mystery of posting them.

It's a funny old world. A sweet young lady is about to try her first case before me, and it will be my last. I have a sense of doom. I hear you say, 'Tut tut, same old Herbie.' But no, I have a sense of doom. I really do. More than usual. And you, for one, know what I am like.

You see, I did do something quite awful many years ago and it has come back to haunt me. I will be dead by the time you get this, and I just want you to understand. It's a funny old world.

A terrible sense of dread has just come over me. I'm repeating myself. Sorry.

I see a young man, a boy really, who I had no power to release, and I remanded in custody, in my days as a young part-time resident magistrate. And as a quirk of fate, I am asked to sit today in Derry in my new status as district judge. All those years ago. I should not have any regrets at all. I complied with my obligations under the law. But now, I think of our parents and our dear old big brother Ernie. Even at my age, I wish they were here. It's not a physical possibility, in any way, but part of me wants it to be. I'm getting old.

The boy is now a man. An angry man, and I strangely feel I deserve what's coming to me. We all do. It isn't bad luck, or being in the wrong place at the wrong time. We deserve what we get, don't we? What do you think, Wilbert? Do we all deserve what we get? Do we die by plan just as we are born by plan? Or, is it all haphazard? You see, I couldn't release him, I had no power. No lawful authority. But again it haunts me. I knew he was innocent. I always did. I sensed it. I could see it. I should have shouted it from the rooftops. But no. I failed him, too, along with the justice system. The boy was innocent. Gustav Valberg was right. Remember good old Gustav? Rumours abound about the rows he had in the jury room with the other jurors.

Now he's back. Not Gustav, he died from cancer. But the boy. I am sure you heard all that news from here. He's back anyway. A new man, and I am about to remand him in custody again. I simply cannot believe it. Did he have to be so brutal?

Well, I think I hear the court clerk coming.

Wilbert, my friend, my brother, I loved you like no other.

Yours,
Herbie.

Valberg had been given a copy of the letter by the new investigation team, as it referred to his father. He shook his head, folded the letter and put it back in his jacket.

He was now on the Strand and near the Savoy. He was looking forward to seeing Christina Maguire but not what he had in his mind's eye, namely the sight of a bunch of solicitors with no rhythm, trying to dance at a party.

CHAPTER 55

Valberg approached one of the reception desks of the Savoy Hotel with some trepidation.

'I have a room in my own name, Valberg, or that of Miss Christina Maguire.'

'Ah, Mr Valberg. We've been expecting you. Yes, your suite is ready and you have nothing to do here as it's already taken care of. Miss Maguire's PA said you would be travelling light and I see that you are. Do you—'

Valberg interrupted.

'Where can I get a drink?'

'You can go directly to the function.'

'Function?'

'Well, the party for Princeton, Braithwaite and Sotomeyer.'

'Oh, yeah. Sorry. She mentioned that. Of course. Sorry, I was in another world there.'

'That's quite alright, sir. Just leave your bag here and I will take care of it. Miss Maguire said to tell you to go on up when you arrive anyway. She said if you are lucky you might miss all the speeches.'

'Let's hope so.'

'Indeed, sir. They're all in the Lancaster Ballroom for now – I'll get someone to show you the way.'

At that precise moment, standing amid all the luxury of the Savoy, Valberg's mood dipped and he had to find another seat to sit down away from the reception desk. He had been advised to do this by his doctor. Stay calm and relax.

Valberg spotted a seat in the foyer of the hotel. He could have been anywhere now. But he had to sit down. An overwhelming sense of depression descended on him and his thoughts became irrational. This flood of darkness and negativity came from nowhere at the most rarest of times. Now was one of those times. Valberg wanted to be dropped to the bottom of the ocean, any ocean. When it arrived, Valberg thought of it as a medical condition, not to be ignored but to be treated with respect. It would be easier to go and get drunk. But he tried to control that. So no matter where, he conditioned himself to stop what he was doing immediately. He did that now. Sometimes the wave of darkness came and vanished just as quickly. But not this one. This was going to be heavy and he wanted to cry. Valberg fixed his stare in front of him but was not focused on anything. He felt a weight pressing down on him, leaving him unable to move. The weight always felt predominantly as if it were on his chest, pushing down and through him. He watched all manner of people arriving at the Savoy and leaving. He was picking up accents and parts of conversations. He was picking up pieces of lives he had never known. He wanted Private Matthew Rankin to walk in and he wanted to hug him. Valberg imagined a conversation with the dead soldier.

'Sir, even when there is truth and justice, and an apology, that's not enough.'

'Why not, Private?'

'Everything is left hanging, if you excuse the reference, sir. Only more blood will do. Like Mr O'Driscoll. He had to be brutal.'

'Okay, Private.'

'There is no cure. There is no moving on. When the void comes it never really leaves. Then some people are lucky.'

'Lucky, Private?'

'Yes, sir. You live with it or curl up into a ball of madness and hate. Exploding now and then. It's so unfair. So random. There is no choice. It's all preordained, sir. Find some faith.'

This was all irrational. Valberg wanted everyone who had died and been murdered in Derry over the last two years to present themselves at the Savoy. Now they were all there and he was sure he could see them walking about, even though he wasn't drinking – yet. His attention was drawn to two young girls, probably sisters, playing while their parents checked in. Valberg began feeling foolish, which for him was a sign his rationality was coming back. But he was still fixated with the two children playing, and it was 1979. The children's father had a copy of the *Times* and Valberg could see a picture of the Ayatollah Khomeini, so it must have been 1979. Iran was in meltdown and so was Valberg.

He thought the recovery was on but it was not. He was getting worse. He still remained stuck to his chair. He felt there was a slug slithering up his leg and he was in a boxing ring unable to find his left hook. He was taking blows to the head and body and still felt unable to move. Then he was sure he could hear a horse coming and the sound of hooves. But he believed he was in a church, and a priest was crying while blessing a horse.

'Go and return victorious,' the priest cried.

Valberg wanted to get his head back to the Savoy, and he believed he was hearing the introduction to *European Super State* by Killing Joke. He remembered Christina said she loved that song, so it allowed him to get up and follow the sound of the music. Or at least he thought he was getting up. A sense of anger was rousing in Valberg. It was directed at his father. How could he have helped Haslette? Why? His father was, in effect, party to the murder of Orla Harkin. How could he have done this?

'How could you, Dad? How could you do that? Why, why, why, but why?'

Valberg was despairing. In his head he called Francis Steen, his old colleague and friend from the PSNI who himself had had a nervous breakdown and was in early retirement with his Patten money.

'Francis, I'm in a spot of bother. Can you help me? I can't get up.'

'Ah, Jon. May the force be with you. Only joking.'

'Francis, can we meet sometime? Just to talk a few things out. I don't trust anyone. I believe nothing and only see the dark side. The dark side of everything and everyone. But not you. Can you help me? Hello. Hello, Francis. Are you there?'

Anxious and alone, Valberg forced himself finally out of his seat and followed the music. But the music had changed now and he was following the sound of Mylo's *Paris Four Hundred*. He remembered he had to go to the Lancaster Room so he looked for the signs, still angry with his father.

Valberg's ears took him towards the music but his eyes searched for the bar as he entered the room full of solicitors dancing with a surprising degree of rhythm to Mylo's music. He could see a band setting up as well but headed straight for the bar.

'Double brandy with coke. No ice, please.'

The music changed again to Madonna's *Ray Of Light*, and then Kylie Minogue's *Can't Get You Out Of My Head*.

As the music eventually faded to a halt and the dancing stopped, Christina Maguire stood at the podium in front of a large backdrop for Princeton, Braithwaite and Sotomeyer Solicitors. Valberg immediately realised that he had not missed the speeches and therefore ordered another double brandy with coke and no ice.

A young woman with a slight hint of a Scandinavian accent to Valberg's ears stood close to him and ordered a double vodka.

'Oh, I don't recognise you. What's your name? I'm Olga Blom. You don't look like a solicitor.'

'Valberg. Colonel Jon Valberg of the Royal Irish.'

'A soldier? Sexy boy. Will you love me long time?'

'That's up to you. If you keep drinking those double vodkas, anything is possible.'

'Where have you come from, soldier boy?'

'Well, I was stationed in Helmand Province but I have just come back from Loos in Belgium.'

'Interesting, Colonel. Oh. Madam is about to speak. Chat later.'

'Anytime, Olga. Easy on the vodka.'

Valberg switched his attention to Christina.

'Ladies and gentlemen, friends and colleagues, welcome here this evening. What an evening! Let us catch our breath as we celebrate a great year for the litigation and criminal division of Princeton, Braithwaite and Sotomeyer. Well done, everyone. My God, someone told me when I was powdering my nose there was a recession out there. Does anyone know anything about it?'

'Yeah, fucking tell Sidney Rankin's family that one, Christina,' muttered Valberg to himself amid the laughter.

'Another double brandy and coke. No ice. Sorry, I owe you for those other drinks. That's three now, is it?'

'No, sir, it's a free bar. Didn't you know?'

'Keep them coming. What's the story here, *amigo*? I'm only a guest.'

'These Masters of the Universe do this once a year. It's Miss Maguire's crime department really, sir. They just celebrate their winnings.'

'Well, why not? Good luck to them.'

'Certainly, sir. Are you a colonel in the army or a policeman, sir? You look like a policeman to me. My name is Henry. Pleased to meet you.'

'Henry. Very pleased to meet you. I like that name. Henry. I like it.'

'I've a bit of Irish in me, sir. I got the full title: Patrick Henry Pearse. I liked Pearse the best, but everyone spelt it wrongly in school. Even the teachers. So Henry was simpler.'

'But you liked Pearse better?'

'Yes, sir.'

'I like it, too. But Henry it is?'

'Yes, sir.'

'Henry. Can I have—'

'Another double brandy, no ice?'

'Yes, Henry, please. *Gracias*. What's she muttering on about now?'

Valberg turned his attention to Christina and all the solicitors in the room captivated by her. Now that the music had stopped, Valberg analysed the gathering. He turned around to the barman and said, 'Henry, how does this crowd of rich, handsome and recession-proof solicitors do it?'

'Not sure. But it seems this recession thing isn't killing everyone, sir.'

'Henry. I think the same man, and I stress man, interviewed all these women for their jobs. They all look the same, don't they? Or is it my fondness for blondes that is blinding me? Legal merit was void. Yeah. But blonde hair, and colouring acceptable, won the day. Or got you the job.

There's a certain look here. Pretty, for the low-life scumbags they represent. A slight hint of perfume and body odour, and the mystery of what is underneath a short skirt, is a must for this crew. It's very settling for a rapist and a murderer to have the scent of a woman in a holding cell. Her perspiring with fear herself. All moist and terrified. Look at them. No-one is overweight or over thirty-five. They are dressed immaculately, even for solicitors. Most of them were even dancing in time to the music and I was hypnotised for a while with their sense of rhythm. Anyway, where's the fat, cigar-smoking partner fond of the smell of his own shite?'

'Sir, he's never here. The crime division is all Her Ladyship's, as she's known, sir. She has another few years in her. Then Miss Blom, the one you told you were a soldier, she's next in line. I see it every year. The subtle changes.'

'So how long were you in the police, Henry?'

'That didn't take long, sir, did it?'

'We can smell each other a mile away.'

'And all the others. We're all ex-cops. All the security. Look around you, Colonel. How do you think you got in here? You haven't just walked into a PSNI crime scene. Everyone knew you were coming.'

'I see, Henry. Sort of sensed heavy security. It was too easy walking in. So the Met, then? Flying Squad?'

'Yes, sir. Nearly twenty years. Then I got a job here. Well, I do the bar at these things and keep a close eye on everyone. I make sure no-one goes over their quota. Her Ladyship will see you when she's finished. Listen, it's just all congratulations. She gets a huge bonus every year. At least a million. She puts this spread on. They're paid nearly as much as professional footballers. But they've a lot more sense.'

'The footballers?'

'Very good, Colonel.'

'So, all cops, then? Or ex-cops?'

'Some military as well. But hand-picked. Like you. Not just any old maverick. Well paid. Well looked after. No questions asked. Some of us on security detail. I wasn't over in Derry but I've heard all about it. Some of the other guys, and girls, looked after Christina.'

'Oh, I see.'

'It's no ordinary law firm. Big money.'

'Yeah, makes the world go round.'

'No limits here.'

'Maybe I'll listen to her then a bit, Henry, and learn something.'

Just as Valberg finished his visual analysis of all before him his mobile hummed on vibrate.

'Excuse me, Henry, I'll just take this.'

'Okay, Colonel, I'll line another up for you.'

'Hello.'

'You know, the first thing you need to do, Jon, is forgive him. Let his soul rest in peace. For your sake. For his sake.'

'Have you found God now? Where are you calling me from, Gerry?'

'Hardly important, is it? So will you let his soul go? Your father's? I can hear Christina in the background. Don't worry. They're good to me in here.'

'Lanarkshire?'

'You think so?'

'Well, the only safe thing for all of us is for you to be in Carstairs. That's the rumour. So is that where you are calling from? Did someone smuggle in a phone for you?'

'Always the policeman. Relax.'

'Gerry, as much as I'd like to chat, I'm not in the mood. But fuck me, you left us skip loads of evidence. There's a lot to get through. Or was it just your justification to try and have us give you some sympathy for killing all those innocent people?'

'Now, now, Jon, enjoy the party. Or are you on a bipolar dive, Jon?'

'But you are in that secure wing there at Carstairs, aren't you? You must be. By consent, I hear.'

'For me to know and you to find out. But it's grand for now, until they get my new accommodation ready.'

'Where's that?'

'The Maze. Don't tell me you don't know?'

'No, I don't. Tell me. Go on.'

'They're building a multi-million-pound leisure suite for me on the grounds of national security. Escape proof I hear.'

'Really, Gerry?'

'Yeah. The bloody hospital and part of the H-Blocks are listed buildings, being renovated all for me. Some conflict-transformation centre that'll be. I've wrecked the last jewel in the crown of British imperialism in Ireland.'

'Gerry, what are you on about?'

'The Balmoral Show. I've just fucked its new location. Jesus, take the Derryman out of Derry and all hell breaks loose. I'm getting my own purpose-built hotel. A prison with one inmate – me.'

'I'm delighted for you. How are you anyway, Gerry? It's a waste of bloody drinking time asking you about anything.'

'Thanks for asking. My mood like yours is up and down. A lot of dark. No light. The usual stuff. And all those new officers asking me questions. New officers. New questions. I'm in a good place this evening so I thought I would call. But thanks for asking anyway. The constant interviews and statement taking is so laborious. All these new funny techniques. Everything filmed. Plenty of tea and no handcuffs. No guns. All relaxed.'

'How are you really, Gerry? Come on.'

'What do you think? City of Culture, eh? The whole world's watching. And not even for Wales ...'

'Richard Rich? You're referring to Richard Rich, aren't you?'

'Sold out Sir Thomas More for Wales and you sell me out for what? A grain of salt?'

'You gave me it. You know that. I'd no choice. You know that, too.'

'A grain of salt. All you believed in and you sold me out for a grain of salt. Planted and tampered with evidence. Jon, you might as well be a B Special or RUC Special Branch. Not a care in the world over perjury.'

'Well, Gerry, some other time. Take care of yourself. I'm sure you will.'

'You, too. I hear clapping, laughter and cheering. Nothing like landing in the middle of someone else's party or function with all their in-house jokes and jibes you don't get. Solicitors. Don't you just love them? Always something in their sights. Always looking for a target. Always focused on something. Like trained snipers or marksmen ...'

'Gerry, you're drifting. I'll go now. Call anytime.'

'Okay, Jon. If you take the job we are divorced. Seven towers. One target. Then there's the red gurnard.'

Valberg paused for a brief moment. 'What?'

'If you cut your hand holding a red gurnard your blood just drips and soaks in unnoticed. And it's so painful. They live in the murky depths.'

'Gerry, you're losing me. Right, Gerry. Bye.'

'If you need any help when it erupts, call me. Or I'll call you, more likely. And remember: think about what you have missed, not what you have found out. And how is Linda? We have so much in common.'

'What do you mean?'

'False-father fatigue.'

'What do you mean?'

'Her mother remarried, didn't she?'

'Well, I don't know.'

'I mean, her father is not her real father. Common now. At least my real father is still alive. Barely.'

'Gerry, can I ask you something? Something I get asked quite a bit.'

'Go on, try me.'

'Did you have to be so cruel? So brutal? Really? Did you?'

'Sorry, Jon, a disturbed inmate is signalling for my attention ...'

Valberg hung up, content in the knowledge he had had the last word.

'Where's the bathroom, Henry? I'll be back in a minute.'

Henry pointed Valberg in the direction of the Gents.

CHAPTER 56

Immediately upon entering the lush Savoy bathroom, Valberg could hear the sounds of what was clear to him was frantic sex in a cubicle. As he used the urinal, he thought of how the world was entirely on CCTV. There were cameras everywhere and nothing was private. Even sneaking away for a few lines of cocaine and sex in the male toilet would be captured on the cameras around the hotel. There might even be a camera in the cubicle. As the groaning got louder and all was coming to a climax, Valberg, curious, lingered so he could see who was doing what.

Valberg didn't recognise the young lady who exited the stall first.

The girl came over to the sink to wash her hands and looked at Valberg in the mirror. Valberg just said, 'Hello.' Another female solicitor beauty, interviewed by the same man who interviewed them all. The girl then looked at him again. This time more closely, but still in the mirror.

'You're the detective. Mr Valberg. Aren't you? I like that name. Christina has told me all about you. I recognise you from the television footage and photographs. Ours.'

'Well, I hope it was good.'

She looked at Valberg and kept her stare on him, 'Well, it could have been better.' She looked over at the cubicle. 'He had to get it out of his system.'

She smiled and called out, 'Hans, I'm going back. See you in there.'

She looked at Valberg again in the mirror. 'See you later, too, Jon.'

255

'Okay. Sorry, and you are?'

'I'm Katrina Shultz. I won't shake your hand. Not just now. Especially after where it's been.'

Hans came stumbling out of the cubicle, fixing his trousers and wiping cocaine from his nose and licking it from his hand.

'Hello. I'm Peter Rosborough. But everyone calls me Hans.'

'Okay, Hans. Nice to meet you anyway. But "Hans"?'

'Oh, they say I talk with my hands, but I don't get it.'

Valberg was getting it, as even on that short exchange Hans was talking with his hands. He had a gesture for almost every word. Valberg thought the guy must be an expert in the Wing Chun style of Kung Fu.

'Okay, Hans, I'll let you get back to the speeches and the party. Nice to meet you.'

'Sure, sure, sure. I'm actually not in this department. Shipping and aviation law, that's my bag.'

'I'm sure it is, Hans. And exciting, too, I bet.'

Hans burst out laughing as he left, still saying, 'Sure, sure, sure.'

Valberg freshened up with some water on his face and could hear clapping and cheering, which seemed to signify the end of Christina talking and an end to self-congratulation and what might even appear as smugness.

***

But there was one further dip into the deepening darkness for Valberg when he had a flashback of Finbar asking him about the definition of a 'person'. This had happened when Valberg was washing his face at Strand Road Station a few years ago. Valberg thought now that Finbar was standing behind him looking at him in the mirror the same way Katrina Shultz had just done.

'Sir, can you help me with this? I know it's not your scene. I'm not sure.'

'What is it, Finbar? Go ahead.'

'Mr Rankin. Sidney. Sidney Rankin, the solicitor, has just mentioned something to me that I don't understand.'

'Finbar. Did you miss the "get to the point" course at

training? What the fuck is it?'

'Sir. What's the definition of a person?'

Valberg started to dry his face.

'A person? The definition of a person?'

'Aye, sir. It's an RTA. A dead body. This guy just handed himself in. We made an appeal on the radio and he walked in within an hour with Mr Rankin.'

'I don't listen to the news, Finbar. What road traffic accident? Where?'

'Up the country, sir.'

'Finbar, you seem to be in a bit of a daze there, and I'm off to the mortuary. Can you be more specific? A person has to be alive.'

Finbar cut in quick.

'That's exactly what the solicitor said – "A divine living human being." His point is that his client can't be charged with anything because the guy might have already been dead. I'm just thinking about it all.'

'Go on, tell me more. It sounds interesting.'

'Sir, Ronnie McKnight left his local country pub at one or so this morning to walk home. He was hit by something or someone and lay, it seems, on the road. Stevie Clarke also left the same pub a bit later. He was doing a quiz. He admits he was drinking. He drove over, he claims, a black bin liner or bag. Or so he thought at the time. Heard a little bump. Thought nothing of it and went on home to bed. His wife confirmed all the timings.'

'Right, okay. Go on.'

'McKnight's body is discovered and we put an appeal out.'

Finbar had got Valberg's attention and interest.

'Right. Okay. So it's on the radio we're looking for witnesses and that.'

'Yes, sir, exactly. Clarke comes in with his car. It's parked outside. There are pieces of flesh, human flesh I think, on the front underside of the car. There's no other damage. Absolutely none. Not a scratch or bump. A forensic crew is on its way.'

Valberg put up his hand requesting Finbar to stop talking and thought, then said, 'I get it, and the solicitor is right.'

'How's that, sir?'

'How are you going to prove that McKnight was alive when Clarke drove over him?'

'Aye, but—'

'No, Finbar. The solicitor has you by the balls, so do nothing. Don't charge his client yet. That's what he wants. Keep them both as long as you can, but don't charge him until someone from the DPP looks at it for you. Don't make an arse of yourself.'

'A divine living human being then, sir. That's beyond all reasonable doubt. A person is a divine human living being, and to prove that Clarke caused death by dangerous driving to a "person" then we have to prove beyond all reasonable doubt that—'

'Look, Finbar. You've got it. Now you, me and Mr Rankin agree. So can I go now, Finbar?'

Valberg thought Finbar was still in a daze and just walked away shaking his head.

Finbar called to his superior.

'Sir?'

'Yes, Finbar?'

'Thanks, sir. Thanks.'

Valberg shook his head and didn't acknowledge the thanks and left the police station.

***

Now, looking at his reflection in the palatial bathroom next to the Lancaster Room in the Savoy, Valberg whispered what he wished he had said to Finbar: 'It's okay, Finbar, I'm glad you asked. No trouble at all. Glad to help. Take care … Finbar … Finbar.'

Then there was a loud bang on the bathroom door, and another young couple stumbled in, drunk, full of life and joy and on their way straight into one of the cubicles again. It startled Valberg and he left, pushing past them, a bit annoyed that the bang had scared him.

CHAPTER 57

Valberg stood and watched the young gathering. All solicitors. Not a barrister in sight, thought Valberg. All healthy, young and neat solicitors, void of the effects of the economic gloom hanging over the world.

Valberg walked to Henry.

'They're full of life, almost naive, and my head has been lacerated in a sanity shredder.'

'Yes, Colonel. Indeed.'

'Henry, I'm hitting the sack. I've forgotten my room number but I hope we meet again.'

'Oh, for sure we will. Just check at reception, but you're in one of the suites.'

Valberg left, still steady on his feet and totally aware of his surroundings. He stood and looked again at the gathering until Christina approached him. She gave him a big hug and Valberg felt embarrassed, but hid it, and played along as falsely as he believed Christina was. She whispered into Valberg's ear:

'The Katharine Hepburn suite. I'll see you up there soon. Here's a card.'

Then she introduced Valberg to her various colleagues, mostly female, and Valberg said his hellos and goodbyes. All part of the interview, thought Valberg. He could see he was being analysed carefully.

Christina walked with Valberg out of the Lancaster Room.

'I know you hate all this social stuff. Don't worry. There isn't much of this. Everyone is just anxious to meet you and I think we are all glad you are alive.'

'Glad? Alive?' queried Valberg.

'The bomb, the Eglinton bomb.'

'Oh, how could I forget? Of course.'

'And so, do we have you?'

'*Have* me?'

'Have you. Do we?'

'How could I refuse? Maybe make me a remand prisoner, just before I agree to a full sentence. Let's see. I've a few more questions, but sure, why not?'

'Great, Jon. I'll be up soon or come down again. I'm all yours.'

'And I'm all yours, it seems.'

Christina kissed Valberg again and she walked back to the party and the music.

Valberg stared at Christina's body tightly enveloped in a blue Louis Vuitton dress. He could still smell her Christian Dior perfume. She took another glass of white wine from a waiter who seemed to be following her.

Valberg watched everyone one last time and his mood began to plunge once more. He looked at Christina and started to sing to himself Tanita Tikaram's *Twist In My Sobriety*.

'Fuck me, Christina. Love drawn red from my hands. That's all you'll ever be. A twist in my sobriety.'

He walked away.

'I need a rest.'

With a hotel full of lawyers, it was always going to be hard for Valberg to avoid them. It was also impossible to avoid their drunken conversations about their cases. Valberg walked straight into one waiting on the elevator and had to endure it all the way to the Katharine Hepburn suite.

'The man who entered the witness box was not the man who left it.'

'What do you mean, Chuck?'

'Look, we destroyed him, Bob.'

'Ah, Chuck. You're a legend.'

'Well, four hours later he was floundering.'

'Jesus.'

'All his medical qualifications, prizes, honours and medals, a sham. Reduced to nothing over one fucking stupid lie. One slip leads to his downfall. A father, a husband, grandfather.

Held in the highest esteem. Now on suicide watch, chasing the dragon.'

'A privileged life now a discredited one. All he'll be remembered for now is one slip.'

'Bob, he was too smart for his own good. A guy who was never in a fist fight and only kissed one girl and then married her. Had a life of awards, committees, groups, and never questioned about anything in his life. You know what he said at one time?'

'What was that?'

'"I couldn't swear to it." That's what he said, and the trial judge emptied him.'

'What did the judge say?'

'He said you are sworn to it. You have taken an oath and you are swearing. That was the end of him. Then he told the truth.'

'Well, you got him, Chuck.'

'Not by design. I kept it simple. Reduce it. Keep it simple stupid. Basic investigation. This guy was socially inept unless he was being praised. His international qualifications and credentials impeccable. All in the trash can now. He tried to keep the death of the child from the coroner. I love forensic pathology. Love it.'

Valberg was saved by the arrival of the elevator at his floor.

The two lawyers kept talking.

Valberg thought to himself that he got something out of the exchange inflicted upon him. He should keep things simple and, perhaps, as Gerard O'Driscoll had said, he should think about what has been missed, and not found. Keep it simple stupid.

Valberg still had *Twist In My Sobriety* in his head and was humming it now on the way to his room. He didn't bother examining his first-class accommodation. He threw his coat and shoes off and lay on the bed, exhausted. He didn't even search for the remote but instead just allowed himself to relax.

Keep it simple, and think about what was missed, not found. He wondered if he could ever stop thinking about all the events of the last couple of years. It would be beautiful if he could allow his mind to wander. If he could find a way to get past the giant red gurnard blocking his way. He would run, and keep running, until complete exhaustion made him collapse. But every time he tried to relax, he became agitated and annoyed, with everyone. He was almost three days without sleep and the hallucinations were getting stronger.

Just as he was about to drop off, Christina came in. She slipped into the bathroom and reappeared wearing a black basque with stockings and suspenders. Valberg said to her, 'Eh? Where did it all go wrong?'

Christina opened a bottle of champagne that Valberg had ignored and drank the overflow directly from the bottle. She gave it to Valberg and he began drinking from the bottle as well.

Christina wore a tight pearl necklace and began the process of taking off, very carefully, the rest of her jewellery while staring at Valberg as he stared back at her.

'Let's not talk, Christina. I'm fed up talking and thinking.'

'Suits me, Jon. Too much talk. Time to relax.'

Valberg lifted himself up, sat on the end of the bed and pulled Christina in towards him. He held her tight and inhaled her smell.

'I want everything off this time,' Valberg finally said as Christina fell over him laughing. 'Fuck. I never laugh when having sex. Do you? Is it not the most fun you can have without laughing, Christina?'

'Turn off the lights, Jon. And take off your clothes.'

'I will if you wear nothing but your eye mask.'

'They're at the side of the bed there, Jon. Go on.'

Valberg eased Christina gently down on the bed on her back and all she wore now was her black stockings and suspenders with her eyes covered. Valberg gently began squeezing her neck with both his hands and Christina didn't object. Valberg then got up and took the rest of his own clothes off, turned out the lights and got back into bed.

CHAPTER 58

Valberg woke up around four; Christina was still sound asleep.

He thought he had been in a forest with his father and could smell the pine. As usual, he didn't know whether he was dreaming or hallucinating. The forest was sweet and fresh. He could smell the bark from the trees and could feel the sticky sap on his hands. He felt the soft ground with a bed of brown pine needles beneath his feet. He knew the only way to get this thought process out of his head was to get up.

Valberg tried to remember the names of the trees on the map that Chief Superintendent Kells had given him. He knew the names would come once he had a visual of the document as an image in his mind. Despite the time, he decided to go into the bathroom and call Linda. About what, he was not sure, but Ian Haslette's murder was troubling him. Perhaps not so much the murder, as Debbie Sloan had confessed all to him, but more about Haslette's room and what was left there.

Linda didn't take long to answer her phone.

'For God's sake, Jon, it's … it's four in the morning.'

'I know. Sorry. But Ian Haslette—'

'Jesus. Let me wake up at least. Right, go on.'

'What was in his bin? I remember looking at or hearing about the rest of the room. And I was there. But wasn't everything tagged and bagged from the bin?'

'Aye. I remember that. It was just rubbish and letters torn up. From another solicitor. He was getting sued I think.

Nothing else.'

'Nothing else?'

'Nothing, just a load of scrunched-up tickets.'

'Tickets?'

'Aye.'

'Tickets for what?'

'I remember the National Trust wording and an oak leaf or something. I think. I didn't look at dates or anything. Tickets for Downhill. Mussenden Temple. Hezlett House. What's this about, Jon? Where are you? And I'm fine by the way, if you care to know.'

'Samuel Hezlett was found hanging from the Spanish chestnut tree at Hezlett House. Sita, Spruce, Ash, Michaela—'

'Jon, stop. It's the middle of the night and I'm on duty at eight. Let me get back to sleep.'

'Keep everything safe.'

'Not for the first time, Jon, you have lost me.'

'Black Glen Pond. There's a pond there surrounded by trees. That whole area was desolate before the National Trust took it over. I remember my father took me there. The pond needs drained. The forest. The trees. The girls. There wasn't even an inquest for them. The forest. The trees. The forest ...'

Valberg was beginning to regret getting into this with Linda. He should have called Michael. He knew if he opened up more, he would have to talk about a date and time that he knew Linda would not want to talk about.

'Jon? Jon? Are you still there?'

'Sorry. Yes. I'll let you go. Thanks. Sorry I woke you.'

'Okay. Don't worry. Are you okay?'

'I'm okay. Try to get some sleep. Sorry again. Bye.'

'Bye.'

Valberg crept back into bed and lay awake, staring at the ceiling and thinking about Mussenden Temple and Downhill and the times he had spent there with his father. He was never going to sleep now and could smell the pine needles falling through his hands. He looked at Christina, completely naked now save for her eye mask. He started to imagine again that everyone who had been killed recently since O'Driscoll returned to Derry was also alive and booked into the Savoy. He imagined them walking about the corridors outside and whispering to one another. He could hear Orla Harkin, Ashley and Michaela Rankin running up and down the corridors outside laughing and playing. All three children were caught in a time warp of innocence without a worry in the world. They laughed as they ran towards each other with their hair flowing and screaming at the top of their voices. Valberg was wide awake and his mind was in overdrive. Fearful of sleep and where his dreams would take him, he decided to get up again. Only this time, instead of calling Linda, he called Michael and realised he was getting an international dialling tone.

'Michael, Michael. It's me – Jon.'

'Sir, I'm away with Jenny. Hold on, I'll go into the bathroom.'

'Michael. Get details on all the children dead or disappeared from about nineteen seventy-nine to now. All of them. Any inquests. Anything. But nothing political. Any deaths. And, Michael, even ones lost then found. Get all the files—'

'Slow down, please, sir. I'm just waking up.'

'Don't tell anyone. Here, take these names down or memorise them. It's easy. Think of trees. Ashley and Michaela. Ashley and Michaela Rankin. Rankin. Mr Rankin's girls. The solicitor. The dead solicitor. And any more. There must be more—'

'Sorry, sir, Jenny is calling me. Hold on.'

'Michael. Stop. Stop. Hold on. Tell no-one.'

'Dead children?'

'Dead or vanished. There must be some database. Work back a little from Orla and keep going. Say nothing to Linda. Or anyone. Would you do that for me?'

'Aye. No problem. I have to go. Jenny hears me talking.'

'Okay. Good man. Tell no-one. Great. Bye.'

'Bye, sir.'

Valberg was on fire.

He got into bed again and Christina began to stir. The only way he could calm himself was to have sex with her again and, afterwards, he eventually fell asleep.

CHAPTER 59

'Christina, I'm off to Spain. I need to talk to the police-man dealing with Carolina's death.'

It was early the next morning and Valberg lay stretched out on the king-sized bed.

Christina moved beside him and he noticed marks on her neck and back.

'What happened to you?'

'You did. Don't worry, Jon, consent is nine tenths of the law. And I do come with a health warning.'

'Perhaps I should, too. Sorry.'

'You were saying her name in your sleep. If you were sleeping. She meant a lot to you. Carolina.'

'She still does.'

'I understand. Domingo is no ordinary policeman, Jon. He is a senior member of the Serious Crime Organisation. Watch him.'

Valberg smirked.

'Fuck me. How many times do I hear that? Watch him. Watch her. Believe no-one.'

'Where are you meeting him?'

'Malaga.'

'Nice.'

'I find that part of Spain, despite the trash-brigade influx, well ... hypnotic.'

'So, Jon, are we cool, then? Are you in?'

'Can I go on probation?'

'You've met Henry and some of the solicitors. But we are no ordinary law firm.'

'I've gathered that.'

'What we do is different. We stabilise positions and re-solve things that law-enforcement agencies cannot.'

'Legally?'

'Lawfully and legally, of course.'

'Well, what could I fix or stabilise?'

'We will get you something. Don't worry. Far away from Derry.'

'The further the better.'

'Jon, it's a great opportunity. Or live in Derry and have life drained from you.'

'I've no intention, Christina, of staying in Derry. With both parents dead, my suspension, trials, tribulations and public inquiries looming, my time is short.'

'Well, make the time. It won't wait for you.'

'Right. I'll await your call and stipendiary arrangements.'

Valberg was only half-joking now.

'You'll be well paid and we'll let you work on your own.'

Valberg rose and started to dress.

'Right, I'm off to Malaga. Keep in touch. I'll not resign just yet. I'll wait on my first job offer from you before I look for my P45 from the PSNI. Or is it a P60? I dunno.'

'Right, Jon. Call or text when back from Malaga.'

Valberg kissed Christina.

'Take care of yourself, Christina. It's a dangerous world you function in. Dangerous people. Watch yourself.'

'I will, Jon. See you soon.'

As Valberg got ready to go he remembered the last time he left his father. He didn't realise back then that that would be the last time he would see his father alive. But he wondered now if he would see Christina again. He got on with his journey to Stansted Airport for the flight to Malaga, recalling Janice Sloan again and her sister. He had been meaning to talk to Christina about Janice and if she ever hallucinated about her but forgot. Another time, he thought. Make the time.

CHAPTER 60

Valberg had arranged to meet Inspector Antonio Domingo of the Spanish Serious Organised Crime Agency at the Kaleido Café, Palmeral de las Sorpresas, Puerto de Malaga. He would not talk to him any longer on the telephone.

The café and the port were new and clean and well away from the centre of Malaga with its cathedral and hordes of rude tourists. Valberg got a taxi, having refused a pick-up from the police, straight to the café from the airport and Domingo was waiting for him as arranged, sipping a glass of red wine.

Valberg thought the new marina was breathtaking, especially the area where he was to meet Domingo. Its construction and layout had been well worth the wait. The white-and-cream structure allowed just enough light to filter through and enough shade for comfort.

Domingo was a handsome man in his early fifties with the blackest hair Valberg had ever laid eyes on. His left hand was bandaged from what appeared to be a recent injury, but Valberg made no comment on it as they greeted each other.

'Inspector Valberg of the PS and I. I got your text when the plane arrived and I came straight here. It is a pleasure to meet you at last. I have read so much about you. We have talked so much on the phone. Please do sit. We can talk in English and forgive me if I dip into Russian every now and then. I use it a lot at the moment. Did you have a nice flight?'

'Fine. Apart from the Belgian manic depressive with terrible teeth I met, who told me he hated the sun but was still going to Malaga. Apart from that. Yeah, sure. No problem. I have some Spanish, as you can guess from our calls, but I think your English is much better. And thanks for meeting me here. It is a bit more pleasant. I'm ashamed that my Spanish is so vulgar and ignorant. It is a disgrace.'

'Don't worry. Well, what can I get you? I ordered this in advance.' Domingo gestured to the wine bottle.

Valberg could see a bottle of Brunello on the table. His personal favourite. Clearly Domingo had done his research.

'Pour me a glass. Thank you.'

As the waiter came over and poured the wine, Valberg was distracted by children and tourists taking photographs in front of what appeared to be a display of front pages from a newspaper.

'What is that, Inspector Domingo? What is the display?'

'Yes. I have been watching. The passing of time. The years. The passing of the last seventy-five years, to be exact. Every year seems to mean something to someone so they take a photo. *El Sur*. It is a display by *El Sur*.'

'Yeah. The paper. I get the English version now and then.'

'Even Franco is in there.'

'Where does the time go, Inspector?' Valberg asked.

'I wish I knew. Then I could stop it running away. Or better, turn it back. But "Antonio" is fine. Call me Antonio.'

'And so is "Jon". Thanks for the wine. It's delicious. Just beautiful. I can inhale it and it takes me back.'

'To Carolina?'

Valberg paused in reflection then took a large drink again of the Brunello and emptied his glass. The waiter was over instantly to perform the refill. Valberg looked at Domingo's bandaged hand and answered.

'Yes, Antonio. Carolina.'

'How did you meet her? The usual way?' asked Domingo.

Valberg smiled and shook his head.

'No. No. Not the usual way. Not an advertisement in the paper, a bar or a nightclub. The post office. *Correos*.'

'The post office?'

'Yes. In Puerto Banus. I was posting a book I had just found in an old bookstore to a friend, and Carolina was in front of me in the queue. I can still smell her. I can still see her. She didn't have her daughter then. At least I don't think so. Well, I stood in the queue and she presented her whole life to a policeman who is never off duty. Her iPhone told me everything I needed to know; that and the form that she had filled out. The code on her phone is, or was, two-three-zero-three.'

'Correct, Jon. Go on.'

'Well, whatever way she was holding the phone I could see her tap in her code, and I read her text messages. And replies. And her emails. There was another woman at the desk causing chaos and delay, but I was in heaven behind Carolina. As she came out of her messages, her number came up on her screen. I didn't memorise it on purpose. But I have this thing, this memory thing. Anyway, I called her at three that morning and we met up. We didn't have sex. We just met up.'

Valberg paused and looked at Domingo.

'I have this sleep thing, too. I don't sleep. And one other thing. There was this really horrible guy looking to post something. I thought him suspicious, but Carolina took pity on him, I think. She helped him seal a large envelope and explained to him what to do. It was a real act of kindness. The guy meant no harm. At the time, perhaps, I was jealous of the attention he got.'

'What was the book, Jon?'

'The book?'

'The book you were posting.'

'Oh, yes, the book. *The Bridge of San Luis Rey.*'

'Mr Thornton Wilder.'

'That's right. I hadn't read it in years and I found it and was posting it to Anna.'

'Anna?'

'Anna Harte.'

'Oh, I see. Anna Harte, your Chief Constable now. My God, she is a fantastic woman. You must be so proud to have a chief of police with her credentials.'

'She is my salvation, Antonio. Without her I am nothing. But anyway, you want to know about Carolina and I want to tell you the truth.'

'Before you go on, Jon, what do you see when you watch these people in front of us? Do you see what I see? Like the man in the post office you were jealous of?'

'I don't know what you see, but I don't see an old man just off a cruise ship with socks and sandals, white skin, pot belly and a cheap sombrero straw hat. I see a dodgy past and shame. I see wife beaters, rapists, thieves and murderers. I see children with drug problems and mental instability. I see the wrong side of everything. Or is it the truth, Antonio?'

'I see that darkness, too. How can we not in our work? It is as inevitable as death itself. The only thing that is certain.'

'What is that?' Valberg asked.

Just then, two uniformed police officers, one female, noticed Domingo and came straight over to him. They became lost in deep conversation as Domingo rose to meet them and take them away from Valberg. The female officer, Valberg could see, was getting emotional and both Domingo and the other male officer steadied her. Behind her sunglasses Valberg could see that she was crying. They were speaking so fast Valberg could not catch the conversation but there was one word he heard and understood – *muerta*.

Valberg watched more and more people stand at different years from the *El Sur* exhibition and have their photograph taken. Perhaps he should do the same before he left, he thought. He also noticed more armed police officers patrolling the area. Valberg, dressed in black as usual, lifted his Ray Ban sunglasses to his head and examined intently the female officer, now in control of her emotions, as she was leaving Domingo.

'More wine, *señor?*' asked the waiter.

'*Si. Mi gusta,*' Valberg said smiling. '*Gracias.*'

Domingo returned to Valberg and apologised immediately.

'*Lo siento.* The girl was very upset and I thought it best ...'

'Oh, no problem. I could see. Can I ask what is wrong with her?'

'She is upset as today is the first day she has seen me since my daughter died.'

'Very sorry to hear about that.'

'It is truly a most horrific situation. But tell me more about Carolina. Everything.'

271

Valberg was going to ask Domingo if the female officer was married or not but in the circumstances he thought he would leave that query for now.

'Of course. Everything. I'll tell you everything. As agreed – policeman to policeman.'

CHAPTER 61

Valberg knew not to mess with Domingo. He had to be the best witness he could be. The witness he would want. So after a few more sips of wine, Valberg began.

'Dyed blonde long hair with dark roots. Five foot eight or nine with her shoes on. Beautiful. Her nails always perfectly manicured. Always. Very little make-up. Orange or red lipstick. She was always spotless, too. So clean and hygienic. I can still taste her scent. She was beautiful. Thirty-four D and always black or red underwear. Never any other colour. She had a piercing just above her right upper lip and always wore a small diamond in it. She never met me without her Louis Vuitton hand case sort of thing that opened out with two mobile phones. One an iPhone and the other a BlackBerry. But when she was with me she turned them off. She had brown eyes and milky Latina pure skin. Her pubis was always totally shaven. I never saw any hair on her apart from her head. She would spend ages in the bathroom when we were at hotels. When she came out I used to think I would melt. She looked like gold porcelain, if there is such a substance. She always had another bag with a change of clothes, underwear and sex toys. She also had a variation of wigs. It amazed me how different she looked just by changing the colour of her hair. There was something dangerous and unsettling about her change, too. We never talked about personal stuff. That's why we got on so well. I never really scratched below the mental surface with her. I certainly did so physically. One time, well, more than once, but one time in particular I thought I choked her to death. We'd both taken some cocaine and I was being particularly rough. The usual misconception on my part. I thought that's what she wanted. My hands were around her neck more often than I care to remember but also around her waist. Her waist was so small my hands would nearly meet. Even after Maria was born. In fact, we lost contact for a year or so but she looked even better after her daughter was born. More relaxed, too. I wouldn't go to her apartment. I let her talk about the child. I listened. Then in the last couple of years, she seemed to be a bit more pensive. More financially aware, if I can put it that way. She mentioned one name.'

'Yes, Jon, what was the name?'

'I hope I have got it right – Urko? Is that right, Antonio?'

'Urko is right. Go on, Jon, don't stop.'

'Well, it was a sexual relationship. No ties or obligations, and I paid for it.'

'Jon, as promised, you have my undertaking and word on that. I, or we, have no interest in you paying for whatever she did to you or you to her. I personally don't care about the *diablo's* powder, either. Can you tell me more about what she said about any Russians, as she thought them to be, or Urko?'

'She was scared. I see that now and I didn't pay any attention. I should have. She called them Russians but was that right, Antonio?'

'Perhaps not. Serbian more likely. Bosnian Serbs. Urko was a mass murderer. A Serb. He was assassinated and then left hanging over the River Guadalevin. He was suspended from the New Bridge, not a very inspiring name, in Ronda. Just a couple of years back.'

'Did he have any other injuries?'

'A very interesting question, Jon.'

'Did he have a cut to his neck, to the palms of his hands, under his armpits and the back of his ankles? Was his body drained of blood?'

'Let me show you this, Jon. And those details were not in the press, by the way. I understand the loss of so much blood, slowly, eventually makes the heart stop pumping.'

Domingo produced an iPad and played footage of Gerard

O'Driscoll standing in the Prado museum in Madrid, staring at a painting.

Valberg shook his head.

'*Blodigt helvete*. Can we get more wine? Two more bottles, perhaps. Then stop me.'

'What do you see now, Jon?'

'You know who this is, presumably, do you?' Valberg asked in the hope of a positive response.

'He knew he was being filmed, Jon. He didn't break in or anything. You can see the time and date on the clock. He tipped the guard, yes, to get straight to Goya's *Saturn* first, but he just stood there. In a trance. He had a tolerance level of about three or four tourists at the most. Then he left. He did this every day for about a month then vanished. We have film of him every single day. No-one had any reason to suspect him of anything. He was not doing anything against Spanish law, or any law then. We were trying to find him then Langley, Virginia, helped us. But by that time it was too late and we heard all about his little visit to Derry. The CIA monitored him but did nothing. I think they are petrified now that he is in custody. The problem is that Urko's sons have sworn revenge on him and everyone connected with him.'

'Everyone? That's not a lot.'

'Mr O'Driscoll was Urko's assassin. A bunch of crazy Croats paid him. Urko was a fugitive from the International Criminal Tribunal for the former Yugoslavia. That court in The Hague. No-one could find him, but Mr O'Driscoll did. It is ironic that my countrymen and women have been praised internationally for finding dead bodies in the Balkans. We have hid our own so well, it seems. No-one can find them. Have you ever heard of Valedo?'

'Valedo? No.'

'He butchered a pregnant woman during the Civil War here. Cut the unborn child out and left the child and her mother at the side of the road. It is just that the many stories I heard about Valedo when I was growing up as a child scared me to death. My father and my grandfather talked about and argued about him. When I read and heard about Mr O'Driscoll, he reminded me of Valedo. He seemed to have that same killer instinct.'

'Was there a split about the war in your family?'

'A split? More like a fracture as wide as the Grand Canyon. But that discussion we can have later, Jon. Back to Urko and O'Driscoll. Both killers. We read and hear about serial killers and spree killers and all sorts of things. The myths become reality. Analysis becomes overbearing. All this pyschobabble. Mitigation. That's all it is. It bores me. Hate and money drive a lot of killers. I wouldn't over-analyse these people. They kill. That's what they do. They kill. They have no remorse. Ireland has seen enough of that. You have an island full of killers.'

'Well, O'Driscoll could have killed me any time he wanted. To my shame, I attacked him when he was in my custody. I deeply regret that now. It has caused me a problem or two. I was also involved in a case of noble-cause corruption. Tell me more about Urko.'

'Urko was hiding out here in Spain. He had many safe houses. Again, that's all for later. What you need to know is that you were identified with Carolina. Followed many times and I am sorry to tell you, Carolina was kidnapped by Urko's sons, tortured, mutilated, raped and deformed. The Carolina you have just perfectly described was not the Carolina we found. Her coffin was closed. Her daughter heartbroken. They probably did not believe you told her nothing. Nothing about anything. And she was murdered. She was totally loyal to you. She wanted you to stay alive.'

'And her daughter?'

'She is well cared for at the moment.'

'I had dreams about her. She tried to teach me some Spanish and I deliberately always pretended I misunderstood her. Her laugh was infectious.'

'Was, Jon? She is still alive. Maybe you will hear it again. Carolina must have thought well of you, as a client, to introduce her daughter to you.'

'Is she in danger?'

'In danger, yes, but well protected. She is safe.'

'Well, that is something, as I don't care about myself.'

'Why not, Jon? You should. Carolina did.'

'Can we get more wine?'

'Jon, you also need to know, my friend, that Urko's sons,

in their minds, must avenge their father. These maniacs believe you have a close relationship with Mr O'Driscoll, that he spared your father and you saved him. Let him go at one stage.'

'That was to protect others. Women and children. It was to avert a bloodbath.'

'Maybe it was. Perhaps whatever you did was rational. Perhaps noble, I do not know. But what I do know is that these crazy fuckers are out to kill you now as well – and Carolina's daughter.'

'Fuck me. They can join the queue.'

'Anyway. We are well protected here. One more bottle between us, Jon, and I have more to show you. Here, look at this. Do you know her?'

Valberg was staring now at iPad footage of Christina Maguire in London. He was wondering if he should tell Domingo that Christina had already given him some of the details of Carolina's murder. He was thinking specifically about the tattooed bar code on her inner thigh.

'It is O'Driscoll's solicitor. His *abogado*,' confirmed Valberg.

'Well, his *abogado* is in mortal danger, too.'

'She is originally from Derry.'

'She is in serious danger, and some of my team are on their way to her in London with our colleagues there to get her to safety. I hope it is not too late.'

'I can tell you, I know with certainty that she is well protected and constantly under security.'

'So was Carolina. My God. So was Urko. He was one of the most protected men in the world. Then he vanished and turned up in Ronda. Hanging from a bridge. Cut and mutilated also. A number of intelligence agencies know all of this, including the CIA. They were even in Derry – or watching it, for sure.'

'Are you really telling me the CIA watched over O'Driscoll when he was back in Derry? When all the killing and mayhem was going on? They just watched, presumably via satellite? This whole thing is mad.'

'Certainly. And people on the ground as well. All over your city, I am afraid, Jon. They let him roam. He was in his hometown, for a short while by his standards, and the Saturn Killer was reborn. We have his medical file, too. He is not well, it seems. Do you know of this? Has anyone in your police told you?'

'Mentally?'

'He had a heavy blow to the head in Angola years ago. After his time in the Balkans. He could die at any moment. Angola was his last mission as a mercenary for the CIA. A mood-altering blow to the head. One minute up, the next down.'

'Couldn't any of us die at any moment?'

Domingo paused. 'We don't have the tumour he has. It is untreatable now. There is no hope for him. And he knows it. He will not trouble your state for too much longer.'

Valberg looked around him again and let out a sigh. He drank more wine and stared at more people at the *El Sur* display. He was content and relaxed as he'd ever been. He had a rush of thoughts and emotions he'd never experienced. It was dealt with all the easier in the comfort of the Brunello.

Staring at the wine, Valberg could see more blood and rage. He visualised O'Driscoll going completely mad with anger, escaping from prison, and killing everyone in his way. He was dying, with nothing to lose. We were only treated to a fraction of what he is capable of; more suffering was inevitable. Time would tell.

However, the news of O'Driscoll's tumour also had the effect of removing Valberg's anger towards his father. It had been boiling in him. He was now doing what Chief Superintendent Kells wanted him to do. He was finding a way to forgive the sins of his father. He imagined his father staring into the boot of Ian Haslette's car and at Orla Harkin's body. She was past pain and suffering – perhaps even dancing with the angels.

Valberg took a large gulp of wine, then focused on the *El Sur* display again. We are timeless, he thought. Not as individuals, but collectively. Life moves on. Compassion and forgiveness are crucial to our existence. Blame, hate and bitterness will drown us. If we are quick to judge and anger, then we will walk hand in hand with prejudice. O'Driscoll had to be dealt with. He had to be understood. That's what Valberg's father would say. So if Valberg could find a way to forgive his father, he could find a way to at least understand O'Driscoll. We are all dying – not just O'Driscoll. All the pain was yesterday. Only tomorrow counts. There has to be a better future. Let the sun in Malaga, comforting Valberg's face for the moment, replace the pain and sorrow.

Valberg was doing all he could to stop falling into negativity. The news about O'Driscoll lifted him in a strange way. It made him focus on his father with less aggression. At the same time, he was overcome with a sense of compassion for O'Driscoll. It was as if the trouble of the last year had been leading to this moment.

'Jon. Jon, my friend. Are you okay?'

'I want to say I'm sorry to hear that. Does that sound wrong to you, Antonio? Can I think and feel that? I can't use the word affection, but there is something about him I want to protect. Why is that? He has killed so many people. Blood on his hands. Swimming in it, bathing in it and drinking it. But I feel ... I feel protective of him. It's like protecting the devil. Well, at least he made a mark. He wasn't a bore, in debt, complaining about bankers. He did something.'

Domingo then paused and could see that Valberg was still staring at the *El Sur* display. He tried to take in what he was saying and finished his glass of wine.

'If we keep drinking this wine, Jon, we will be singing and hugging each other next. So let's stop for now, shall we, and take this up later.'

'Before we leave, can I get a picture?'

Domingo laughed.

'I knew you were going to ask. Can I have your mobile, then, and what year?'

'You pick one, Antonio. I really like the idea of this display.'

'Here, let's go for two thousand and three.'

'Okay. I'll not ask why, but two thousand and three it is.'

Domingo took care of the bill and the two men left and walked in the direction of 2003 *El Sur*. Valberg pretended not to notice the ever-present armed officers in the area and proudly stood at the display.

'A good year, Jon. Let's hope for more,' said Domingo as he took the picture.

Valberg, despite all that he had been through, and in contemplation of what was ahead of him, managed a huge smile for his photograph.

He felt content and relaxed in Spain and knew Domingo would have more questions for him and he for Domingo. This was especially in relation to the Derry councillor murdered in Malaga. But not now, thought Valberg. Time to relax, recalibrate and decompress.

CHAPTER 62

'Mr O'Driscoll, thanks for seeing me. You got my letter and I got permission from the Governor here at Carstairs. Carstairs, Lanarkshire. What a place.'

O'Driscoll studied Diana White meticulously. A young, beautiful girl with brown hair and the whitest teeth O'Driscoll had ever seen sat on the other side of a protective glass partition. Her teeth were so white they reminded O'Driscoll of the young girl he saved in Angola from rape and certain death.

'Okay. What is it you want from me? What can I do to help you in your studies? That *is* why you are here?'

O'Driscoll wasn't being obtuse. He looked genuinely perplexed.

'I just want to know how you killed him.'

O'Driscoll shook his head in disbelief at what he was being asked. But he knew who Diana was talking about.

'I can tell you how he died. The cross fell on his head. Right on the front of his skull. Crushed it completely.'

O'Driscoll pointed to his forehead.

'He saw it coming, screamed in terror just before it hit him. I've already told the lawful authorities and it's all on CCTV security footage anyway.'

'He's the man who raped me. Repeatedly. When I was sixteen. He destroyed my family and has left my father in a vegetative state.'

'I know that, Diana. Why are you really here? What do you want? I'm truly confused. Why don't you just continue with your studies? Become a nice qualified solicitor. You got in here on the basis of this paper you are supposed to be writing, you told me through your correspondence, about injustice. I know all about you. I know all about injustice. So don't worry about that. I saved a child once from rape. I wish I could have saved more, and you. Stick to the law.'

'Law. That's a joke. Why I ever thought I could be a solicitor, I don't know. Who would think I would be any good at that?'

'You would. Your clients would, I am sure. Isn't that enough? If you believe in God. God will know. Wouldn't he? Not a bad clientele. Stick to the law, Diana.'

Diana was eighteen, and O'Driscoll knew full well she had excelled in her studies. Despite her obvious attractiveness, O'Driscoll also believed no-one could get close to her. O'Driscoll was examining her teeth again. It indicated good oral hygiene, he thought. Her nails were perfectly manicured as well. She looked more like a junior partner in a law firm than a student. She wore a tight, black knee-length dress and was the picture of health physically. Mentally, O'Driscoll assumed, she was not so healthy. Perhaps like him. He wondered if he could use her in any way at all.

'It can be an honourable profession if you let it, the law,' O'Driscoll insisted.

'Teaching, journalism, medicine. Honourable? What's honourable in this decrepit day and age?'

'Very wise and commendable, Diana. But if you twist the knife inside you it will only damage you. Look at me. Look at me, Diana. Would you like to come in here?'

'Well, the law failed me, too'

'Not the law, Diana. People. Individuals. There was a trial.'

'It was worse than your trial. Only this time from a prosecution point of view. I've studied everything about you. I know you're a model prisoner now. On remand, no less, and you have consented to be here. Look, they were useless in my trial. But they let him go. Why? Who's to blame? The police, the so-called prosecution counsel, or the PPS generally, or the judge? Or all of them? You blamed everyone, Mr O'Driscoll. I'll not get a public inquiry, but you're going to be the star of your own.'

O'Driscoll stared intently at her but remained expression-less.

She moved closer to the partition and lowered her voice.

'Teach me how to kill. The way you did. I'm a crack shot already. I'm in Milltown Gun Club. I'm a natural, I'm told. I know how to kill, but teach me how to kill the way you killed.'

O'Driscoll sat back and shook his head behind the screen separating him from Diana White. Then he raised his voice.

'So you have come to learn Latin. Teach yourself Latin, Diana. Not Oxford Latin. The old Latin. Then come back and talk to me. If you've come about revenge you need to dig more than two graves. Confucius was wrong.'

'Help me kill them.'

'Diana, I can help you with what it's like to be stoned to death under Islamic law. That's what it will be like for me watching you killing people. I couldn't save an adulteress once. I had to stand back and watch. All quite legal if you accept it. That's what the rest of your life will be like if you kill.'

Diana stayed silent.

'Perhaps study that, Diana, and see if you are still on the morality scale for killing. I'm telling you. Stick to the law. Before you kill, wash yourself with lotus water, camphor water and pure water so that your own body will be ready for burial after what will be a self-execution. A whole new concept.'

Diana looked at O'Driscoll intently.

'If you then confess to your killing, see if you can manage to wriggle out of your own pit of death,' O'Driscoll said with some forcefulness. He then abruptly got up from his seat and called the guards, saying he wanted to go.

Diana called after him.

'Help me, Mr O'Driscoll. Help me.'

O'Driscoll ignored her as he was ushered away. He was thinking about Diana's rapist and was getting angry. Leaving now was the best option. O'Driscoll could see that this young woman, this girl, who was bent on revenge on all those that failed her, was evil in mind. Murder, death and bloodshed.

O'Driscoll said to the guards, 'That girl will get a first-class degree in law. She'll learn Latin easily. Just as easy as learning to kill.'

As he was ushered away, O'Driscoll thought of Sidney Rankin's son who had also visited him recently and was also once a member of Milltown Gun Club. Dominic Rankin, O'Driscoll had discovered, had no interest in the law, either. He would not continue in his father's footsteps. Sidney Rankin and Son Solicitors was now defunct.

O'Driscoll turned to one of the guards, Richard, with whom he had become very friendly.

'Isn't it strange how one death can lead to multiple deaths? Or one injustice leads to another injustice? One death isolated then snowballs. The killing circle goes around and around, and I have two perfectly innocent people who can finish all of this. Quite extraordinary, Richard.'

'How are the headaches, Gerard?'

'Not as bad this week. Last week was bad, Richard, wasn't it?'

'I will do everything you ask, Gerard, when the time comes. I promise.'

'That's good of you. I'm told I could go any time. It's like a hammer waiting to fall. Waiting to strike. But I don't feel physically weak. Sometimes the pain cripples me for sure, but no sickness really. Not yet. But if I read the entirety of the internet again on tumours, I might just die anyway. Then there's the cyclizine and the morphine when all that starts. I don't want to think about it.'

'You're going nowhere, Gerard, for the moment. You're as fit as a fiddle. Look at you.'

'Thanks, Richard, for walking me back. I'm okay now. I'll read and think a bit. Perhaps think more and work all this out and make a decision.'

'Okay, Gerard, we can chat later. Get some rest. That girl was beautiful. Bye.'

O'Driscoll was let back into his cell and he sat on his bed looking around him now, thinking more about dying and the tumour in his head growing bigger by the day. He knew once he started medication he was finished. So now was the time for rational thought and analysis. He closed his eyes and thought about Diana White again and what she must have gone through. Did she deserve her revenge the way he felt he deserved his? Her desire to spill blood made him question what he had done.

It also made him go to the darkest place he could go. That was to the riverbank of the Foyle in the spring of 1982. Was he suffering from false-memory syndrome? Did he kill everyone recently just to profess a false innocence? Was his barbaric behaviour a reinforcement of innocence or an attempt to plead innocence when he was in fact guilty? These were terrible thoughts and they usually led to outbursts of intense and dangerous anger. An anger he couldn't shift when it descended on him. O'Driscoll struggled to recall now exactly what had happened, and he started to imagine as reality what had been said to him by the police and alleged at court. Everything was confused and muddled.

He called, 'Richard, Richard.'

His cell door was opened.

'What is it, Gerard?'

O'Driscoll stared at the wall in front of him.

'Lock the door. Turn out the lights. Just make sure the door is locked, Richard. Thanks. It's not too late I know but I want to sit in the dark.'

Richard backed out of the room and locked the door. He opened the slim spyhole and looked in on O'Driscoll, frozen and solid, still staring at nothing in particular.

O'Driscoll sat in the dark, mapping out a course of further death and execution in Derry. He might even have a couple of willing participants to put his plan into operation. He was intent on making his own contribution to Derry's 2013 City of Culture celebrations. The newly opened Ebrington Square, home of the old army base, would be such a perfect stage for a public assassination.